Chapter 1: Th

CW00448001

Up in the tree lines, in the deepest areas of woodland, existed a kingdom which was home to creatures with wings. Fairies, to be exact. The thicker branches were hollowed out to create a cornucopia of houses. A fairy's house was filled with warmth, family, and friends came and went without issue. Wooden beams ran across the ceilings, and each house was decorated with objects that made the fairy inhabitant feel most at home.

The magic surrounding the kingdom made every non-plant species shrink in size when they crossed the threshold. It prevented those that lived inside from being detected by the outside world, the power only waning a little once every hundred years. Outside of this area, a fairy was the same size as the average human.

It was said, in all the history books, that they had once lived alongside humans as elves until the first massacre for their wings. The stories told of a night when humans seeking magic had raided the elven homes and ripped their wings from their backs. They didn't know what the reason was for this sudden betrayal, but back then, the fairies hadn't evolved any offensive magic to help them under such an attack. Their only choice had been to run, as quickly as they could, and escape to the safety of the woods where they stayed protected for the centuries to come. Since then, they had dispersed further into smaller woodland settlements while the original tree city became the metropolis of their kingdom.

Fairies were found with the use of five main elements; light, shadow, plant, water, and ice and these laced their way into their kingdom. Light magic created the lanterns and hearths going through the nights, while shadow magic shielded them from eyes beneath their kingdom that would look up into the trees. Ice magic made sure they could store water and keep it fresh for consumption within the homes, thawing as much as they needed, when they needed it. Water magic allowed for the homes to stay dry while manipulating the freshwater to fuel the fruit on the trees, and on the smaller branches which grew separate fruits. These smaller branches with different fruit growing were not natural, but due to the plant magic which flowed through the community. The community and lifestyle were sustainable but would only work so long as all types of magic worked as one.

The fairies themselves were able to use and link with all the different elements of magic, however, everyone leant towards a stronger affiliation with one element over the others. This affiliation was obvious from birth as the element affected the colour of the fairy's hair, skin and wings. Light magic led to yellow wings, blonde hair and a yellow glittering shimmer on their skin; shadow magic led to black hair, wings, and shimmer, water magic led to blue, plant magic led to green, and ice magic led to white/silver. Each element had an elder fairy representative on the kingdom council which made decisions for the whole community, decisions that would make sure the elemental balance remained. So long as the elements remained split evenly throughout the community, the elemental magic would keep their community going.

It was a design that allowed them to work together in harmony.

Well, that was the theory…

One young fairy had always seen a different side of the community that was meant to work for everyone.

Lily Rosales was born to a male ice fairy named Isa, and a female plant fairy named Terra. Her parents had been normal in every sense of the word, they didn't even differentiate away from the stereotypical traits of their element either. Her father was sometimes very logical, and her mother preferred nature to others of their kind. Her father worked with the elders to manage the elements, making sure they kept aware of which elements may be suffering for any reason. Her mother worked with the cultivation of the fruits on the trees and spent a lot of her time out on the branches where natural sunlight peeked through the canopy of the trees.

There was nothing about those two which suggested there would ever be an issue with a child they bore together. But, life was a strange one, and it brought to them an unexpected challenge when their daughter was born without wings.

A fairy without wings. It was laughable! A ridiculous notion! How could one live in a community based on being able to fly to one's front door or the city hall?

Some even said it was a bad omen. That having a child who could not keep up with the community would have a knock-on effect on the carefully kept balance that kept the wheels of their lives turning. Any child born previously without wings had been disastrous when using magic. There were many records of the wingless trying to use magic and creating huge problems. Tales were told about them using light magic and creating enough heat to cause fires in the wooden community or water magic getting out of hand and flooding the homes.

When she was just a babe, Lily would often create little things spontaneously. A random sneeze would cause a plant to grow rapidly and shatter the pot it was in. Her crying in discomfort or need for resources would cause lights to glow and flicker or blow a tap off the sink or cause leaks in the water storage areas.

This wasn't anything strange for a baby though, it was common for fairies before the age of five to have difficulty in controlling the magic around them.

What was strange, was Lily Rosales had outbursts of magic that weren't linked to the main elements. Objects would move when she was throwing a tantrum, things would disappear, and sparks of colour would dance around her when her emotions took over. It made her very easy to read as a child and her parents were always ready to deal with whatever she had to throw at them.

For a fairy born without wings, Lily was at least lucky to have had the parents she did. They didn't treat her like she was troublesome to have around even if she couldn't leave the house unless they flew her out of the door. They didn't act like there was something wrong with her even though the absence of wings made it painfully obvious. They taught her everything from the ground up, they took time to help her grasp the magic that was overflowing from her and they did everything they could to keep telling her that there was nothing wrong with having no wings. Her mother helped her learn in her early years how to create vines and wooden tendrils from the environment so that Lily could climb up and down their homeland without needing to fly. Her father took up running with his small child to help encourage her fitness levels so that she could keep up with others who could fly straight up.

She never could keep up though.

No matter how quick she could get up and down those branches, the kids would just fly from branch to branch to keep out of her reach. After a while, Lily began to realise that this wasn't just a game of chase. They just didn't want her to play with them.

As she grew up a little more, the avoidance was the last of her worries. Lily grew accustomed to being left out of games and sleepovers. Instead, it was the names which got to her more. Wingless freak. Unwanted. Useless.

Abomination. The latter was one that she had overheard from adults, and, while she didn't know what it meant at a young age, she knew it was bad from the way the adults said it quietly and with bitter voices. The adults always looked at her with some strange anger that she didn't quite understand.

Other than her parents, Lily didn't get much acknowledgement from anyone. But, she found that she was able to exist quite happily with her own company; however, once she was ten years old she didn't have to be alone.

When fairies turn ten, they are taken down below the tree line and out of the protective magic to take part in a ritual. Under the light of the moon, they sit within a pentagram made of the five elements and they recite words passed through generations.

These words would draw in their lifelong companion animals. There were usually up to three of them and could be animals such as songbirds, squirrels, rabbits, stoats, beavers, and mice. Other possibilities were available such as; cats, rats, bats, ravens, and snakes, but they usually resonated with witches more than fairies.

"What if I'm not 'fairy enough' to get one?" Lily had asked nervously to her father who was tying her long white hair up into pigtail buns either side of her head.

Her father paused, his silver eyes meeting his daughter's identical ones. They were already so full of worry about her differences to everyone else. No matter how often he and Lily's mother tried to make sure their daughter's confidence remained intact, there were too many young fairies yelling negativities at her during playtime for them to truly contend with.

It didn't stop him pressing his lips to his daughter's forehead in a reassuring gesture before he pulled back to smile at her. "You are more fairy than anyone, just look at how much magic you've already mastered! Those potential companions will be fighting for the chance to be bonded with you."

Lily giggled a little as he bopped the buns, signally he was finished.

"You ready, sweetie?" Lily's mother asked as she walked through the foyer of their home, her leaf green hair pulled into a braid down her back.

Lily nodded with a nervous smile.

"Good. Come on then" Her mother leant down to lift her daughter, she was getting to the size where she wouldn't be able to carry Lily around for that much longer. For today, though, her mother didn't want to make Lily climb all the way down the tree they were housed in.

When Lily was taken out of the protective boundary, her mother placed her on the ground beside the pentagram which had been set up. Lily glanced around the woodland in wonder, this was the first time she had ever been out of the shrinking magic border. She couldn't help but smile at how big she felt.

"Lil? You remember everything you need?" Lily's mother asked.

Again, a gentle nod.

"Ok. Well, I'm going to be right up there, if you want me to come and carry you back up when you are done, just give me a call."

"Ok, Mommy. I'll come back with the best of friends!" Lily chimed, trying to pretend her nerves weren't there still. With one small wave to her mother, Lily watched as she spread those gorgeous lime green coloured butterfly style wings and flew back up into the trees.

Lily envied her parents' wings so much.

Biting her lip gently, the child turned around to face the pentagram and let out a shuddered sigh.

'Please let this work,' she prayed silently.

Stepping into the pentagram, Lily sat herself down, letting her light green dress splay out around her legs. Closing her eyes, she began to recite the words she had been practising for the past couple of months in the run-up to her birthday.

'Emoc ot em nionapmoc, dnib flesruoy htiw ym luos elihw enim llahs dnib ot sruoy. Klaw rehtegot htiw em litnu ruo tsal nward htaerb'

Seconds ticked by and nothing showed. Lily could feel tears sting her eyes. If she had to go back up to her home without a companion... being wingless was bad enough, having no companion as well would only make her even more of a freak.

Suddenly, there was a crunch of movement in the undergrowth. Lily's eyes snapped open as she spun around to look in the direction. Her eyes settled on two sets of eyes, one yellow pair, and one green pair. Slowly, they came closer and, in the light, she could see that two black cats had chosen her.

Felines rarely showed for a companion bonding with fairies, especially black cats. They were drawn to the magic of witches.

But Lily didn't care. She had managed to get her companions. She had been enough for something!

"Erm... hello?" Lily stammered.

The smaller of the two cats bound forward and jumped up onto Lily's lap while the other walked slower and nudged against her outstretched hand, licking at her fingers gently.

The two cats showing up that day to bond with Lily would surely only add to the negative view the community held of her.

Witch. Imposter. Monster. Mutant.

These were just a few extra words added to the list of names given to her following that day. But, at least she had the two cats to support her alongside her parents.

The following few days allowed the strength of the bond to increase and the animal companions found their voices around fairies. Their personalities could shine through with their words and their actions. They were also granted the ability to grow wings to follow their companion fairy up and down the tree lines. It was strange to be a fairy without wings when your companion cats could still grow them and fly around next to you.

Oscar and Kiki tried not to use their flight abilities though. They knew, intimately, how much it bothered Lily that she was wingless, and they didn't want to add to that.

Oscar was the bigger of the two, he was a large muscular black cat without any markings. He walked with confidence and often had a look of judgment in his eyes as he watched the world around him. He also developed sarcastic comments in response to any mocking that Lily received in the attempt to take the edge off their words.

Kiki, on the other hand, was a little menace with too much energy. She was only a kitten, but she still charged back and forth over moss-covered branches outside, creating moss stains on her little feet which were white, standing out like socks against the rest of her black fur.

It didn't take long for these two to become Lily's best friends, and for Kiki to become a large form of entertainment to the girl.

Other than the cats and her parents, only one other showed any kindness towards her. Jared Linwood, son of the black fairy elder. Jared never spoke to her much, only a small statement or two. But in schooling scenarios where the younglings were required to move up and down the branches quickly, Jared would pick Lily up and fly her there. He knew well of how she was viewed by the adults and knew the teacher wouldn't wait for her.

They weren't friends, Jared's mother would never have allowed that, but that black-haired, black-eyed fairy brought a refreshing light to her days whenever he helped her.

Some days were worse than others though.

Some days, if her talent for magic hadn't been so quick, she may not have made it much further through life.

One day when she was twelve, a particular group within the class Lily was part of lingered behind the lesson after the teacher had gone. They had been in the canopy of the trees, learning to enhance their light magic with the rays of sunlight that peeked through the leaves.

Lily had arrived late, as usual, having had to climb the trees to reach them. And, as usual, she had to make her way manually back down them. At least these days, she had Oscar and Kiki to keep her company on the journeys. Kiki spent a lot of time sitting on Lily's shoulder while Oscar walked beside her, often trying to use their wings as little as possible in a show of solidarity with their little girl companion.

"What do you reckon Ma has planned for tea?" Kiki's voice was high and almost chirp like making her always sound excitable.

"Whatever it is, it better be plentiful" Oscar commented flatly in his silvery voice "Going up and down these branches makes me so hungry!"

"Everything makes you hungry, Ozzy." Lily giggled a little, leaning down to scratch behind the larger cat's left ear.

"You could just not come," commented a voice from behind her. Lily recognised the honeyed voice of River Barrett.

She was a blue fairy with a narrowed glare to her blue eyes. River was the daughter of the Council's blue fairy, and she talked and acted like she was more important than others... especially Lily.

River was always flanked by three others; the children of the other elders aside from Jared Linwood. There was the green fairy's daughter, Chloe Irving, the white fairy's daughter, Crystal Parisa, and the yellow fairy's son, Blaine Lior.

The children of the elders were her main tormentors, and Kiki hissed the moment River's voice had sounded.

"Get lost!" Kiki spat from Lily's shoulder.

"Still hiding behind those moggies... you're so pathetic" Blaine rolled his eyes as his own companion, a majestic stag deer, pawed at the ground, challenging the little black kitten. Kiki growled, pressing herself closer to Lily's neck.

"At least she's not hiding behind her parents, acting like that makes her some kind of great entity" Oscar growled warningly, eyeing up the blue jay companion of River's.

Ever since she'd gotten the cats, this had been a common occurrence. They spoke out for her more than she ever did herself.

"We don't act like we are great, we just know we are better than her" Crystal piped up in a sickeningly sweet voice that didn't suit the malicious glare in her young white eyes.

"She's a freak. No one wants her in class!" Chloe added indignantly, pushing her jade fringe from out of her face.

Lily felt his stomach twist heavily. At this point, she believed those words. She was a freak, and hearing it now made her hang her head.

"See, she knows we are right." River drawled "She knows it would be better just to not bother coming."

The four laughed as Lily turned to walk down the branch, Oscar hesitated, looking like he was ready to pounce at River's throat. Thankfully, he decided against it. With one last growl, he turned and trotted after Lily, coming level with her feet.

"Ignore them. They're nothing but cockroaches!" He growled up to her, though his words didn't soothe the tears that stung Lily's eyes.

River wasn't done. As they walked away she cackled "That's it coward, run home to Mommy. Don't bother coming back tomorrow!" Then she smirked towards Crystal and in an undertone added, "Why don't you add some ice to speed up her runaway?"

Perhaps they thought it wouldn't be an issue as they had seen Lily create her own ice slides and skate down them effortlessly. Or perhaps they didn't care what the outcome was. All Lily knew was that it was a very different experience creating your own ice, as compared to ice suddenly appearing under your feet as you were moving.

Her body lurched as her foot slid out in the wrong direction. Her head hit the branch as she fell and, even though she had reached out with both hands, Lily slipped off the side of the branch and fell.

She had never fallen from one of the branches before, not without her parents there to catch her. Air rushed past her ears. She barely heard the cry of Oscar and Kiki. The speed of air hitting her made it difficult for her to breath as she fell. Her tears and the wind stung her eyes. She couldn't think straight. Panic seemed to rid all thoughts from her mind.

Suddenly, her dress was pulled on and she glanced over her shoulder.

Oscar and Kiki had jumped after her, spread their wings and grabbed the back of her dress. She was heavier than they could manage though, no matter how hard they were beating their wings. Her weight was dragging them down with her.

"Come on Lil, we got you!" Kiki strained.

"Get yourself to the branches!" Oscar yelled.

"But..."

"No buts! Make those vines obey you!" Oscar snapped.

Lily had been able to manipulate vines and branches but to do that precisely enough to catch her as she fell through the air... Well, she didn't believe in herself enough for that.

"Lily!" Kiki's voice snapped through those doubts and fears.

Reaching out a hand towards the main tree trunk, Lily created a vine which shot out towards her outstretched arm. It missed. Again, she attempted with no avail. And a third time. She couldn't get the timing right.

"I can't do it!" Lily cried, her tears beginning to trickle out of the corners of her eyes.

"Keep trying!!"

The attempts were weaker as fear took over.

Then something did catch her wrist. It wasn't a vine. It was a hand. Lily's eyes snapped around, landing on the familiar black shimmering skin of Jared Linwood. He had flown beside her to catch her at the right speed.

After he had caught her wrist, he reached closer to grip her under her shoulder. With a flap of his black feathered wings, he led her to the side and placed her down safely on the closest branch.

"Are you... ok?" Jared asked awkwardly once Lily was seated securely on the branch.

Lily sniffed, reaching up to wipe the tears from her cheeks. "Yes... th-thank you."

Jared shook his head a little, standing next to her as though he wasn't sure of what to do now. Everyone knew he got told off for interacting with her. He was probably torn between staying with her and avoiding that scolding from his mother.

His conscience won out and he sat a little way from her. "What happened?"

"Nothing."

"Nothing my fluffy butt!" Oscar touched down next to her and his wings vanished. "Those vicious liches did it!"

"Ozzy..." Lily sniffed "They were just..."

"Just nothing! They almost killed you" Kiki spat.

Jared shifted awkwardly, he knew who the cats were talking about. "I'm sorry," He mumbled.

Lily shook her head quickly. Being apologised to felt weird, and when it was the only person ever nice to her, it felt wrong. "I'm fine, it's ok."

The cats hissed again in disagreement.

"I just want to go home," Lily added, trying to move on from the subject.

"I'll um... I'll take you?" Jared offered quietly.

Lily shuddered a little and quickly shook her head; she didn't want any more reasons for those four to pick at her, and Jared being around her for a long time would only spell worse things for her as well as him.

Instead, she picked herself up to her feet and, after thanking Jared again, she headed back home.

For the next few years, this was her life. The mocking followed her everywhere and how she had fallen ungracefully, how her dress had flapped high enough to flash her undergarments was added to the things she was ridiculed for. No matter what she tried, she couldn't break into any social group, she was scared to try being friends with Jared and so, relied solely on the cats and her parents for company.

Chapter 2: Birthday Surprise

Due to her lack of friends, Lily Rosale's birthdays were never that different from the one before. She had come to enjoy the birthday treats that her parents made her and the way the cats sang to her so badly.

Her fifteenth birthday came with no new surprises that morning.

"Haaaaaaappy biiiirthday to you! Happy birthday! Happy birthday!" Kiki sat on her forehead and sang in a very off-tone, shrill voice that she was exaggerating. "Now wakey-wakey so we can eat your cakey!"

"Ki, it's the crack of dawn" Lily groaned, reaching up to push the small cat off her head.

"Yup! It's a beautiful day! Hey!"

Kiki yelped a little as Lily moved one lazy arm up and pulled the feline down into a hug, partially out of affection and partially to shut her up for a moment.

"Lemme go!" Kiki struggled, wriggling until she was released.

Lily rolled over in her single sized bed and buried her face back into her pillow. But she was not going to receive any freedom from Kiki. The small cat jumped onto her shoulder blade and began kneading.

"Lily, get up! Your dad wants to see you before he goes to work" Kiki whined close to Lily's ear.

Lily grumbled sleepily into the pillow.

It didn't take her long, however, to drag herself out of the warm embrace of her duvet. She pulled on her dressing gown which was white with a grey fluffy trim on the interior to keep her warm. The early morning sunlight that peaked through the sky-lights in the hallway made the shimmer of her skin sparkle. It gave her pale skin a silver glow. Yawning widely, Lily walked into the kitchen and smiled as she saw her father finishing off his breakfast of fresh fruit.

"Morning Dad," Lily mumbled.

"Ah, it lives!" Her father turned his head to smile over at his daughter who resembled him so much these days.

They shared the same silver eyes, pale skin which glittered with silver dust, and white hair; Isa Rosales' cropped and smart, pushed back in a traditional cut, while Lily's was messy from sleep and daring to reach her hips. They also had the same slightly rounded chin and long pointed ears. Maybe if she had had wings, Lily would have sported the same white-feathered type as he did.

"Thought you were going to sleep the whole morning away." He chuckled.

"I was," Lily yawned again as she sat down on the breakfast bar next to her father. "Kiki woke me up with her screeching."

"Excuse you! That was my best singing voice!" Kiki commented in mock indignation as she hopped up onto the main kitchen table. She sat herself down beside her father's companion Felix, a grey squirrel which was cleaning its tail waiting for her father to finish his breakfast.

"Yes, we all heard it too." Her father chortled, reaching over to pull his daughter into a hug "Happy birthday Lily," he added in a merry tone.

"Thanks, Dad."

"Oh, you're up!" Lily's mother's voice sounded out as she bustled into the kitchen. Terra Rosales was a slim green fairy with large butterfly wings which were folded up delicately behind her as she walked, carrying a small present in her left hand. "We thought we were going to have to wait till tonight to give you this" She swept over to Lily, her long lime dress flowing around her ankles. Her mother held out the present to Lily, her arm passing by a golden streak of light from the side window making her skin glitter green.

Lily smiled as she took it. "Thank you," she chimed brightly.

Birthdays for Lily were never huge events where she got presents a-plenty. Usually presents on birthdays came as happily given treats from others in the community; those who could make clothes, jewellery, ornaments, furniture etc, would give them to the fairy celebrating their day of birth.

The community, of course, didn't want to be seen involved in giving Lily treats like that. But every year, Lily's parents were able to create something with a great deal of learning and practise. All the companions tried to help as well, usually with fetching materials that could be used for the next present.

Lily's mother's companion fluttered onto Lily's shoulder. Bella was a tiny but brightly beautiful hummingbird with mostly green feathers that matched Terra's hair. "Open it Lils!" Bella chirped.

"Yeah!" Kiki called with a purr.

"You all know what it is..." Lily chuckled softly, noticing the fond smile that her parents were wearing and the way all companions had turned attention to her. Even Oscar had sat upon the sun-soaked window sill. Despite that comment, she ripped the brown paper off the present and let a delicate necklace drop into her hand.

"Oh... wow!" She whispered out in awe as she picked up the necklace to dangle it in front of her face. It was a thin silver chain that glittered like her skin, with a large teardrop blue-green opal hanging from it. As the sun's rays hit the jewel it glistened like the surface of a still, unpolluted oceanscape. "It's gorgeous!" she breathed, her eyes watering a little in gratitude.

Her father, now getting up from his seat, walked over to Lily and gave her a very tight hug and kissed the side of her head. "Happy birthday Lil. I'll see you tonight" He walked over to his wife and kissed her softly with a smile "See you later Terra," he said softly before glancing at Felix and motioning to the door. The squirrel hopped off the table, and after a detour onto the kitchen counter to nuzzle Lily's hand and get a kiss from her on the top of his head, Felix jumped after her father and headed out of the front door.

As the front door shut behind them, Lily's mother started to clear up the bowl that her father had been using. "We're going to have a huge meal tonight, I've managed to get a few favours in from the harvest and I'm going to make strawberry and lime cheesecake," She said as she cleared the dish easily with water magic.

"Really? Awesome!" Lily grinned. Strawberry and lime cheesecake was her favourite dessert, but usually, they couldn't get enough strawberries to use them all for one dessert.

Her mother glanced back at her daughter and chuckled "Here, let me." Lily had been fumbling to try and get the necklace open and around her neck. She took the silver chain and walked around the counter. Once Lily had bundled up all her white locks and pulled them up out of the way, her mother quickly and easily hooked the necklace around Lily's pale neck.

Lily looked down at the jewel twinkling against her chest, it shone more than her skin and she couldn't help but grin at the sight of it. Her parents must have taken most of the last year to perfect making something like this.

"It's really beautiful Mom!" Lily raised her hand to run her fingers over the jewel as Kiki jumped up on the counter to look at it closely. Oscar wasn't as bothered, he had probably been the one who had patiently sat with her parents in the finishing process being asked his opinion. Even to her parents, Oscar was sometimes brutally honest, but it was always with Lily's best interest in mind.

"It suits you, I'm so glad we chose that opal. We debated a ruby or amethyst, but Oscar thought the blue colour of that would suit you better" Lily's mother mused as she stepped back and looked at the necklace with a fond approval before heading over to the large, overflowing fruit bowl and began to pick various fruits out for her and Lily's breakfast.

"I love it Mom," Lily exclaimed as she observed the trinket around her neck before getting up and walking over to Oscar when he sunned himself "Thank you, Ozzy."

"Only the best." Oscar purred gently.

"It's so pretty," Kiki complimented.

Giving Oscar one last affectionate scratch behind the ear, Lily turned to walk back to the counter and sat herself down as her mother placed a bowl in front of her.

An array of mango, orange, banana, kiwi, pineapple, and pear sat chopped inside with a generous amount of sweetened evaporated fugacapra milk. Lily's mother always made sure that they had enough milk for her to create many kinds of food for all of those within the house.

With a soft thank you, Lily dug into her breakfast. It may have been early but getting up on her birthday always succeeded in making her feel more confident even if just for the one day.

This year, her birthday had fallen on a day when she didn't have to attend any form of learning. Lily was tempted to spend it on the far edges of the kingdom, out by the thin bridges that connected them to the other cities that came their way for information from the elders. The bridges were simply a very thin stretch of the barrier which reached out to another part of the woodland where more fairy homes were situated. Generally, these bridges were void of people, and so Lily could sit with Oscar and Kiki, watching the movement of the large woodland beneath her or experimenting with another idea of what she could make happen with her magic.

She didn't have to worry about River, her gang, or anyone else bothering her there.

"Oh, bloombursts!" Lily's mother suddenly exclaimed, causing Lily to look up from the spoonful of mango she had picked out as her next mouthful. "Your father forgot his lunch" came the explanation.

She was holding a small box of food that had been prepared for Lily's father. She glanced over to the window as though to judge the position of the sun in the sky. "I'll have to dash to get it to him before I get to the harvest today."

"I could drop it off to him?" Lily offered helpfully. She didn't really like visiting her father at work. He worked in the central hall, where the elders often held their meetings.

"Are you sure?" Her mother sounded apprehensive. She knew that the reception Lily got in their main city hall was not a pleasant one, and she didn't like the idea of her listening to such things on any normal day, let alone her birthday.

Lily nodded, however, putting on a brave smile "Yeah. I was going to head to the bridges anyway, so I can drop it in while I go past."

With the necklace hanging against her chest, Lily felt like she could ignore whatever the whispers said for a brief visit into the city hall. She would have a free day and then a fantastic dessert tonight to look forward to. Plus, it would only take a moment to drop off a box and leave again.

Still, her mother hesitated, a pang of resigned guilt moving over her features. Finally, she gave Lily a strained sort of smile and placed the box down on the counter "Thank you, sweetheart." She kissed her daughter's temple lightly "I'll see you tonight ok?"

"Yup!" Lily chirped, making sure to keep any concern about going to the city hall off her face. She didn't want her mother to feel any guiltier than she already did; her parents were always doing their best to keep Lily out of the community's line of fire. Not that they could protect her from everything, but Lily knew how much they had altered their lifestyles since her birth.

Another quick kiss and her mother had bustled back into the bedroom she shared with Lily's father to get ready for work. It barely took her any time, having only needed to get her hair into a braided bun so it was out of the way and to pick up her harvesting gloves, and soon her mother's green butterfly wings were unfolding themselves while she walked through the entrance.

"Enjoy your day sweetie!" Her mother chimed.

"Thanks, Mom! Have a good day!" She called after her mother who waved to her from the kitchen door before heading out of the front door, Bella the hummingbird following quickly.

Silence fell over the room, only Oscar's satisfied purring on the windowsill could be heard alongside the clinking of Lily's spoon hitting the bowl as she scooped out the last few mouthfuls of evaporated milk.

"You didn't have to offer," Kiki commented in an off-hand voice. "I know you always want to do what you can, but River and her gang are bound to be there, making themselves out to be more important than they are."

"I know, but it's just a quick visit. We'll be out again before anyone can say anything." Lily said, getting up to wash her bowl up "Besides, they can't do anything physical to me somewhere that public, they have their façade to keep up."

"Yeah, they have to pretend to be such perfect children" Oscar grumbled from the window "Otherwise their parents would get schtick for raising the little rats the way they have!"

The larger of the two cats was always very cold to the topic of the Elders and their children. Ever since that day they had sent Lily off one of the highest branches in the kingdom, he had shown no care to hide his opinion of them.

"Exactly," Lily agreed. "If we ignore them, we won't have any problems. I'll go wash and change, then we'll go out early; maybe they won't even be there this early."

Inwardly, she hoped with everything she had that they weren't. Lily knew that even if she didn't react to their jibes, the words still drove the pain further into her soul. In the last few years, she had been mocked over so many little things that they had affected her even if she didn't say it. The most obvious was the fact she no longer wore dresses; because her panties had been mocked so many times from that day of her fall, she couldn't face giving anyone else another chance to flick up a skirt or dress.

When Lily came back from bathing and changing, she was wearing a pair of white cotton pants, loose and easy to manoeuvre in, and a dark green vest top. The necklace was tucked just under the neckline, hiding the trinket from view so it didn't catch any unnecessary looks.

"You guys ready?" She asked, finishing tying her hair as she walked into the kitchen again. She had pulled the now brushed hair over her right shoulder and was binding it into a tight braid to stop it from catching on anything outside.

Both cats bounded off their respective surfaces and trotted over to her, Kiki nuzzling against Lily's bare ankle as Oscar walked over to the door. With a smile, Lily walked over to pick up her dad's lunch as well as her own and placed them in a small green cotton bag she took from the first drawer on the left of the sink.

The day outside was beautiful. It was a day in early autumn, with a warmth that crept even into the shadows. A yellow hue had begun to show on the leaves outside of the magical barrier, giving the canopy a beautiful glow as the sun shone against and through them. Within the barrier, the leaves retained their green colour, sustained by the magic of the community to keep them optimal all year round.

The moment Lily opened the front door, she placed out a hand and, with next to no concentration, grabbed hold of a vine which grew down from the branch above. She had become rather adept with all magic which could help her get around the community, and most importantly, save her if anything dangerous happened to her again. Lily hung from the vine long enough to let the cats fly out and to shut the door behind them, then she silently willed it to pull her up onto the solid branch.

The moss on the bark was soft and spongy against her feet. The sun had given it a warmth which made her unable to resist curling her toes into the embrace of the green folds.

"What a day!" Oscar said as he landed beside her and made his wings vanish as usual. "Lunch on that sunny bridge is going to be luxurious!"

"Feeling like napping today?" Lily chuckled.

"Well, I was out hunting last night in the main woods," Oscar said with a yawn. "I didn't find anything cool enough to bring back though."

"The woods aren't well travelled enough to find anything that cool" Lily reminded him as Kiki landed on the other side of her. "But I wouldn't mind lying in the sun for a while," she added, setting off up the branch with careful and light-footed movements.

Compared to any other fairy, Lily was obviously used to moving through their home on foot. She was graceful as she climbed what she could, and her magic was seamless to aid the three of them over gaps and up elevations that were too large for her reach. Lily had slightly more muscle than the average fairy now as well, giving her a toned look as she pulled herself up onto the thick branch protruding out from the main trunk where the city hall was situated.

The central tree of the fairy city was a large oak tree whose branches reached out to entwine with the trees surrounding it. The trunk was thick with a maze of official rooms within. There was a door to this internal city hall on every bough that protruded from the trunk. The quickest one to take to see her father was the third up from the bottom on the east side of the trunk. Lily had to swing across on a vine to reach the east side of the tree, but it was a better choice than walking through the whole set of rooms within. Once she was inside, all she would have to do was walk past the Elder meeting room and up the small set of stairs to her father's office.

Pulling the door open, Lily stepped inside.

The city hall wasn't lit by much natural light as most homes, instead, there were balls of light magic hovering on the walls of the corridors. It was like looking at stars in the night sky, though the amount of them made the walkways and rooms bright and welcoming. Lily never felt welcomed, but she did appreciate the beauty of the light magic.

Her bare feet took her quietly over the smooth wooden flooring. She was as silent as the cats' soft paws which pattered along beside her.

"They've started already?!" A voice suddenly sounded from the door Lily was passing. Lily stopped in her tracks. She recognised the sullen voice of Jared Linwood's mother, Layla Linwood, the Shadow Elder. Lily's silver eyes glanced to the door behind which the voice had sounded; the last thing she wanted was for them all to be leaving the room while Lily was in the line of sight.

There wasn't any sound of movement within, only firm voices. The urgency seemed to make it harder for Lily to keep herself walking past, she couldn't help but be curious what the pressing tone was about.

Stepping closer to the closed door, Lily raised her finger to her lips telling the two cats not to make a noise.

Inside the five Elders seemed to be alone in their discussions.

"My companion followed a pair, they were headed to a large building protected by magic." A gentle voice sounded. That voice belonged to Clara Lior, the Light Elder. "He couldn't go inside but he watched for a while and saw more entering."

"There are still a few years before the century is up though?" The plant Elder, Douglas Irving said.

"They will need to make sure all their youths are ready for it though. Were those entering young?" Water Elder, Livius Barrett's stern voice added in. There was a moment of silence before he continued, whoever he had addressed must have simply nodded. "They must be setting up a training facility to make sure they make the most of this century."

"You think they would make their young join in?" Clara's voice seemed wary of thinking such a thing.

Outside, Lily's brows had furrowed a little. Who were they talking about? Could it be that they were discussing the first sign that this century's massacre, there were still five years till that was due? As far as she was aware, that was the only thing that could be related to in terms of centuries.

"Witches don't care about age." A new fifth voice spat. That must have been the Ice Elder, Lily thought, having never actually met that final elder. "They will want as many people gathering wings as they can get."

A heavy silence fell over the room. Lily could feel the tension mount on her shoulders even from outside the door. Her silver eyes glanced to the cats either side of her, the fear she felt in that moment reflected out of their eyes. Everyone had hoped that this would be the century where it just didn't happen.

Lily went to move away, but the voices starting again inside caused her to stop again.

"Do we have any idea which city within the kingdom they are starting with?" Livius asked.

"If we did, maybe we could increase the defence there and reduce the casualties?" Douglas added.

"No," came Layla's voice "If Clara's companion is right, there's no chance of getting inside their gathering to find that out. They would pick out a fairy companion in an instant, and our wings would give us away."

"We'll have to keep a watch from the outside and see what we can observe." Clara agreed.

They began to speak about possible rotations of who could observe the witches from the outside without gaining too much attention. Small companions seemed to be the best bet, they would be able to linger just out of sight but hear what occurred outside of the gathering building.

Outside, Lily jumped as a small cough sounded behind her. Her face pulled tight into a grimace as she turned to look over her shoulder. River Barrett stood there, her arms folded and a sickeningly gleeful look on her face.

"Eavesdropping?" She hissed in delight.

"No...I..." Lily stammered.

"You're going to try and deny it?" River chortled derisively "You really are such a pathetic little rat. No, don't get up. You should live on your knees." She added, reaching out her bare left foot to knock Lily back down as she attempted to stand up and away from the door.

Lily couldn't have even pretended that she felt rage over such actions any more. Instead, she seemed to accept that being on the floor was where she now belonged.

This was punishment for listening to things she was never meant to hear.

The excited look in River's eyes was terrifying. Lily couldn't even bring herself to look up at them properly. She was going to report her, and Lily was going to have to deal with the wrath of all five Elders. Whatever she was thinking to bring that cruel glint into her eyes couldn't be something good for Lily.

"Come here!" River snarled, reaching down to take a painful grip on Lily's upper arm. Ignoring the hisses from the two cats in protest, River pushed the door open and strode in, dragging a paling Lily with her.

Before a word could be uttered, River chimed up, still gripping Lily's arm very tightly. "She could be disguised to get inside."

Her stomach felt sick the very second the words left River's mouth. Was she insane?!

"What?!" Lily yelped.

That thought seemed to be shared by the Light, Water and Ice Elders, though Layla Linwood and Douglas Irving seemed to look at her without any care for what she had to say.

"Don't be stupid, girl. Get out. This had nothing to do with you" Layla waved her hand dismissively as though trying to banish a servant from the room.

"I would ask you not to speak to my daughter like that." Livius Barret growled towards the dark-haired fairy, his butterfly wings quivering in a dangerous fashion. Layla Linwood simply glanced at him coldly.

"Well, it's a ridiculous idea," She stated blandly.

"Not really." River's hummingbird companion piped up as he fluttered from her shoulder and sat on the table before the Elders "Logically, it's a pretty good option. Not only does she not have wings, but she has two cats, a typically witchy companion."

"Wait... no..." Lily started.

"And she's of the right age." Everyone seemed surprised to hear Clara's deer companion cut Lily off as he trotted over to Lily and looked her up and down. "If her hair and eyes were changed and the shimmer on her skin was lost, she looks just like the ones I've seen going inside."

He wasn't wrong.

"But, I don't..." Lily started again pitifully, but no one was listening.

The chatter among the Elders and their companions became excitable at the factors pointed out and they turned to each other to discuss the new prospect.

Lily darted a glance at River who looked triumphant. It was apparent that she would have done anything to put Lily in a tough and potentially dangerous situation for the fun of it. But Lily couldn't believe that the Elders were even entertaining the idea!

Were they going to jump at the chance to get someone inside the witches' den in order to give them insight into the coming storm even if that meant sending a socially anxious fifteen-year-old?

I seemed that way from the phrases which caught Lily's ear.

"Magic could easily cover her shimmer and change her hair," Clara was saying.

"It would be easy for one of her cats to bring information to the woods" The Ice Elder was adding in a logical voice.

"And," Layla Linwood added darkly "If she got caught, it's not like she knows much."

"Or her loss matters..." Livius Barrett interjected almost venomously.

His words caused Lily to shudder slightly; something about their lifelong attitude towards her told her that this was going to be quite a big factor in the decision. If she failed and never came back, the community wouldn't miss her.

'My parents would' Lily reminded herself as the sinking feeling of pointlessness came down over her like a wave of darkness.

It was a painfully numbing feeling that seemed to plunge her heart into ice. She had become used to the blank feeling where all thoughts puttered out into nothing and her inner voice became too pathetic to be able to argue through that silence. Though, that was better than when the other little voice came up; in this state, it would have perhaps queried whether her parents really would miss her. That voice was the toughest to deal with.

None of the Elders was paying her any courtesy now. They were talking avidly among themselves. Lily wondered quietly if she crept back out of the room, would they just carry on without her attendance? Maybe if she wasn't there, they wouldn't be encouraged to discuss this senseless idea and would contemplate something much more appropriate.

After a glance at River who was watching the Elders with a greedy look on her features, Lily took a couple of slow steps backwards with trepidation. However, the narrow black eyes of Layla Linwood flicked to her and she scowled.

"Where do you think you are going?" She snarled. "No one said you could go anywhere."

At these harsh words from the Shadow Elder, Lily stopped moving and hung her head down, her icy eyes looking at the spot of her shirt under which lay her new necklace trinket. River giggled at the scenario, clearly receiving a great amount of pleasure from the fact they may actually be sending Lily out of the community.

Lily didn't register the rest of the conversation occurring between the Elders. Instead, she stood, her eyes transfixed on that one spot of her shirt while berating herself mentally for stopping to listen at the door. If River hadn't caught her there, she wouldn't have had a chance to think up this foul idea!

After what felt like an hour, the talk seemed to die down and Lily was addressed once again.

"You will do this task, Lily Rosales." The Ice Elder, whose name Lily still didn't know, concluded. "At least for preliminary information."

Lily gulped. Had she just had her death sentence signed?

Out of the corner of her eyes, as she looked up, Lily could see the way River's mouth was twitching at the edges. She looked like she was trying to conceal an obvious look of glee, as though all her birthdays had come at once.

The Ice Elder turned to her own companion, a chunky beaver who looked like he was rather spoiled with his food intake, and Clara's deer companion. "Go and fetch Mr and Mrs Rosales; so, we can tell them where we are sending their daughter."

Without argument, the two animals bounded off, the door which Lily had entered through opening automatically to let them pass.

"You'll have to use a different name, yours is far too floral to get away with" interjected Livius Barrett with a grumble as though he didn't want to provide her with any ideas which would allow her to survive for long. His face softened as he looked at his daughter with an adoring smile "Thank you for providing us with a solution River. Was there anything else you came for?"

"I just wanted to pop by and say hi before I went off with the others" River smiled sweetly at her father.

"As sweet as always." Livius smiled. "You don't need to stay, so you go enjoy your day."

"Thank you, Daddy! See you tonight!" River glanced at Lily and the sweetness turned to triumph before she turned fully, her long blue dress flowing around her ankles as she left.

The silence that fell was brief, but Lily felt like it was crushing her. She retreated to staring at her necklace again. It was the door clattering open again that broke the silence quickly. Lily's father was power walking through with angry worry etched on his face.

"Lily!" He strode over to her and spun her around, looking down at the teenager "Do not tell me you've agreed to this!" He had obviously been told the decision that the council had come to, but the beaver that waddled in after Isa Rosales appeared to have not told him that this was River's idea and Lily had not spoken a single word yet.

Even now she couldn't get the words to dislodge from her throat. So, she settled for shaking her head.

"No, she hasn't!" Kiki called from her side, finally finding her voice "She hasn't said a single thing, but they are signing her up for it anyway!"

Her father's eyes turned to her, and then to Oscar who nodded his head gravely to confirm the little feline's words. His icy eyes flashed dangerously as he straightened up and pulled Lily closer to his side with one arm. She had never felt smaller; but she felt safer pulled there, like a baby bird still tucked under its mothers' wings before it was ready to try flying.

"She will not be going!" Lily's father snapped defiantly.

"She has no choice." Layla Linwood spoke coldly, as though his words meant nothing to her.

"She's fifteen!"

"Exactly, the perfect age to be going over there and not being discovered." Douglas Irving cut across him. "She is the only one of us that can do this, and the needs of the community greatly outweigh one teenager."

Lily's father looked like he couldn't believe what he was hearing. "You lot wouldn't do this if it was your own children" he spat accusingly to the gathering before him "You wouldn't dare let them wander outside the barrier!"

Behind them, the door clattered open as Lily's mother barged in looking flushed from the speed she had flown.

"Isa! What is this rubbish I've just been told?!" Her voice was high and frenzied as she strode over to her husband and daughter who had both turned to look at the entrance. "This rodent said that they've decided to send Lily off to some witches coven to spy on them?!"

"Rodent?" The beaver companion had caught up now and looked thoroughly indignant as he walked back to the council table "How rude!" He muttered as he tapped his wide tail against the table top in an annoyed fashion.

"That's what they seem to be insisting..." Isa Rosales confirmed with a very cold tone.

"Well... I...." Terra Rosales started, her cheeks burning as rage grew in her. Biting her tongue to keep herself from exploding there and then, she looked down at Lily and forced a smile that only made her look intimidating. "Go wait outside Lily" It wasn't a request.

Lily nodded mutely and pulled herself reluctantly from the safety of her fathers' side.

"We have not dismissed her," Livius snarled.

"I don't give a flying rat's backside!" Lily's mother roared at him, causing his eyebrows to raise and Lily's legs to break out into a light jog until she reached the threshold of the room and slammed the door behind her.

Leaning her back against the door, Lily sunk to the ground with a shiver. "This is not happening" she mumbled to herself.

"It'll be ok," Kiki commented, nuzzling into Lily's side soothingly.

"Yeah, your parents will make them come to their senses!" Oscar added, sitting in front of Lily and placing his paw on her knee. "You'll see!"

Inside, Lily's mother had certainly lost her temper now. Lily could hear every word even if she didn't want to.

"Outrageous!! Have you no shame?!" Her mother was shrieking at the ominously quiet council of Elders. The responses were too quiet for Lily to make out, but her mother's voice told her that her fury and fear was not being calmed.

"Good of the community my ass! You've never cared about her!"

Lily's chest tightened. Even without them saying it to her parents, they knew that the Elders wouldn't see it as a loss if Lily didn't come back from a task like this.

"We can't even begin to imagine what exists out there! Things will have evolved, beasts... the Macellavir!"

Lily shuddered at the name. The Macellavir was said to be a two-legged beast which stomped through the undergrowth of woods and forests looking for lost souls to feed on. No one quite knew what it looked like, but the stories described a towering form with a wolf skull over its face to keep the true form hidden. They also described how rot and moss would grow over its skeletal body making it look more like a rotting tree when it stood unmoving watching its prey. It came out only in the darkening evenings and nights, which was why they were always told to do their companion ritual in the morning so that they would be safely back by the time the sun began to fall.

"Oh please, that's an old wives' tale" Layla Linwood called dismissively over Lily's mother.

"How do you know? When was the last time anyone of us or our companions was outside the barriers at night when we weren't doing a companion trial?!" Her father demanded. "And that's hardly far from the borders!"

"They were never real. They were just a story to scare the kids into behaving, just like the bogeyman." Livius drawled with a roll of his eyes.

Lily gulped silently, her throat feeling like it was closing on her airways. Oh, the nightmares she had had during her childhood of the Macellavir until she was reassured that it was not real. And now her father stood there claiming they had no proof it wasn't real… right when Lily was being told to go out there.

She trembled while she looked towards the ground with her silver eyes filled with terror. Oscar and Kiki both moved in closer to her on either side, attempting to comfort her.

"It's ok. It's just a story," Oscar whispered.

"Yeah, they are just trying to make a huge case so they don't send you to the witches place" Kiki agreed, though Lily could tell that neither was completely certain of what they claimed.

Her parents were indeed trying to make a huge case for Lily not to be sent. They brought up the lack of knowledge they had on witch customs and the dangers of being found out. They brought up the fact that witches needed instruments to perform magic while fairies did not. Everything that could possibly go wrong was raised, and each one sounded like it was met with a solution or dismissal.

By the time the door opened again, Lily's mind was as numb as her bum while she sat on the solid wood floor. She didn't even need them to tell her that she was still being sent, and she knew that there was nothing she could add that would help her. None of the Elders cared whether she wanted to do this.

Looking up, Lily saw her parents appear in the doorway and they looked positively anguished. Her mother's cheeks were drowning in angry tears and her father looked like he had lost any logical thought in his mind.

"They're foul! How can they?!" Lily's mother was muttering as she reached down to grab Lily's arm and pull her to her feet. "She's not going!"

"No. She's not!" Her father agreed as he slammed the door shut behind them and led them out of the room and ushered them from the corridor.

"What's happening?" Lily asked.

"We're going home, and you are not being sent anywhere!" Her mother snapped stubbornly, walking hastily while ignoring the sounds of the Elders wrenching the door open behind them and yelling after them that it wasn't Terra and Isa Rosales' choice.

Chapter 3: Preparation & Departure

Lily was not allowed out of the house in the next few days. Her parents had kept her under house arrest as though that was going to protect her from the decision that had been made.

"We'll take it in turns to have days off work" Her father had planned as though this would stop officials coming in and dragging Lily away in the middle of the day. Perhaps it was even working initially, every time someone came to urge Lily into preparing for her journey they were chased off by whichever parent was still home.

The two cats kept telling Lily that they would give up eventually, but the logic and the pessimist within her knew the reality. If this was the best plan for the Kingdom, then they wouldn't stop coming until she had started on the journey.

If they were going to have given up, they would have done so already. Instead, the Elders seemed to have leaked the information to many of the central city and more citizens were turning up day by day on the doorstep to plead with Lily's parents to stop being protective. It was the ones who were sympathetic but logical that her parents struggled to make leave. Apparently, the reality of the situation was beginning to sink into them as well, but none of the family spoke outwardly about it when they weren't hounded by others.

At least, they didn't until six days after shutting Lily in the house.

Her mother had walked into Lily's bedroom to let her know that dinner was ready and to get washed up, but before any word could leave her lips she let out a shriek instead. The sound caused Lily's father to come running through the house, his feathered wings flexing behind him.

"What is it?" He asked before gasping as he followed his wife's line of sight "Lily!"

Lily stood in her bedroom with a sheepish and guilty expression on her face, except, she didn't look like Lily Rosales now. Her hair was a soft chocolate brown and the eyes which screwed up a little expecting punishment were a gentle but deep green colour. Even the shimmer on her skin was gone, replaced with flattering freckling over her pale skin.

"What have you done?!" He demanded instantly.

"I… well…" Lily started, glancing at the bowl which she had been mixing magic in. "I was trying to make a less strenuous way to change my appearance rather than constantly focus magic."

"You are not going!" Her mother yelled.

"Mom…" Lily tried to interject, but she faltered at the sight of fear swimming in her mother's green eyes. Gulping back the lump in her throat, she started again "You know they aren't going to stop coming to get me to do it; it's the first time they've ever thought I'd be useful."

"But you are…" Her mother was cut off by Oscar who yowled loudly as though to stop her talking, though this got him a very vicious glare sent his way.

"I just thought that when, if," Lily corrected herself quickly, "they wear us down, I should be as ready as I can be… so I can definitely come back."

It pained her parents for them to see Lily already resigned to such a dangerous plan. It wasn't that she was being brave, it was simply that she didn't see that she had any choice. Lily was the outcast of the Kingdom, everyone other than those in this house would be all for her being the one in danger. And there was literally no other fairy who could do it as there had never been another without wings.

"Besides," Lily tried to force some kind of cheerfulness into her voice now, voicing the only piece of optimism which she could think of about the prospect of going out of the boundaries of fairydom "If I managed to pull this off, not only could I save people, but some people might actually be willing to look and talk to me when I'm older."

"Oh…" Her mother breathed out a small sob. This was the first time in many years that Lily had spoken about how her rejection by society affected her.

After glancing at Oscar and Kiki, both of whom looked like they were resigned to the unspoken decision in the air, Lily's father sighed. "Are you sure about this Lil?"

Lily let her shoulders shrug slightly "It's not like there's really much choice, so I just want to be ready. I don't want to be found out."

A heavy silence filled the room, broken only by the sniffs of her mother who was trying to keep her sobs from properly starting out again.

"So, you've been experimenting with potions?" Her father queried with a raised eyebrow.

"Well, not quite. It looks like a potion, but it's mostly water magic with the right levels of light and shadow mixed in to make it something I can drink for a lingering effect." Lily commented, sounding a little less nervous. This was something she had played with a lot when she was younger but had given up on the idea of changing how she looked after realising that no matter what she looked like if she still had no wings it wouldn't help her.

"Well, it's nothing I've ever seen done" Her father smiled softly, it was forced but he was clearly trying to keep his tone light rather than add to any concerns unspoken between them all. "You'll be able to convince a lot of people if you pick up skills this easily without teaching."

Lily smiled softly up at her father, silently grateful for the message he was passing on. If she did do this, he would believe that she would do it well and come back to them without a problem.

It was certainly difficult for her parents to accept, but two days later when an official turned up to parley with them for agreement, they let them cross the threshold of the home. That day it became set in stone that Lily Rosales was going to be heading out to the witches' boot camp.

And she wasn't given long to prepare either; seven days.

The first day was spent standing in front of the Elders again, then telling her all the things that were expected of her. They lectured her on the behaviour that both she and her companions should display, though as Fairydom had only seen Witchdom once a century in a battle for the last god-knows-how-many millennia, none of the Elders really knew much about this subject.

"Your companions shouldn't speak and should act like normal cats unless it's clear that Witch companions can speak. They also should not fly, I don't believe there's ever been a record of a Witch's companion flying when they have been seen." Clara Lior explained after a lengthy debate over what they knew for sure and what they didn't.

Out of all of them, the Light Elder seemed to be the only one who thought this actually had a shot at working. The others seemed to be more of the mindset that it just didn't matter if it didn't.

Lily, who hadn't spoken throughout that day, simply nodded to show she understood what Clara Lior was saying to her. She was white-haired again, the potion only working for a span of twelve hours so far, and she stood without her companions who had been ordered to wait outside. They had a habit of trying to stand up for Lily where she wouldn't speak up, so they weren't welcome to interrupt the instructions she was given.

By the time she came out of the Elder council room, Kiki was stalking up and down the corridor growling and hissing while Oscar stood by the door like a guardian statue with a glare in his expression.

"So…" Kiki snarled, obviously very angry about being left outside. "What did they have to say?!"

Lily bent down to run her shimmering fingers through the small cat's short black fur, trying to soothe her. As she scratched behind the kitten's left ear, Kiki relaxed a little, though she quickly caught herself and lifted a paw to bat Lily's hand away.

"Don't do that!" Kiki grumbled, causing Lily to smile fondly.

"Let's head home, Lil can tell us on the way." Oscar piped up, padding across to them and nuzzling his head into Lily's right thigh as she crouched there in the corridor.

On the way back, with the cool autumn breeze relaxing her muscles somewhat, Lily went over what had been ordered of her.

"So, we can't talk?" Kiki asked indignantly "But what if someone is horrid?"

"Nope, not unless we hear their companions talking as well," Lily said.

"Can we scratch them instead then?" Kiki chortled.

"Ki…"

"Of course! If they are mean, we can bite and scratch them… that's normal cat behaviour" If Oscar had a human expression, he would have been smirking evilly as he spoke now.

"Guys, be nice"

"Only if they are" Oscar grumbled in a warning.

"Anyway," Lily continued, quietly feeling as grateful as always when the felines stood up for her when she didn't have the strength to do so "They also tried to tell me about witch customs, typical spell work and all that, but it turns out that we only have their attack magic recorded in the history files and those are all incredibly vague as they were recalled from people who survived the century attacks."

"That's not helpful!" Kiki snapped. "How are you meant to act like a witch if you've got no idea how they act in the first place?"

Lily shrugged.

"I guess they are hoping that because you are so quiet, you'll just be the silent one at the back and observe everything without being paid attention to?" Oscar interjected thoughtfully. "I mean, if you look like them, you'll just be the quiet kid who can slip away from groups to look around."

Lily thought about it for a moment before shrugging again, this time a little more like she was resigned to that if that was how her fate would go.

"If they leave me be for being quiet then it might be an ok experience?" She mused, hopping across to the next interlocked tree branch. "I can just learn more magic and find out the information without any hassle."

"That would be easier than going to school here" Oscar chortled. Lily's lips twitched into a smile, a small glimmer of hope rising in her chest. If it did work out that way, if it was a simple case of her blending into the background and finding out something that could save her parents without her getting caught, she would be very happy with her lot.

"Lily?" A male voice sounded out close behind her causing her to spin around on the balls of her feet. Her silver eyes didn't really need to confirm who the awkward, low voice belonged to, but she was stunned to have actually been approached by Jared Linwood. He only ever interacted with her to help her out of a potentially dangerous situation.

Jared was about a head taller than her, and he still kept his black hair short and cropped close around his ears. Lily noticed that the top of his hair was a lot messier now than it had been when he was younger.

"Erm… yes?" Lily's voice was always weaker when she spoke to anyone other than her family and companions if she spoke at all. Jared was no smoother though, his wings flicked nervously behind him, the black feathers rippling a little in the breeze. Lily never would understand how the son of an Elder could end up with no people skills and no desire to be around others for long. But, perhaps having a mother so strict had made the guy feel it was safer to just stay away from anything that could get him in trouble?

"They, I mean, the elders… they forgot to give you this," He said in a timorous voice holding out his right hand to her.

Lily's eyes dropped down to the object in his open hand. It was a prettily designed stick. She felt her eyebrow raise as she stared at it in silence.

"Witches use wands? They um… told you about that… right?"

Lily shook her head dumbly.

"They left out a piece of vital information like that?!" Kiki cried, causing Jared and the stoat companion on his shoulder to flinch and jump in surprise before looking down at her.

"They should have told you, Jared was sent to go pick this up" The stoat sounded reproachful as her fur bristled a little. "You don't think they sent you so it would be too late to get to her?" She spoke to Jared who had an understanding and somewhat ashamed expression on his face.

"My mother is..." He stopped himself before he could finish that whisper, his body shuddering as though he had caught himself before he could do something that would bring on an onslaught of suffering after.

"Your mother is being cruel if she knowingly was going to let Lily walk into this without something so critical!" Oscar growled "As are all the other Elders. Oh, one day I'll scratch them so deeply they'll never heal."

"Oh! Do a letter on each face so when they stand in their order they spell something rude!" Kiki piped up excitedly.

"Good idea!" Oscar chortled, ignoring the judging look he was receiving from the stoat.

"Anyway. At least we caught you" the stoat, whose name had never reached Lily's ears, spoke loud over the two cats chuckling evilly together on the branch while debating what they could write out that was incredibly rude but five letters. "It's been made with your hair in the centre, your mother provided it, so hopefully you'll be able to target your magic through it easier to keep up the pretence."

Lily blinked at the wand again before reaching out and taking it. It was light to hold, and it seemed so slim and breakable. But it was engraved carefully, becoming thinner towards one end.

"How?" She breathed.

"What?" Jared seemed to be surprised when her silver eyes looked up to meet his own black ones.

"How am I meant to target magic through there?"

For a moment, Jared stammered over a word before he looked at his stoat companion and then back at Lily. "I, I don't know" a small awkward flush rose under the black shimmer on his skin. "I'm sorry." He added quickly at the mixed look of both confusion and worry that crossed Lily's face.

Lily shook her head. "It's ok. Thank you for bringing it to me." She couldn't help the little twitch that pulled on the right side of her lips. Once again, Jared Linwood had come into her path with something that would save her from potentially severe danger.

Raising his hand to awkwardly scratch the back of his neck, Jared glanced away "No problem. Erm... good luck, be careful." With that he was gone, his wide wings giving a strong beat to lift him from the branch and take him back to his home.

"You're blushing." Oscar's voice stated bluntly, causing Lily to snap back to reality and force her eyes off the black feathered wings.

"Am not..." She grumbled before turning back in their direction of home.

The following six days were all spent inside, trying with all her might to learn how to make her magic to direct itself through the end of the wand that was given to her. It was constant practice and by the time she had gone to bed that final night she hadn't got anything but light to appear at the tip of the wand.

"I'm so in trouble..." She had mumbled to nothing as she fell asleep that night, both the cats already snoring at the end of her bed.

The morning Lily was going to leave her cosy home and set out on the mission she had been given, she did not find herself faced with much of a send-off. Not that she had expected one, but this fact seemed to be something that her mother had focused on.

"They forced her to do this and they can't even turn up to give her one last word of luck or advice" Lily's mother bristled as she stood by the front door. It was likely that she was focusing on what annoyed her about the situation to prevent herself from crying again.

"I'm glad they didn't turn up!" Kiki mewled with a small growl. "Those elders are the last thing we wanna see before leaving!"

Oscar nodded in agreement as he pawed at the ground. They were both waiting for Lily who had taken the potion she had matured for longer effects, and to change into what they could only guess was a fitting attire for a witch.

When she finally emerged, Lily wore a mid-length flowing dress that hung off her shoulder and had long flared sleeves. It was fully black in colour, the only colour in her attire now being the glittering blue-green jewel on her necklace.

"Stop tugging at it" Lily's mother sighed lightly as she watched Lily pull on the hem as though trying to make it grow longer and cover more of her pale skinned legs.

"You know I don't like dresses," Lily grumbled.

"I know, but this is the only kind of record they had of what witches wore" Her mother started kindly.

"Yeah, a century ago…"

"Your mother modified it as best she could to make it look modern, but we can only guess what they wear now" Lily's father sounded out behind her, his hand reaching out to brush Lily's now brown hair out of her face as he came to a stop in front of her.

"I know." Lily conceded. "Sorry."

Her mother smiled weakly and moved over to Lily and wrapped her arms around her shoulders. "I know you don't like dresses, but we couldn't risk it."

Lily nodded mutely. She couldn't believe that she was actually going to do this. She had never been away from the safety of her home for long, and now she was going to venture further than anyone ever had done previously. Well, not in the last few centuries anyway. Fear gripped her. It seemed to fill her stomach with a lead that made her body feel heavy and unbalanced as she pulled back from her mother and attempted to give her a reassuring smile.

Lily couldn't quite do it, so she turned to her father instead and wrapped her arms around his waist to give him a hug goodbye as well. She took the few moments that her face was hidden to furiously blink away the prickling at the corner of her eyes.

She was terrified. More afraid than she had ever been in her life, more afraid and uneasy than River and her gang had ever made her feel. But she had decided to not let her parents worry any more than they already were.

"I love you both" Her voice was muffled against her dad's chest, but both of them were smiling woefully at her when she pulled away and picked up her small bag of stuff.

"Love you too sweetheart," they said in unison before looking at the cats "Look after her ok?"

"Of course!" Kiki flew up onto Lily's shoulder and stowed her wings.

"Forever and always" Oscar assured them as he sat smartly beside Lily's right foot, looking up at her with his green eyes fondly. She was so glad that she didn't have to do this without these two, Lily was certain she wouldn't have the strength without them.

With one last look towards her parents, Lily turned to open the door and summoned a long vine to move through and wrap around her wrist and arm. She paused only to allow Oscar to jump up and steady himself, back feet on her bag and front feet on her free shoulder. Then, she stepped out the door and dropped towards the ground, the vine steadying her descent to one that was graceful and steady.

The woodland floor was quiet when Lily's feet came into contact and the cats jumped down from her shoulders. It was very strange to be outside the barrier which protected their home. For one, she felt like a giant. Up in the kingdom, she lived inside a branch, down here she could have snapped that same branch but trying to climb it with the height and weight she had now.

For a while, she just stood there looking around the woodland. It was a beautiful bright day, so the sun picked through the canopy and illuminated the undergrowth with golden strips of light. The ground was littered with fallen leaves of the autumn days and the orange and red hues from above made the sight before her somewhat magical in its own rights.

The fear within kept her feet rooted to the spot though. She had no idea what was out here, what kind of creatures lived out here and what kind of people she might meet.

"Come on. We got your back!" Oscar nudged the back of her calf, giving her a gentle push to get her legs working.

"Yeah, we might not be able to talk when we get there, but we'll always be with you!" Kiki added.

Lily smiled softly, feeling the lead in her stomach ebb away a little as her right leg moved to take that first step, followed by another, and another, until she had fallen into a slow but steady walk away from the kingdom she had called home for so long.

Chapter 4: The Witches' World

After a few minutes of walking, Lily couldn't deny that the fearful feeling in her stomach was waning fast. The woods were, well, they were beautiful to walk in. The sunlight of the late morning made the different colours in the bark covered trunks stand out and the colours of the undergrowth were crisp and fun to walk through. Birds twittered overhead as they hopped on branches or flew to a safe distance from where Lily and her cats walked; they were obviously not like the companions she was used to; these birds would see a cat and see it immediately as a predator. Out of the corner of her eye, she could see both cats turn their heads to glance up at every movement by something smaller than them. It was easy to forget that they were, in fact, predators when they sat laughing with her daily.

It took about an hour of slow walking to start seeing the edge of the woodland, the light between the trunks getting brighter by the second. At the edge, Lily had to raise her hand to shield her eyes. She had never seen the sunlight without some of it being masked or blocked by leaves and trees, but here it swallowed the world before her for the moments that her now green eyes adjusted to it.

"Whoa..." Kiki breathed down by Lily's left foot.

'Whoa' was the only word for it. As soon as her eyes had adjusted and Lily could make out what was in front of her, she felt her jaw gape open. The sight before her was nothing like she had ever known, nothing she had ever imagined.

She had been told to venture to the right of the witches' congregation first, so it didn't look obvious that she was coming directly from the woods, but the Elders had not told her that there was something like this waiting for her!

Down the hillside where the woods started, there was a large mass of organised rock, stone and carved wood. There were chunks of metals that could never have occurred naturally seeming to hold the wood to the stone, or maybe they were just for decoration? As she walked down the hillside, her eyebrows furrowed into a confused expression, Lily couldn't keep her eyes off the first structure. The one that ran around the outside of the settlement. It was at least ten times the height of her, and it seemed to be made purely of grey stone, though there were rectangular holes in the sides of it at different heights. As she got closer, she realised that there was light through those holes and some kind of clear material that reminded her of the ice they used to cover the gaps in their homes to allow sunlight inside.

Coming to a stop, she looked up at the structure with an eyebrow raised while dawning understanding moved across her face. Witches lived within stone homes. Though not naturally occurring stone, it was like the building she had seen in the history books that all those related to mankind had lived in.

Lily was surprised they hadn't moved onto something more... well, pleasant.

As she looked around, she noticed that there seemed to be no end to them as she walked further inside. It was some kind of town, with the stone buildings reaching different heights, some towering over her threatening to outgrow even the oldest oak tree, others sitting timidly in the shadows looking run-down but somehow friendlier. This city was likely as large as their little area of woodland; the first witch settlement on a border between races, just as theirs was one of the first Fairy cities they would come to in the woodland which was said to span to the ends of the world where the stone grew up to meet the sky in a boundary at the world's edge.

People moved around her and flitted from one building to another, some carrying bundles of things Lily couldn't make out but all being followed by at least one companion animal. Cats, rats, bats, dogs, ravens, ferrets, frogs, and even a couple of stoats or mink could be seen trailing after their respective companions.

Strange. Lily thought that the numbers of witches were meant to be low; but from what she could see, every single person that resided here was a witch.

She felt sick at the thought, and with a subtle glance to the cats by her side, they were thinking the same thing. If all these witches were a part of the training to target the fairies, there would be a much bigger war than there ever had been previously!

"Nice shoes!" A voice sounded behind her, causing Lily to jump viciously, her feet actually leaving the ground a little as she scrambled away from the voice and turning around to find the source. Beside her, Kiki had yelped and ran a little away before turning and Oscar had spun on the spot, hackles raised and hissing angrily.

To all their surprise, they were faced with a creased face of a girl who looked around Lily's age. She was laughing hysterically at the response she had been given and waving her hand in front of her as though that would help her calm down. Her chest rising and falling heavily, Lily simply watched the girl with her eyes still wide with unease. She noticed that there were three rats clinging onto the front of the girl's jacket to stop them from falling down into Oscar's reach.

The girl before her had a happy rounded face that was framed gloriously with messy curls of auburn hair that reached her shoulder blades. Her shirt was oversized, falling off one shoulder, with a cute drawn rabbit on the front who had an eyepatch and held an anatomically correct heart in its front left paw. Beneath it in beautiful italic writing read *My heart for yours?*

"Sorry, sorry!" The girl choked out as she began to get her breath back. "I've never seen anyone jump that high in surprise!" She giggled standing up straighter so that Lily could see the thick black choker around her neck with small chains and a black star hanging from it.

Lily must have seemed stunned into silence, but the girl merely smiled brightly up at her before motioning to Lily's feet again.

"Your parents some of those hippy types? I've not seen people use such rustic material for shoes before." Her smile wasn't mocking, but her words caused pink to pepper Lily's cheeks in embarrassment as she looked down at her own feet. The things that had been made for her feet were wound together from fine strips of wood and then a tiny layer of ice was used to keep them shiny.

"Erm... yeah?" Lily's voice was incredibly quiet. Was she going to get caught out for her shoes?? This early on?? Fairies had no need or urge to wear shoes in their kingdom, so they hadn't even known where to start with them. "I don't really like them," she added as an honest thought.

"Well, I can help that!" The girl commented, and Lily only had time to look back up before the girl had pulled a wand out of a pocket in her puffed out short skirt and waved it in the direction of Lily's feet. "*Consilce.*"

Lily couldn't keep her eyes from widening in horror as she looked down. But all she was met with was the sight of her shoes condensing and the material rippling into something much softer on her skin. Soon enough, she was looking down at her feet which were now within slim slip-on shoes rather than ones that hugged her ankles like before. They were black and gleaming, matching her dress and standing out against the grey of the stone floor of the city.

"Wow..." Lily couldn't keep her lips shut this time.

"I know... I should be able to do that without my wand," The girl had started saying "But my wandless magic often goes wrong so I prefer using it to be safe."

Lily looked back up as Oscar and Kiki moved over to sniff at the new shoes curiously.

"Wandless magic?" Lily tilted her head a little with a bit of hope tickling her heart.

"Yeah, my dad says my bloodline should mean I can use it." The girl looked sheepish now "Can you do it?"

Without thinking, Lily nodded though she received a claw to the side of her now visible ankle from Oscar. "Well," She tried to rectify quickly, "I can do some, but I've always been a slow learner."

That was a lie, but it seemed to bring a brighter smile to the girl's face again. "A kindred soul!" She chimed happily before sticking out her right hand in greeting "I'm Diavian Blythe, though you can just call me Dia!"

Lily reached out to take the hand, noting that it was covered in a multitude of small bandages. "I'm Li..." Damn, she hadn't decided on a name "Liliana. Liliana Roselyn; though my friends call me Lil or Lily" She invented hastily.

The girl named Dia didn't seem to have noticed Lily's hesitation and shook her hand almost gleefully. "Pleasure! Say, you aren't by chance heading for the coven centre out of town, are you?"

Lily raised her eyebrow as she let her hand fall back to her side.

"It's just, I didn't like the idea of going alone. I bet most signing up will be able to use wandless magic and be so much better than me." Dia was continuing "But if you were going, we could go together and maybe it'd feel better? I dunno, it's just what I was thinking." Her voice began to trail off at the sight of Lily simply looking at her without any reaction.

"Yeah, ok" Lily agreed quickly but nervously. It would be a very good idea to go into her destination with an actual witch, at least she could just be the quiet one to follow in the wake of this bouncy redhead.

"Really?! Alright!!" Dia really seemed like a bundle of sunshine, it was strange to think that someone like this could be one of the witches who would kill fairies in a few years' time. "Did you need anything from here first?" She asked Lily looking around the entrance to the city, there wasn't much here aside from a couple of places to eat and lots of homes.

"No" Came Lily's answer, still highly nervous of giving anything else away and letting it out that she was no witch.

"Alright, let's go then!"

Lily could never have been prepared to deal with a girl like Diavian Blythe, but she took Lily's hand and tugged her from the city entrance in the direction of the so-called 'coven'.

Dia talked the whole way, not seeming to mind that she either got one-word responses or no response at all.

"This is Snow, Idella and Gary. They're so playful and they always come to give me a cuddle when I need it." She was saying, pointing to the white rat, brown rat and grey rat in turn. "My dad says that they're the weakest companions other than frogs, but they're the best friends I could hope for, you know?"

Lily hummed in agreement. She knew nothing about witch companions, let alone whether they had any difference in strength.

"What are yours called?" Dia asks, looking to the side at Lily to show her that she was expecting an answer this time.

"Oh. Kiki is the smaller one with socks, and Oscar is the larger one." She motioned to them, both trotting along silently either side of her as she walked. So far, they hadn't heard any of the rats utter a single word, so Lily assumed the cats were sticking to the plan of keeping their tongues held too.

"Cute names!" The auburn-haired witch looked down at the cats and gave them a happy wave with her left hand. "Nice to meet you both!"

A low rumbling purr came from Oscar but that was all they could respond with.

Before any more could be said, Lily stopped and found herself looking up at a large gateway which towered above her. It was another stone structure that ran around what was inside, like a fence, though Lily couldn't make out how far it went. It was far too high to think about venturing over and, dotted along the top, there appeared to be large figures standing sentinel.

These same sentinel figures were found at the gateway, one either side of the gate and standing at a colossal height. Lily tilted her head back to look up at the faces. How tall was that? Close to fifteen feet? They were cat-like in form, their giant paws flexing against the floor and their regal faces turned slightly into the pathway where the people would pass. Their fur was grey, but plumage of feathers sprouted off them in different areas. The sentinel on the right had green and yellow feathers, they sprouted from its back and over its two front legs while the green feathers on its head made it look like it was wearing a headdress. The sentinel on the left had a similar headdress style with its feathers, but they were of a deep violet and magenta mix. It had feathers down its sides over the rib areas and instead of a feline tail, it had feathers of the same hues splayed out like the tail of a peacock.

"Custosphinga" Dia whispered in awe as she looked from Lily, wondering why she had stopped, and the sentinel creatures.

"Wha…" Lily stuttered "I've never heard of them?"

"Really??" Dia looked utterly stunned, causing heat to prickle the back of Lily's neck. Had she messed up? "Damn, you from like a farm out in the sticks or something? Your parents really kept you sheltered, huh?"

"Erm… yeah." Lily didn't have to try to look sheepish now, her face was obviously awkward.

"Wow. Well, I'll help where I can! Us slow learners gotta stick together!" Dia grinned brightly before turning to look at the sentinels again. "Custosphinga are basically guards. They were bred to be dutiful and to be able to see the true physical form of those who pass. You know, to keep out any race like fairies or Draconian if they were hiding their wings, scales or horns somehow."

Lily's eyebrows furrowed. What was Draconian? And did it mean that these sentinels would be able to see what she was? Dread filled her in an instant. All other thoughts were lost from her mind. Her green eyes glanced immediately to Kiki and Oscar who were looking up at her, trying to keep their demeanour from becoming obviously nervous.

"So, we just walk past them?" Lily asked with her voice surprisingly steady, though as quiet as always.

"Yup! Come on, they won't do anything to us witches." Dia assured her while linking her arm with Lily's and leading her towards the gateway. Lily tried to keep her legs moving evenly, trying not to show any display of hesitation. She didn't want the sentinels to have any reason to single her out. Though, as she grew closer and could see their eyes, their large red eyes with silver pupils that ran like an 'S' down the centre, Lily knew that she was being viewed all over.

The few seconds that it took to walk past the sentinels seemed like an eternity to her. Her heart was pounding in her chest and the hairs on her neck raised with the feeling of being watched, being seen pure and naked under the gaze of red and silver.

And then, the feeling of their stare was gone. Dia was guiding her further past the gate and into the courtyard leading to the coven.

How Lily had managed to walk past she didn't know, but the relief that spread through her made her want to sink to the ground and rest. But this had only been the first hurdle, the next was right in front of her.

What she faced now, was a huge stone building, longer than it was tall with some spires up high above the centre of the building. From the look of the windows, the building had three floors in most places and four in the central part that reached up higher into the air. The stone wasn't grey like the outer wall, they were white and beautiful, and the ground floor windows and doors were arched and regal.

The courtyard that they stood in was well kept, not wild like the woodland that Lily had grown up in. It was pristine, grass kept at an even length and trimmed back off the stone pathways that led to the doors in the building. Rows of flower beds lined the stone wall that ran around the edge of the courtyard and around the main building.

"Wow! It's awesome in here!" Dia sounded excited beside her, and although she was still filled with dread, Lily could see why. The building truly was stunning in a way Lily could never have described; it wasn't cold like the grey stone from the city. This white stone was oddly inviting, warm and pleasant as it reflected the afternoon autumn sun.

"Come on. Gotta register!" Again, Dia was pulling Lily by their linked elbows towards the main door. Did this girl just have no awareness of how nervous Lily was right now?! Did she have no delicacy?? She pulled Lily along like she was just as excited as Dia was for this. It really made Lily's stomach turn a little to think that Dia was so eager to learn magic which would one day allow her to rip wings from fairies, potentially from Lily's parents.

Taking a deep shuddering breath, Lily tried to calm herself. Having Dia pull her around was allowing her to get places she needed without having to know what she was doing; yes, that would be useful to her. Lily could use that. The logical argument chanted inside her head like a mantra to keep herself from pulling away from the auburn-haired witch and moving away from her in fear. The entrance foyer was huge, the roof arching upwards with artwork painted across the ceiling. The tall windows let the sunlight bathe the interior in a warm light that made the white stone of the walls seem to glow while the brown wooden floor simply glinted from its obviously recent polish.

As if this bright stone image wasn't enough, there was a pair of double doors to the right side of the entrance leading into a small and more dimly lit room. The lighting in there was not from the windows, Lily realised as she was dragged through the doors, mahogany shutters were pulled closed over the windows to block out the sunlight. Lily was stunned to see fire dancing along the cornices at the top of the walls. It was blue in colour and it flickered completely out of reach and forever burning without fuel.

In the blue flickering light, Lily could see a desk in the centre of the small room where both a tall, slim, hooded figure sat in the chair, and a strange hunched creature the size of a hare sat on the left side of the desk. The creature watched them with beady black eyes that reflected the blue fire around the room. It was a slimy-looking creature of pure black, with four legs and a fifth limb sticking out of its chest with six curled talons at the end of spindly digits.

Lily shivered, revolted by the way those creepy black eyes stared at her. Though, she found it no less creepy to focus on the figure completely shadowed by the hood.

Something about it felt like she was being seen through to her core.

"Well, hello there, sweeties" The voice that came from the hood was surprisingly charming. It was a tantalising singsong voice that brought an amazing feeling of calm and joy over those who heard it. It was the total opposite to the feeling which was given from the visual image of the room. "Here to sign up for some glorious learning?"

"Yes, ma'am!" Dia chimed while Lily merely gulped nervously and nodded. "I'm Diavian Blythe and this is Liliana Roselyn. Three rats with me, and two cats with her!"

"Splendid! Would Blythe be similar to Bermet Blythe?" The hooded woman trilled.

Lily glanced to the side at Dia who shuffled uncomfortably but smiled still. "Yes, that was my great grandmother."

"Oh, how wonderful! You'll be a pride of this school then, just like her."

"I-I hope so."

Lily's stomach felt heavier by the second, if Dia's great grandmother was the pride of this school then that would have been about a century ago when the last fairy massacre was, in which case, it was probably because she had ripped a record amount of wings off or something.

"Well, this is wonderful! And you're already friends so I'll place you both in room thirteen in the Purple Spiocus house which is the second house you come to when you exit the main building out the back." The hooded woman was explaining, though she still hadn't risen from her seat. Instead, she motioned to the creepy creature to her right which had stretched out those talon-ended digits and the centre of the hand seemed to glow a sock orange colour "Just place your hand against his, and you'll be able to enter your rooms without any worry throughout the time you are here."

Lily definitely didn't like that idea. Her disgust at the concept of touching the creature must have shown on her face as her eyes glanced down to the cats for reassurance. Unfortunately, they were supposed to be acting like true cats so the sight she was met with was Oscar staring avidly up at the white rat on Dia's shoulder, and Kiki batting at Oscar's tail as it flicked from side to side.

Dia went first, seemingly without any worry in the world. Her hand outstretched and placed itself palm to palm with the creature, and after a moment she pulled back with a smile at Lily. Well, it hadn't hurt her. Though maybe it would sense Lily wasn't a witch.

Swallowing heavily, but aware of the two pairs of witch eyes on her, she stepped forward and placed her palm against the creatures. There was a pleasant heating sensation against the centre of her palm that lasted all of three seconds as though a flame had been lit beneath, then it vanished leaving her skin cool. Turning her hand to look at the palm, Lily was honestly surprised to find that there wasn't even the slightest mark left behind.

"Marvellous! The lessons don't start for another couple of weeks, so just make yourselves at home and have a good look around, girls!" The hooded woman was chiming cheerily before raising a hand that was covered in a black silk glove to motion them to the door.

Lily honestly couldn't believe she had not only got past the sentinels at the gate but had somehow not been detected by whatever that creepy creature was.

"Awesome! We get to be roommates with someone we already know!" Dia seemed to have both figured out and accepted that Lily was not talkative, but she took Lily's elbow again anyway and started dragging her through the school in search of the back where they could find the dormitory houses, the cats trailing along behind them as they went.

"Dia," Lily started quietly. "How many roommates are in a room?"

"Just the two I believe, why?"

"My parents never told me much about this place," Lily covered quickly, though she couldn't help but feel more pressured by the minute. If she was honest, she would have liked to have had a room to herself. She would have liked to be able to talk to Oscar and Kiki on an evening to talk through anything they had found out.

Maybe though, if it was only Dia and the rats, there would be some way for her to be able to tell the cats when to take the information back to the woods.

Dia laughed brightly "Did your parents teach you anything?"

Lily had to stifle a look of irritation and instead shrugged as she was pulled along by her elbow "Mostly how to tend to fruit and vegetables." She would have to keep going with a story that made it sound like she was neglected being taught most of the extensive magical information about the witches' world, as though her parents had just taken all that as a given in the world and had thought it best only to teach her how to handle the land.

"Ah, so basically you're a farming daughter?"

Lily nodded without verbally committing to anything.

"Well, you'll have a lot to catch up on then" Dia chortled as she finally reached the door out to the rear of the large building and pushed it open.

The outside here was just as well kept as the front, but the pathway that extended from the door split off six times to six incredibly tall, long and beautiful buildings that ran along the tall grey stone outer wall, three on the right side and three on the left. Like the main building, they were made of white stone and they had smooth white pillars stretching from ground to roof at each corner. Ornamental engravings were designed into them, creating grab holds for vines to cling to as they grew up the walls, each dormitory bearing different flowers giving them an obviously different aesthetic. It seemed that the colours of the flowers that climbed the walls were there to match the colour spiocus the dormitory was named after.

They walked up to the path to the building with purple wisteria climbing up its side. In front of the main entrance stood a large stone statue of a winged horse with a spiral horn sticking out jagged from its forehead and its muzzle looking like it was the skull with skin ripped back a third of the way up the face. Tilting her head, Lily glanced up at it with a concerned look moving over her features. What was that?

Before she could think further on that, she felt a burning against her palm again. Turning her hand to face upward so she could look at the palm that had been touched by that black creature in the registration room; on it had appeared a glowing purple spiocus, a small body rippling in purple spirit essence was unfolding on her palm, it had front legs which uncurled from its body and large ears that poked out from behind a strange mask that hid its face from sight. From the corner of her eye, Lily could see the purple glow on Dia's palm as well. In front of them, the eyes of the horse-like statue glowed the same colour and slowly the stone creaked as it moved to walk to the side and reveal the door.

"That was cool!" Dia grinned, while watching the spiocus on her hand as they walked inside. The interior was less interesting than the outside, filled with long corridors with doors adjacent to them all the way along. From the look of the spiral staircase in the centre, there were around seven or eight floors.

They had to go to the second floor to find room thirteen as there were eight rooms per floor. As they walked towards the room, both girls looked down at their palms which had burned once more. The spiocus had yawned, the mouth appearing from underneath the mask and a deep orange number '13' shining in the depth of the dark mouth. The door to their room clicked to signify it had unlocked at their presence.

With another sideward glance to the cats, who were both looking anxious, Lily stepped inside after her new roommate.

Chapter 5: Quintegia

The room inside was spacious, with decent sized single beds placed foot to foot at the end of the room leaving a large space that held a pair of comfortable chairs in front of writing desks. Either side was the mirror image of the other, except the left side of the room had a mahogany door which opened out into a washroom which was glorious to behold.

Dia kept dragging Lily around for the rest of that afternoon. She said that they were exploring the school but that seemed to involve poking her head into every door she came to and then telling Lily what resided inside. Lily was more interested in looking around at where everything was and trying to commit it to memory. Oscar and Kiki had gone for a wander now they were inside the school, perhaps it was because they had deemed that something cats would be more than likely to do or maybe they had followed the rats lead as the three had stayed inside the dorm room. Witch companions appeared to be a lot more alike to their wild counterparts.

Both had noticed that others walking out of the registration room were carrying bags with them. It occurred to Lily then that she must have seemed strange arriving without any possessions and was grateful to her luck that she seemed to have bumped into the only witch who also didn't have any. Dia didn't mention it, didn't ask Lily as to why she hadn't had anything. But Lily figured that it was because she didn't want the same question directed back at her.

The dynamic of Dia babbling and Lily listening in a polite silence seemed to form between them quickly. Dia talked about all sorts of things, about how she wanted to learn how to use magic without her wand because her whole family had been able to, about what her rats were like and how old they were; it seemed that Witches had the same companion ritual at the same age as Fairies did. Lily wondered if that was something that dated back to when they lived aside one another. Dia talked over dinner about her favourite foods, and she wondered aloud if the food itself that had been served to them by magically-moving utensils at the end of the canteen hall had been created by magic or if there was a kitchen hidden somewhere. Lily had nothing to contribute but the way she looked at Dia made it obvious she was listening with a curiosity that didn't seem to be fading any time soon.

Lily had decided that the more knowledge she could get the better, and if Dia was so willing to talk then Lily didn't think there would be any reason to stop her.

The following morning, Lily had gotten up at the crack of dawn, too nervous of this whole situation to sleep properly.

"Kiki and I are going to spend the day really wandering around, seeing if we can check out the other dorms or rooms to see if there's anyone talking about anything big." Oscar whispered to her as he sat on the side of her bath. Kiki remained outside so she could meow loudly if Dia woke up so Oscar could stop talking out loud.

"Ok." Lily nodded, enjoying the warmth of the water. Back in the fairy kingdom they never got the heat of their water up this high and frankly, it was beautiful. "I was thinking I'd pop to the library and see if there is any information about this place, so I don't raise too many questions."

"Good idea; Dia seems easy to fool but others might get suspicious when you know nothing about witches" Oscar agreed as he lay down and pawed the surface of the water. After a moment, he added, "Are you doing ok, Lil?"

Her green eyes turned to the large cat and a small smile pulled on her lips at Oscar's sign of care. "I'm so scared. I thought this was just going to be a group of witches being trained, not a proper school that I'm going to have to try and convince hundreds of people I'm not an imposter!" Her voice trembled as she spoke her thoughts out loud. "I can't even fit into the race I'm born into, how am I meant to fit into something like this?"

Oscar sighed and walked around the edge of the smooth bath until he was at the side where Lily's head rested. He bent down to nuzzle her wet hair. "You were better than any of the others back home" He purred while licking the temple of her head. "You could do things they couldn't imagine with your magic, and look, you even developed a mixture of magic that changed your look for half a day at a time!! If anyone CAN do this, it's you."

"But…"

"No buts, Lil. I know you don't believe in yourself, but Ki and I do. We've watched you for the last five years, and we plan on watching you for many more." Lily turned her head to kiss Oscar's nose.

She didn't know what to say to that, she didn't believe him, but she knew better not to argue with him. So, she fell into a comfortable silence letting her head flop to the side and rest on his side.

Oscar didn't urge her to move soon, he let Lily soothe and calm in the water which did not go cold. She could have spent hours there. But within the hour Lily was out of that water, dressed, and stood in the library glancing around wondering where she should even start. From the amount Dia seemed to know about this place, Lily figured she should start with the school information first.

The library was a huge domed room with three floors, the two higher floors had bookcases lining the walls while the ground floor had four aisles of deep mahogany bookcases. Lily took a full walk through the library, gazing at the sections. The ground floor had sections for: history, structure spells, flying enchantments, flying theory, mythical creatures care and use, ancient legends. The first floor was dedicated to spell-work and the top floor was potions.

Returning to the ground floor, Lily made her way along the far-left aisle which had history books lining the bookcase along the wall. There were all sorts of books; *History of humans. The divergence of the human genomes. Magical Revolution: An Expanse of Jobs. The Great Magic War.* Finally, Lily came to a smaller section on the historical architecture and creation of the school. She picked up a few of those books and walked across to one of the study tables at the end of the room where long windows let streaks of morning gold wash over the chairs.

The first book, *Building Quintegia,* just told her how the building was made. What magic was used to build the structure, what magic was woven into the stone around the fencing wall and what was used to keep the water hot and the flames alight. Maybe it wasn't what she was looking for, but Lily couldn't help but be fascinated by everything she read. The flames had come from a specific type of small dragon and magic had been used to engrave that flame into the walls of the school. According to the book, this had been the last of those dragons to have been seen in five millennia.

The second book told her something similar just written and compiled by a different author. But the third book, *Quintegia: The Art of Learning,* described much more that would be useful to Lily now.

> *'Named for its founder, Quintina Byrne, Quintegia has in time become one of the greatest schools for witchcraft. It has turned*

out the highest achievers throughout history with many noted and celebrated people rising to high standings in society. The school itself remains to this day a place both of learning, and of fundamental culture structure.'

The start of the book wasn't the most interesting of reads, the introductory first chapter spoke about the wonders and glory of the school. Other chapters talked about the greatest warriors and the most intelligent that had passed through there. However, it was the chapters on the structure of the school that Lily focused on. It explained that the main lessons revolved around four main topics; spells, potions, creature care, and flying. Lily noted as she scanned the kinds of things usually taught that most of it was not stuff that could be used to fight in a war against Fairies.

Lily then turned to a chapter on the dormitory houses out the back.

'Six dormitories exist, they are located out the back of the main school building in rows along the fence walls. Three on the left are the girls' dorms, three on the right are for boys. Each house is named for the different colours of the species Spiocus. Purple Spiocus, Red Spiocus, and Black Spiocus represent the girls' dormitories, while the Blue Spiocus, Yellow Spiocus, and Green Spiocus represent the boys' dormitories.'

Lily blinked down at it; this creature called a Spiocus was still not something she understood. Getting back to her feet she walked to the aisle filled with books on mythical creatures, scanning a few until she found Spiocus in the index of one book named *Spirit Creatures of Modern Times*.

Sitting back down she skimmed the pages until she reached a description;

> *'Small spirit-like creatures that float through walls and cause jokes and pranks. They love to cause mischief and are often responsible for accidents. They can be tamed, but only by someone who will give them plenty of chances to reap havoc throughout their lives. Their general characteristics are small bodies and huge flapping ears with rippling spirit colours surrounding them like fur. They have long tails that propel them through the air away from the scenes they cause, and their faces are covered with masks that represent the innocence level of their potential jokes.'*

Lily's green eyes danced over the drawings that were found flicking and glowing over the edges of the page around the writing. They were just like the Spiocus that had glowed on her palm except they were more intricate in detail and somehow much more beautiful. Closing the book and placing it to the side to take back to the dormitory with her later, Lily turned back to the original books.

The information about the dormitories continued on to explain that each dorm had its own mythical creature as a mascot and that a stone carving of these creatures stands before the door of the dorm house and will only move aside when someone approaches it with the glow of the right brand on their palm. These statues were originally brought in to prevent any uninvited visitors. The brand on the palm was brought in later so that no words or keys needed to be used as, often during exam periods, students would be laden in books and would struggle to get to any keys or door handles.

> 'The dormitory houses soon gained casual names: Moreq, Canton, Trean, Nocto, Ales, and Macella, in relation to the chosen mascots. The mascots of the dormitories were chosen to be six legends which matched up with the six colours of the Spiocus colours.'

Blinking down at the page before her, Lily focused on the word 'Macella'. Her stomach twisted with unease and she quickly got up once again to find a book that would explain and describe six legendary creatures spoken of throughout the world. Sure enough, upon skipping through the pages, she found one with the heading 'Macellavir' and she couldn't suppress a shudder. It couldn't be written here. It was a tale told to Fairy children to keep them in the kingdom boundaries. It wasn't… it couldn't be real.

> 'A two-legged beast which stomps through the undergrowth of woods and forests looking for

lost souls to feed on. No one quite knows what it looks like, but it is said to have a dragon skull over its face to keep the true form from being shown, and rot and moss grow over its skeletal body making it look more like a rotting tree when it stands unmoving.

It has a specific taste for human descended races. However, there are no documented reports of this creature to ever have existed. It is likely that this was simply a legend that started with humans and followed the generations down the races' evolutions.'

The words that reassured her that this was still just a legend made Lily sigh heavily in relief. So, the mascots were just make-believe legends. Thank all that was powerful in the world. Leaning back in her chair, Lily blinked up at the ceiling trying to calm her rapidly beating heart. At least she wasn't in that dormitory, if she had to look up at the stone replica of a Macellavir that she had feared all her childhood, she wasn't sure she would be able to keep it together.

After a moment or two, she turned her attention back to the book, flicking through to find the other five legends. Cantonitrua was the legend used for the yellow dormitory; it was apparently some kind of large dog-like creature with yellow straggled fur and a forked tail that all carried electrical charges. The red dormitory was linked to the Alesrex, the fabled King of the Dragons which was said to resemble a lion/dragon hybrid. The book described that it had grey scales covering its body, tail, and legs, but there was a deep red mane of fur that framed its rounded face that sported two pairs of different coloured eyes. Trean, or the Green Spiocus dormitory, was named for the three-headed snake legend, Treanguis, while the blue dormitory was named after the skeletal manta ray that swam through the night skies named Noctosseus.

Finally, she found the legend which stood outside her new dormitory in the form of a statue. The horse creature was rumoured to be the winged horse which death can be seen riding through scenes of tragic wars. It looked like an ancient unicorn that had gone very wrong, its colours weren't portrayed on the stone statue, but the tail, mane, and eyes had all taken on a glowing purple colour over what would have been a silver mane and golden honest eyes in a normal unicorn.

Lily took the book on legends and myths to the canteen with her while she had a late breakfast. The canteen was open almost all day, with a couple of hour breaks while they changed up the menu between the three meals. It didn't appear to need staff, the food refilled itself and the utensils served up to anyone who came over with a plate or bowl. There were so many kinds of food to choose from, food that Lily had never seen before. Meat. The meat was a new one. Fairies didn't eat meat up in their kingdom. They survived with vegetables, fruit and dairy made from the milk of a Fugacapra; a winged goat which they bred specifically. So, Lily discovered meat for the first time that morning, and if she was honest, she wasn't sure about the salty taste that came with whatever meat it was. The diet of Witches was richer in taste and sauces though, there were spices and herbs that Lily had never come across.

The afternoon found Lily back in the library, each time she read something new it sparked up another tangent of thought which she wanted to read into.

By the time she left later that evening, Lily had piled into her arms as much as she could carry; three bulky books and four smaller ones. They were mostly about the school history and the creatures, but one of the larger books went through the basics of spell work.

Walking out of the library, she took to walking through the small corridors towards the exit to the dormitories. Turning the corner onto the hallway with the exit, Lily felt something crash into her shoulder and knock her a little, sending the books in her arms tumbling to the floor with dull thuds.

"Put some shoes on freak, maybe you'll be able to get out of the way quicker!" A scathing female voice caused Lily's eyes to glance down at her feet, only realising now that she had forgotten to put those shoes on. Turning her green eyes to the female who was walking past her, Lily could only take note of her overall image. She was a beautiful girl with long layered light brown hair which swayed as she walked. She wore a long black robe with a belt tied around the middle to accentuate her body shape, and from the brief look of her face, she wore an expression that showed she thought herself much higher than someone who didn't wear shoes in school.

The first impression made Lily think of River Barrett. Great, another one like that. Well, she thought as she crouched down to collect up the books, at least it wasn't anything new to deal with.

"Hey, you alright there?"

Lily jumped a little as a new voice sounded behind her and someone stepped beside her crouched down. Her breath caught in her throat at the close proximity she found the male in. She could see every strand of stubble on his square jaw, and the green of his eyes seemed to glitter in the evening sun that peaked through the windows of the hallway.

"Um..." She stammered. As of yet, she hadn't spoken to anyone today considering the library books were checked out by an ink quill that acted alone.

The male chuckled softly, "Smooth. Here, let me help." Without waiting for any more response, he reached out a strong arm and picked up the three larger books before Lily could reach for them.

"Thank you," Lily whispered quietly as she scrambled to grab the four other books and get back to her feet. She could feel his eyes watching her from where he still crouched but Lily couldn't force herself to look at his face. She wasn't sure why, but somehow, she was scared that from this close, someone would be able to see through her.

"My pleasure." Finally, he had pushed himself to his feet, Lily's books still held against his chest. "How about I walk you the rest of the way?"

That offer caused Lily's eyes to snap up and blink at the male who was about a head taller than her. His hair was incredibly short on the sides, but the top was messy and brushed slightly to the left giving him a messy fringe. However, it was the kind smile that really took her aback. Even when Jared had helped her back home, he had always rushed off to avoid the vicious backlash from his mother. So, the bright kind smile that she was faced with now was something incredibly new.

The young man had started to walk down the corridor and Lily had no choice but to jog to catch up with him.

"You, erm, you don't have to do this" She stammered.

"I want to," he smiled again, as though trying to reassure her. "I thought the lack of shoes was cute, and that girl knocking you was a liche move." Lily felt her cheeks heating in a flush at that; she had never been referred to as cute for anything she did outside of her family. She opened her mouth to reply but couldn't find any words, so she shut her mouth again. "So... you got a name?" The guy asked tentatively, opening the door and holding it open with his foot for her to pass through.

"Liliana."

"Well, nice to meet you, Liliana. I'm Finnigan, but everyone calls me Finn." As Dia had, this Finnigan didn't seem to mind that Lily didn't say much. "Which dorm are you in? I'm in Nocto or rather, the Blue Spiocus dorm."

"I'm in the purple one. Moreq?" Was she remembering the casual names of the dormitories correctly?

"Oh, nice! The winged death unicorn; that statue definitely looks the coolest out of all of them. Ours doesn't quite work, it's just a weird skeleton."

"Well, it is a flying skeleton of a manta ray." Lily started after what she had read that day "Though, how does it move out of the way?"

The Morequcor stepped out of the way as a horse would, she would assume the Cantonitrua, the Macellavir, and the Alesrex would step aside in a similar way, and that the Treanguis slithered like a snake, but she couldn't imagine how a manta ray skeleton would move.

"They were pretty clever about that," Finnigan replied, seeming to be very happy about the fact Lily had actually asked something rather than just giving him another short answer. "The statue was carved as part of the front wall, so it basically swims over the door and then back off it as the students with the brand get close enough. Yeah, it's pretty cool to see." He added, noticing the raised eyebrows on Lily's face.

"I can imagine." She glanced over to the dormitory with the manta ray skeleton over it.

"One day I'll show you?" Finnigan asked.

"Oh. No, that's ok." Lily said quickly, her cheeks growing darker as she reached to take the large books from Finnigan. "Thank you for these." With that, she bustled off to the stone Morequcor which stepped out of her way with nothing but a small glow of its eyes responding to the brand on her palm.

She didn't breathe easy until she walked back into her room and let herself rest back against the door behind her. Lily had never spoken to someone for that long, and she didn't even know how to handle something like that.

"Whoa! Lessons haven't even started Lil?"

Lily almost dropped the books again at the voice of her roommate. She was not used to this whole 'not being alone' thing!

"Makes sense that you were quiet, you're a bookwyrm!" Dia chimed with a laugh as she watched Lily walk over to the desk to put the books down. "Not a bad thing, mind! You can help me out; I'm not a reader per se, I'm much more into practical stuff. Found anything interesting in them?"

Lily didn't answer. Instead, she was staring down at her bed with confusion. There was a pile of mostly black clothing folded there.

"Erm… where did they…?" She started.

"Oh," Dia flushed a little and rubbed the back of her neck sheepishly "I just thought because you didn't bring bags like me, that you could do with some clothes as well. I went back into town to get some material to turn into clothes."

Lily picked up the top piece of clothing and let it unfold in her grasp. It was a long-sleeved shirt with a simple design on the front of a black cat in front of a midnight fog.

"I didn't know what you liked…"

"It's amazing," Lily whispered, feeling oddly emotional "Thank you."

Dia grinned. "My pleasure! I made you some better shoes too, I noticed you'd left yours behind this morning so thought you'd want some more comfortable ones." She motioned to the area under Lily's desk and she saw that there were four pairs of shoes of different styles underneath.

"I just… forgot the shoes this morning" Lily admitted as she sat down on the chair beside her desk. "And I got mocked for it on the way back."

"Uncool!" Dia exclaimed before pushing Lily to recount the story of the day. This girl really was quite pushy, but it seemed to pry more words from Lily than anyone outside her family had done previously.

Once she had recounted the day, Dia had decided that she didn't like the brown-haired girl, but she seemed more focused on the messy-haired guy that had helped Lily.

"Finnigan? As in Finnigan Byrne?" She demanded.

"Erm, maybe? I didn't ask his last name. Why?"

"Byrne! As in, a descendant of the founder of this place, Quintina Byrne?! Damn!" Dia looked like she wanted to laugh "You get in good with someone like that and this school will be smooth sailing for you! Was he cute?"

The question stunned Lily who simply blinked at her roommate. "What?"

"Come on, dish. Was he cute?" Dia asked again. Girl talk had never ever been something Lily had imagined herself being involved in. And she hadn't even thought about it when she had looked at Finnigan briefly; nor did she know what was deemed as attractive in the witch world.

"Erm, I dunno. I mean, I suppose his eyes were quite pretty" She said thinking hard about his image "They seemed to sparkle?"

"Ooooh!" Dia squealed a little causing Lily's eyebrow to raise "Sounds like you liked what you saw!"

Lily flushed dark, feeling incredibly uncomfortable with a notion such as that. Dia seemed to take the flush as confirmation and spent the rest of the evening teasing Lily until they finally were tired enough to go to bed.

Lying there, Lily did think about Finnigan, but not in the way she had been teased for. If he truly was the descendant of the woman who had founded this school, Lily should keep her distance from him. If he was connected to any high ups, he would be a very dangerous person for her to have around. No matter how kind he had been. No matter how bright his smile had been.

Lily surely could not risk it.

Chapter 6: First Day

"Come on! I want a seat at the front!" Dia exclaimed six days later, on a bright morning.

The rest of the week had gone by without anything else occurring. Lily had spent her time going through basic spell books and practising a few of them with Dia. Dia, it turned out, was not kidding about her liking the practical side of things; she would get incredibly bored when it came to the reading and theory of the spells, but she jumped into practice immediately. This led to things in their room exploding or flying randomly across the room, but that just brought laughter to both girls' lips.

It was very strange to laugh so easily with another person. But Dia made it so easy. She was so open and so bright that Lily soon got caught up in it. Dia's mistakes also made it so that Lily felt less self-conscious trying out the spells as well.

After those few days, Dia seemed to have decided that she was comfortable and that Lily was officially her friend in this school. And now, she bounced the end of Lily's bed excitedly, causing the two cats to growl in warning while Lily whined in protest.

"The sun's only just coming out!" Lily grumbled.

"Yeah, but we can get to class early and get good seats!" Dia insisted, now taking hold of Lily's left foot through the covers and shook it. It was an idea that Lily didn't really like. To be sat right under the nose of a fully-grown witch who would be able to watch her at such a close range, she was sure they would see through her sooner or later.

But she doubted she'd win the debate, so Lily just let out a small groan before pushing herself up from her pillow to look at her roommate. Dia was already dressed in a lace skirt that looked more like a tutu and a long-sleeved shirt which was tucked into that. The shirt had a purple Spiocus that moved around, the sewed pattern moving easily over the grey base colour of the shirt.

In this week alone, Lily was amazed at the creativity of the magic Dia could use. She could create such fun clothing from mere scraps from the local town, and the shoes she had made for Lily were so much more comfortable than the first pair she had. Lily still didn't like shoes though, and she couldn't help but glare down at them slightly in distaste once she was washed and dressed. How witches could just wander around with their feet and toes cramped away in these tight bound casings, she didn't know.

She followed Dia down to the canteen for breakfast, leaving the cats to fall back to sleep on the bed now becoming drenched in the morning sunlight. Both Oscar and Kiki were falling into a more normal set of cat behaviours easily; they slept a lot more and they wandered in and out through the open window. The purple wisteria plant vines were thick enough to allow the cats to clamber up and jump down from.

Lily missed their company, but she knew that if they were constantly by her feet they would raise a lot of questions. The companions of witches didn't seem quite as intricately bound to the soul of their witch as fairies experienced.

They had a quick breakfast, mostly because Dia kept hurrying Lily and Lily was too nervous of her first lessons to have much appetite. So, after a couple of slices of heated bread which Dia called toast, they headed out of the canteen and back to the room where they had registered to pick up their timetables for lessons. The creepy black creature was the only thing in there, and it scrambled across the table and cabinets in a very awkward fashion, as though its slimy-looking limbs were not working properly. It trilled and growled to itself while moving, taking a few moments to realise someone had entered. When it did, Lily felt her palm heat up as those beady black eyes looked at them. It was like the brand on her palm was being analysed. The creature scampered across the main six piles of paper until it stood by the pile second to the right. Its fifth limb took hold of two of the papers and held them out to the girls.

"Awesome! Thanks!" Dia stepped closer and took the papers, handing one to Lily before scanning her own. "Please tell me we have the same; you got Distortion with Warlock Mayai and Tinctures with Sorceress Panga this morning?"

Lily nodded.

"Cool." Dia grabbed hold of her wrist to drag her out of the room and up the main flight of stairs to the second floor where the first lesson was meant to be. The corridors were long and filled with rooms, though Lily couldn't figure out what they would all be used for.

Relying on Dia to lead her the right way, Lily looked over the lesson plan in her hand. Monday had Distortion and Tisane lessons in the morning with Flying and a free period in the afternoon. Tuesday was free in the morning with Elixirs and Maceration in the afternoon. Wednesday morning was dedicated to Creature Handling, while the afternoon had Enchantments following a free period. Thursdays had a second flying lesson after a free period first thing and a whole four-hour afternoon of Tinctures. Finally, Fridays had Transmutation first thing through to lunch, then Charms and one final free period.

"There's a lot of free periods." She observed, not really expecting a response. But of course, Dia would always take up the opportunity to speak.

"Yep! Though don't go thinking that those are to relax! I heard a neighbour talking and they said that they had to use all those free periods to practice spells and to go over theory just to keep up with the pace."

Lily frowned at the paper. That would not leave her much time to look around for information she was here to find.

"Oh! Here we are!" Dia exclaimed, pulling Lily's thoughts back to reality before they could begin to make her worry again.

The classroom inside was, of course, nothing like Lily had ever experienced. There were desks and chairs all facing forward to look at a desk at the front where the teacher must sit, Lily assumed. It was a very cold and lifeless area to work in. But she was still dragged to the table at the front by the left wall and didn't argue while sitting down with her wand on the desk in easy reach. As she sat down, the paper appeared in front of her alongside an inkwell and quill.

Slowly the rest of the class shuffled in, some looking as excited as Dia, others looking bored already.

Finally, the teacher entered. He was a gangly man with a serious look on his sharp-featured face. Warlock Mayai came to stop by the desk and turned around, turning up to make sure his brown hair was still smoothly brushed to the side. Immediately, Lily felt very nervous as his eyes scowled around the room to look over all those who were attending.

"Good morning." His voice was low and almost monotonous "I'm Warlock Mayai, you will have me for two of your classes this twelve-month semester, and one class in the following semester. Today, though, I will be going over the basic rules of spell work so that you are all brought up to the same speed as one another."

"Oh, joy." A voice whispered behind Lily, though she didn't look around to see who the female voice belonged to. It was a familiar voice, which only made Lily less willing to turn around.

Warlock Mayai didn't seem to have noticed the whisper though and had instead turned to the board to write down some points.

"The five basic rules were put together by Master Baird and Crone Starrett three centuries back after experimenting with as many kinds of magic routes they could think of..." His voice was already boring. Lily had never really done well in her lessons back home, but none had sounded this blank when they talked. It was like listening to a textbook read aloud by something that had no soul.

The Baird and Starrett rules in a nutshell were: something cannot be created from nothing, a substance or object cannot be vanished into non-existence, spells do not work properly without incantation, and spells cannot create true love nor create true life.

"The only things that look like they are summoned out of thin air, are light and water." Warlock Mayai was continuing as quills scratched to note his words down. Dia was already bored and doodling on her sheet. "That is, of course, because light and water exist around us and the magic simply pulls it in from the surroundings so that we can use them."

Lily had never had to write for her lessons in the past, so she wrote down what he said in small snippets to make sure she kept up.

"This use of light and water will be the basis for visual distortion which will be the first half of this distortion component in your learning. So, first up is to make sure you all are able to create both light and water at will."

Lily gulped; she knew she could create both happily without any incantations. She would have to keep herself from willing either into existence with her usual methods.

"Today will be on the spell *Luxina* for light; next week we will tackle the water spell *Ominoa*." He continued without worrying to stop and see if anyone had anything to say. "The incantation for both is simple, but to actually draw in enough light and water from the surroundings to be multiplied and utilised is a difficult feat. So, we will begin with you putting your quills down and picking up your wands until you've got the first incantation down."

Even though it was a two-hour lesson, the majority of it was spent with all students staring down at their wands muttering the incantation over and over again.

"*Luxi!*" Dia was half shouting now, only gaining a small glow at the end of the wand. Lily wasn't doing any better, in fact, she was struggling to make the magic happen without relying on her fairy derived magic.

"You guys are pathetic," That voice behind her sounded again, and this time Lily did glance around. It was the same beautiful girl with long layered light brown hair that had knocked her books down in the corridor.

"Don't be a Liche!" Dia snapped back at her.

"I'm not, just telling the truth" The girl drawled "Can't even make the basics work." Unlike them, she had a bright shine of line coming from the end of her wand and it didn't seem to waver even as she let her focus shift more to them than the spell.

"Tch." Dia grumbled, turning her back on the girl and looking down at her own wand, trying again to try and prove herself to be better than that. It didn't work.

Lily shook her head. "Ignore her, we'll get there."

"How can you just ignore that?" Dia half snarled, though all she received was a small shrug from Lily. It was easy to not comment back to someone like the girl behind them, it was just another River Barrett from home. Lily had long since stopped arguing against these things and had long since started believing the words. This time, however, she was comforted by the fact that she could have created a much larger and brighter ball of light if she had been able to use her usual methods. She was just struggling to adapt it to witch-style magic.

By the end of the lesson, there hadn't been much improvement and Dia was in a thoroughly bad mood. Lily walked along beside her, feeling exhausted by the day already, but was glad that the girl decided to get a seat towards the back of the second class of the morning. This classroom was on the ground floor, at the far left of the building and the interior was wider with more spacious seats. Each seat had a small table just off to the side of it which had paper and quill waiting, but what was more interesting to Lily was the deep-set metal bowls.

Tisanes must have been something to do with potions and those bowls must be for mixing whatever Tisanes were.

Sorceress Panga was already in the classroom and waiting at the front, fidgeting her hands almost nervously. Despite the shy aura, Lily suspected she would feel more comfortable under the gaze of this lady than she had done under Warlock Mayai's eye previously.

Dia sat beside her with her arms crossed, clearly not looking forward to more basics in case she couldn't get them right again. Thankfully, Lily noticed the sour-voiced female was not in her class this time.

"Hey there, mind if I sit?" Another familiar voice made her jump and she looked up, a small flush playing on her cheeks as she met those glittering green eyes. Finnigan Byrne was smiling down at her and Dia, another male waiting beside him to take the fourth seat.

"Um." Lily started before looking at Dia who was smirking openly at her.

"Of course, you can!" Dia exclaimed, reaching past to hold out her hand to the two boys. "I'm Dia Blythe, Lily's roommate."

"So, you're the chatty one of the two, huh?" Finn chuckled, shaking Dia's hand. "I'm Finn, this is my roommate Rainer, though I call him Ray whether he likes it or not."

"Rainer's my last name, but I don't think I'm going to fight the nickname with him raving on." Rainer rolled his eyes but grinned in a manner that suggested he didn't really mind while shaking Dia's hand as well. He shared a slightly awkward wave with Lily but didn't comment.

"I told him about you," Finn explained as though that was normal "So he knows you're shy."

An awkward smile pulled on her lips. What was Lily meant to say to that? A thanks of some kind? Or was he mocking her in some way that she didn't understand?

"How have you been?" He asked as the rest of the class settled themselves down.

"Erm... I've been ok." Lily couldn't keep herself from smiling a little at the genuine look in his eyes. "Though, the class is starting."

"Ah, a teacher's pet too." Rainer chuckled, running his fingers through his long black fringe. "You always did like the bright ones."

"Hush up!" Finn smacked his friend lightly, but Lily simply let out a small sigh. As if someone like Finn would ever like her, and she would likely prove in this lesson that she was hardly bright.

She flushed as she realised the thoughts she was having. There was no chance of anything occurring, he was a witch and she was a fairy. And he was a Byrne! A descendant of the one who started this school to make sure they were able to fight and kill Lily's kind! She had to keep some distance otherwise he might figure out what she was up to.

"Good morning everyone!" Sorceress Panga was saying "Welcome to Tisanes. For those who aren't aware of this brand of potion-making, Tisanes are potions used to cure most effects of Tinctures and Philtres which you will also be learning during your time here. Tinctures have a positive mental effect on the drinker, while Philtres have a negative mental effect."

"Wonder if a tincture could make us quicker learners" Dia whispered to Lily who couldn't help but chuckle.

"That'd be useful. But we'd have to learn to make it first."

"Damn. That's true."

The two girls exchanged amused looks before looking back towards Sorceress Panga who was discussing the more in-depth differences between Tinctures and Philtres. It seemed this would be an introductory lesson that involved no practical and just theory of the uses and differences of the three types of potions which Sorceress Panga would be teaching them over their time here.

By the end of the lesson, Lily was convinced that their first morning of lessons every week would be a chore to get through. Warlock Mayai was boring as anything to listen to, and Sorceress Panga seemed to take far too long to explain anything.

"I thought this was going to be great," sighed Dia as they left, raising a lazy wave to Finn and Rainer as they walked off. Lily missed the smile that Finn flashed her way because her eyes were trained on the ground.

"I wonder if flying will be any easier," Lily's voice was as quiet as always, but within a week Dia seemed to have developed a habit of listening out for it.

"Probably not! We have to learn how to make the objects fly before we can even learn how to fly them!" She sounded exasperated. "I think we'll be spending all of our free periods trying to get the incantations to work properly."

"At least we can practice during the free periods and in the room if we practice together?" Was that hope in Lily's voice? She knew she needed to look around, but she also needed not to get kicked out for being useless at magic.

Dia looked delighted at the suggestion, perking up immediately. "Yeah! We'll practice so much we'll be top of the class!"

Lily nodded.

"Let's get our energy up for the afternoon!" And once again, Lily found her elbow taken hold of, Dia dragging her into a faster pace towards the canteen so they could get a larger lunch.

She knew it was wrong to think it, but there was something very enjoyable about Dia Blythe's company.

The afternoon was a lot more fun. Warlock Parvoz was a youthful man with incredibly short brown hair that couldn't be styled. He had a bright smile as he stood out waiting for them in the front greens.

"Come on, all of you! We'll get started as soon as you are all lined up here!" He clapped his hands together happily.

"It's a good thing it's a nice day," Dia mumbled receiving a small nod of agreement from Lily. "It won't be soon enough though I suppose. Will we have to come out here even when it's cold and raining, do you reckon?"

Lily looked up at the sky and shrugged softly "I would imagine so? We can't really fly around inside."

Dia laughed brightly. "Now that would be fun! Though, knowing me I'd probably break a window or something."

They laughed together until the rest of the class filtered out of the building and lined up before the male who waited patiently. At long last, they were all there and Warlock Parvoz seemed to bounce a little on the spot as he began the lesson.

"Flying!" He began, "It's a fantastic feeling when you manage to get the right piece of equipment for you and you're up in the air with smooth grace."

Lily felt a pang of pain in her chest that she was greatly familiar with. The pain that she had every time she looked at the other fairies flying around while her feet were planted solidly on the floor. This time though, there was a feeling that she had never felt before that mingled with it. What was that? It was a strange warming feeling that seemed to cuddle her from the inside. It gave her heart a very light feeling while at the same time causing it to beat heavily inside her chest.

Hope. Nerves. Excitement.

If she could pull this off, would she really be able to see what it was like to fly?

"Now, obviously, unlike Fairies and Draconian, we are not natural flyers. However, over time we have come up with methods to use different equipment to successfully fly." Warlock Parvoz was saying "The most commonly used are brooms, footwear, cloaks, rugs, and boards. Others have been used but balance and manoeuvrability on them were found to be incredibly awkward."

Walking over to a large bag by the side of them all, he picked it up and walked along the row of students getting them to place their hands inside and pull out something from it. Lily did as she was told, opening her hand to find a small pair of boots in them. Beside her, Dia was holding a tiny cloak in burgundy colour. They exchanged quizzical looks, neither knowing what they were meant to do with something so small.

Parvoz was soon explaining, thankfully. With a flick of his wand and a muttered incantation, the objects held in everyone's hand grew to their proper size. "We will be practising how to apply flying spells to the objects you have picked out. Then we will learn how to fly with all types until you discover which one you are most comfortable with."

"Now, the incantation for the *Volantratio* spell is '*Volantra*'," Warlock Parvoz continued happily. "It's performed with a clockwise twist of the hand during the last syllable of the incantation. Like this... *Volantra!*" At the precise moment of the 'tra' in the word, he twisted his wrist to the right. The curved board in front of him shuddered and then rose in front of him to hover in mid-air.

A ripple of excitement moved through the class. Apparently, flying was something that interested many who couldn't fly naturally, Lily thought.

"Right, now it might take a while for you all to get this, but once you've got a spell to stick permanently, you'll feel much better about the idea of letting it carry you a long way off the ground." He chuckled "I've fallen out the air on a badly enchanted rug and broke my legs, so I wouldn't recommend rushing into the air."

The class rippled with laughter, but it was probably a good warning that came with a personal touch, unlike the textbook warnings that you could read.

The incantation was not an easy one to pull off, as expected, but now that Lily wasn't concentrating so hard on not using fairy magic, she found it easy to focus herself. Or perhaps it was due to her sheer wish to fly that made her mind clear perfectly for this; not worried about what anyone in the class was doing.

"Volantra." She twisted her wrist as she spoke clearly, and on her fifth attempt, the boots hovered up into the air in front of her.

"Whoa! Nice one Lil!" Dia sounded incredibly impressed to her side. Lily grinned, for the first time, towards someone other than her family. She could never have explained the warmth she felt having someone outside her family beside her getting excited over her efforts.

"Thanks" She smiled almost shyly, though she couldn't stop her own smile as the auburn-haired witch bounced in a giddy fashion.

"You gotta tell me how you did it though!" Dia was saying, as her cloak had fluttered around on the floor as though the wind was failing to pick it up.

"I just…" Lily paused, what did she do? "I just didn't think about anything except the spell, I suppose?" Well, that was a lame explanation. Obviously, Dia thought so too as she laughed a little.

"Well, that's helpful." She teased.

"Sorry, I'm not good at explaining things."

"No, but I suppose a week ago you weren't into the whole talking thing, so I'll hedge my bets you'll be good at teaching me by the end of the year here."

Lily blinked in surprise at the cheeky grin she was faced with. She'd never felt the sickening feeling of guilt claw at her chest like a vicious monster. It twisted her gut to think that this girl had been so willing to be friends with her and was even planning to still be friends with her by the end of the learning here. Would she still think that way if she knew what Lily was, and what she was here for?

Squashing that feeling back, sealing it behind an emotional and mental wall, Lily attempted a small smile. "I'll do my best."

Thankfully, Dia either didn't notice the hesitation in Lily or had just put it down to her shy nature. Lily continued to try and help Dia, and by the end of the two-hour lesson, the cloak was hovering smoothly in front of her.

"Fantastic work!" Warlock Parvoz exclaimed with a clap of his hands. They all lowered their wands from the things they had hovering. "I'll monitor these and see how long they remain in the air for. We will probably do more of this practice later in the week, just to be safe, but it looks like this will be a class of talent this year!"

As they walked away, Dia grinned brightly, practically skipping at the fact she had managed to get her cloak flying properly. "You'll help me figure out the *Luxina* spell too!"

"I still can't do it, though..." Lily mumbled.

"I'm sure if you find the right book and we practice all free periods, you'll have some pointers." Dia's encouragement really had a wondrous effect, and before Lily could think more into it she had nodded and found her feet leading her to the library again.

Chapter 7: Wild Witch Agrios

Sure enough, the right book did help Lily figure out how to get the *Luxina* spell to work properly. The book in question, *Basic Spells: Incantations and Their Tricks. Volume 1* had been incredibly useful, and Lily had checked it out immediately for a long-term loan. She also found the sister series of these books which described the bulk of basic potions in the same way so had taken out the first volume of those in advance of the following day.

Kiki and Oscar kept themselves quiet over the evening as they had done the previous week, and they took to only following Lily into the bathroom to talk when they could get away with it. This had previously been a brief thing, so far neither of them had found anything within the walls of the school. But, Lily was very glad to hear their voices nonetheless.

But that night, Kiki followed her without news but instead to exchange general thoughts next to the sink while Lily washed her face.

"So, you got the magic to work ok?" She asked early one morning while sitting on the side.

"Yeah. Well, working enough for no one to think I'm not just a less-than naturally-talented witch." Lily assured her quietly, aware of the fact Dia was in the room they shared.

"That's good," Kiki sighed in obvious relief. "We had been worried. I mean, we didn't know if fairies and witches could use each other's magic, so we were very worried you'd hit a problem when the lessons started."

Lily reached out to pet the white-footed cat's head lightly, now and always touched by how much they cared for her. They shared the same concerns and they understood her worries. "I thought the same, but there's still time for me not to be able to keep up with the spells they give me." She admitted.

"Well, you do what you can to keep up with everyday stuff here; Oscar and I will do the digging. You might find stuff in the documents or the lessons, so don't let yourself fall behind" Kiki moved onto her back feet to lean up far enough to nuzzle Lily's upper arm.

A bright smile graced Lily's features as she leant closer to press a couple of kisses to the cat's little black nose.

Lily did as she was told, trusting that Oscar and Kiki would come and let her know whatever they found. The following morning, however, Kiki stayed with her while Lily sat in her bed from sunrise reading through *The Basics of Potion Making: Volume 1*. Lily suspected that the little cat wanted to keep her company but also thought that if the cats were never around to sleep then Dia would get suspicious. After all, cats were meant to sleep for the best part of the day.

What she learned from the book was exactly what they learned later that day from Warlock Fausia. Elixirs were potions used to change the base metals of materials and often used in building, constructing, blacksmithing and other jobs like this. Maceration potions were in short, potions which soften and break down substances they are left on.

Both during her reading of the book in the morning, and during her note-taking in classes as Warlock Fausia went through the basics, and the details of which potions specifically they would be covering in this year, Lily couldn't figure out why these would be taught in a school that was soon to be sent to kill Fairies. The only thing she could come up with, was that these were potential jobs for people after the war?

Still, it was incredibly innocent compared to what she had imagined being taught here. But then, most of the spells and potions she had browsed through in her books didn't seem dangerous. Perhaps that was just the early stage stuff?

She kept rapt attention in the classes just in case she heard something out of the ordinary. But Warlock Fausia didn't seem to let on any air of threat; in fact, he just seemed to have an underlying passion for the manual trades. He seemed stern and stoic, even kind of terrifying with his tall height and mussed-up brown hair with grey flecks, but there was a glitter in his eyes when he spoke about the uses of Elixirs. Because of that, his lessons were certainly going to be much more interesting than Warlock Mayai's had been the day before.

The following day, in their first Creature Handling class, Lily found the teacher she definitely liked best so far.

Wild Witch Agrios was waiting for them with her short blonde hair practically glowing in the early morning sun. She was a muscled woman who didn't seem bothered by the fact her green vest top did nothing to cover the scars and burns that littered her skin.

"I bet you've all been bored out of your mind with the introductory lessons so far this week!" She started with a bounce in her knees, bobbing up and down a little as though unable to stand still. "So, I'm just going to jump straight into it; all you need to know as an intro here is that I go by Aggie, and my assistant over there is Ferny..."

"Ferntide!" The male with a strawberry blonde ponytail flushed, turning back to the large potted plants he was stood by.

"Yes, yes. Young mister Ferntide." Agrios chortled, clearly enjoying the reaction she had gotten. "He's not a teacher, but he's very good with the animals. So, if you can't get hold of me with a question then he's your best bet! Just don't sneak up on him from behind, he spooks easy!"

Again, she laughed brightly. Lily caught the male assistant shifting nervously out of the corner of her eye though he didn't look around or protest.

"So today, I thought we'd dive right in with a creature which won't scare anyone off and may even delight a few. The creepy crawlies can wait until you've built up your stomachs a bit." Without informing them what creatures they would be seeing, Agrios ushered them to follow her as she moved over to where her assistant stood with the plants.

As potted plants went, these were huge. Small trees that were kept in pots for ease of transport most likely.

"Oh look!" One male at the front whispered as they got closer.

"Where?"

"I don't see…"

"Pupuacrin!" Agrios exclaimed happily, motioning towards the branches of the small trees.

"Pupu-what-now?" Lily muttered in confusion, causing a laugh to snort out from Dia beside her. Lily glanced at her wondering if she should have known what these things were. Was she showing her ignorance of this world again? Gulping back the fear she was giving herself away, she simply turned back to the trees and squinted at them. Hopefully, Dia wouldn't think any more of it.

As she continued to investigate the trees, she noticed some of the green and brown colours moving around. Focusing on those she soon came to realise that they were little creatures. Little fluffy creatures with a set of fore- and hind-wings with long apex tails reaching out to almost twice the length of the little creatures' bodies. They were incredibly well camouflaged, curled into balls on the branches.

"Now, these are very curious little creatures so long as you don't make too many loud noises around them" Agrios said, happily reaching into the branches and gently picking up the first creature she could reach.

In her hand, the small creature uncurled itself and took hold of her fingers with eight fluffy feet. It stabled itself and looked around at the class. As it did so, Lily could see that it had two large bright blue eyes and long pointed ears that had long tufts of fur poking up from their tips.

The Pupuacrin really was painfully cute.

"Their fur is used in many potions, usually the ones that are involved in Tinctures. Pupuacrin fur is never found in a potion that has a negative effect, and absolutely never used in poisons of any kind." Agrios was explaining as she walked along the line of students, stopping to allow them to reach out a tentative stroke of the little creature.

Lily found her fingers running over its left ear and a small smile pulling on her lips as it blinked lazily before turning to sniff at her finger. Agrios smiled brightly at her as the Pupuacrin licked Lily's finger.

"He likes you," Agrios commented quietly before moving on to show the last of the class. "The general structure of these lessons will be that you'll examine the creatures and then while you learn to interact with them, handle them or restrain them, I shall talk you through their physiology and care. The following week, you shall work with the same creature and show me how much you have learned about that care."

A few at a time moved forward for Agrios or Ferntide to help them identify the Pupuacrin in the branches and to urge them into their hands. There was one Pupuacrin per pair or trio of students.

"Mind if I join you two?" Asked a voice from behind Lily and Dia, making them both jump in surprise. Spinning around, Lily found Finnigan Byrne smiling down at them. She hadn't noticed him back there, but why did he keep coming over to be around them? Oh god! It occurred to her for a moment that maybe he knew what she was. But it made no sense why he would be smiling at her if he knew.

Her silence was broken by Dia who smirked at Lily before nodding almost eagerly. "Sure thing, Finn!" She agreed, motioning for him to come with them as she took Lily's elbow and pulled her to the trees so they could get a Pupuacrin.

The Pupuacrin turned out to be a glorious distraction from discomfort. Wild Witch Agrios had not been lying when she said these were curious creatures. Once the little creature had sniffed at Lily's fingers with its little twitching nose, it began to scamper up her arm with a surprising grip in its eight tiny paws. It became interested in tangling itself in her hair while Finn and Dia spoke together; Lily overheard a few snippets including Dia explaining that Lily didn't speak much and Finn claiming that he didn't mind.

She didn't get it. Witches weren't meant to be nice or accepting, or anything of that nature.

Frowning a little, she attempted to pull the Pupuacrin from her brown locks.

"You'll have trouble getting all eight of those paws out at once." Lily snapped around to see Agrios smiling in amusement. "Here, let me help. Unless you want it to nest there?"

Lily blinked before shrugging lightly "It's not the worst deal." She mumbled, gaining a hearty laugh from her teacher.

"You're an animal fan?" Agrios asked.

"Well, I lived in an area surrounded by all sorts. Though most weren't particularly wild" Lily half explained, trying to keep everyone's theory that she was a farm girl.

"Ah, good! I'll always welcome an animal fan rather than a people fan!" Agrios finally pulled the little creature free of Lily's hair and placed it back in her hands before smiling and wandering off to the next students.

Wild Witch Agrios could be seen a mile away as an animal lover rather than a people lover. She spoke with such passion about the little creatures while they were being handled and while the class wrote about them in easy to hold handbooks while the creatures flitted between person and tree branch. It didn't feel like they had spent a solid four hours out there, the class was interesting and Agrios made it feel exciting even when she was talking about the maintenance of the Pupuacrin's tiny claws which supposedly had to be trimmed in captivity every two months unless they had the correct branches to scratch into.

By the end of the week, Lily knew that Mythical Creatures would probably be her favourite of all the lessons. They already knew what the other lessons would be like with Panga and Mayai, but Sorceress Meadowtail was even worse for Enchantments. She could obviously not care less about her lessons. Master Orva for Charms on Friday afternoon was passionate, but he held strict intimidation about him which made the whole class feel nervous.

"You reckon first weeks are always meant to be that boring?" Dia sighed heavily, flopping back onto her bed late on Friday night. Lily shrugged. "I mean, sure there's room for introductions, but Orva basically just lectured us on common courtesy for two hours straight!"

Lily picked up Oscar who was lounging on their windowsill and pressed a couple of soft kisses to his head.

"I hope they get more interesting though. Could this place have picked a set of any more boring people?! I mean seriously, how are they meant to get so many of us interested enough to even want to learn when we've got Mayai who doesn't seem to have a personality, Meadowtail and Fausia who clearly don't want to be here, and Panga who looks like one glare from a student would cause a breakdown!" Dia's rant seemed to be full throttle and filled with disappointment.

Lily, who had expected much worse, was still more confused than disappointed. Not one single class that their teachers had described seemed like it would be even a slight threat to the Fairy Kingdom.

Perhaps they were wrong about the gathering of witches here, maybe this was just a school. Maybe the war stuff was somewhere else in the world of witches? Though, how she was meant to get away from a school long enough to find out was a mystery to her.

"It's a damn good thing I got you. You seem to have a dab hand in deciphering books to then tell me what I missed dozing off!" Dia was grinning at her now. Lily pulled her mind quickly back to reality and pushed a slight smile onto her face in response.

"I'll do my best. The theory makes sense, but the practical... well..." Her expression was a little sheepish, she had severely struggled with the initial spells they had been given in Enchantments and Charms.

"We'll work on them tomorrow! Have them aced by next week so that smug little liche can stop smirking at us." Dia grumbled the last few words. Lily knew exactly who she spoke about. It was that brown-haired, beautiful female who had knocked her in the corridor that day. Thanks to Master Orva, who actually took a register, they had found out that the girl's name was Kelsie Fulton.

"She is pretty skilled," Lily added, dropping herself into her desk chair and settling Oscar on her lap.

"So? Doesn't give her any right to lord it over us!"

Lily raised an eyebrow. She couldn't stop herself. From her experience, those who were better at something than she was had always lorded it over her and seemed to be to do so and no one other than her cat companions had ever spoken out about such behaviour.

"How does it not piss you off?"

"Erm, I don't know. I'm used to it?" Lily offered.

"Well, get unused to it! I swear, Lil, I've never met someone as subservient as you!" Dia shook her head with a sigh. Lily blinked in surprise at that but Dia continued "We'll keep practising and show that Kelsie girl up for good! Right?"

The look she shot Lily was so resolute, so determined, that she could do nothing but nod slowly in agreement. Dia beamed.

"Good! We'll start tomorrow, can I use the bathroom first?"

Again, Lily nodded.

Once the door to the bathroom was shut, she looked down at Oscar who had a gleam of amusement in his eyes.

"I like her." He stated simply.

Chapter 8: Inconsistencies

Over the next few weeks, Lily didn't learn of any threats within the school. Even with Dia and her pawing through the spell books in their spare time, both to perfect the spells for the lessons and to learn a few others that seemed interesting or that might come up later... she learned nothing.

But, Lily did find herself having fun.

Oscar and Kiki took turns to take information back to one of the Elders' companions. They passed on the fact that none of them had found a single suspicious thing; the books Lily had read didn't seem to give out any information unless it was related to the subjects that were taught, and while she had been practising and reading into spells they hadn't learned yet, they didn't sound like anything that had been used against fairies in the past. Definitely, nothing that could harm or kill.

What they didn't pass on was, the laughter that had been pulled from Lily's lips when they practised spells, the fact that not just Dia, but Finn and Rainer were more than happy to talk to Lily unlike everyone had been back home, the interest and joy that sometimes moved over Lily's face when they were in the flying or mythical creatures' lessons.

Oscar and Kiki could easily see how much joy and confidence this school was bringing Lily, even if it was wrong and dangerous.

For the first time in Lily's life, she had friends. True, there were still people here who didn't get on with her. Kelsie Fulton was one such person, though there were others who sneered at Lily and Dia. It still amazed Lily that Dia always said something back, usually more defensive and more angrily whenever it was Lily who was the target.

One night, about six weeks after meeting the girl, Lily found herself asking about it.

"Why do you always snap back at them?"

That day a hex had been aimed at them from a group of girls, the group who had gravitated towards Kelsie and her sophisticated aura. They hadn't been taught hexes, so it had missed and had very little effect. But it didn't stop Dia from yelling at them from across the courtyard causing a rather large scene.

Dia was still fuming while sitting on her bed.

"They tried to hex us!" She growled.

"They missed."

"That's not the point! They tried, so why did we get the detention because I wanted to break their damned noses?!"

Lily sighed softly; she still didn't get it. It just settled in the thought that when you spoke back things got worse.

"At least detention won't be such a bad punishment," Dia sighed, raising a hand to rub her shoulder absently.

"No? If it wasn't bad it wouldn't be a punishment." Lily commented.

"Maybe, but they can't resort to anything illegal so I'm sure we'll be fine" Dia sighed as though accepting the punishment and letting her hand fall back from her shoulder. "It'll probably just be boring as hell! Though if we have to serve together we might be able to have a laugh."

Lily didn't comment, but she had a feeling Dia would be the kind of person to make her laugh no matter the situation. Lily had never laughed so much in her life before now.

The detention, it surmised, was cleaning out stock rooms for potion ingredients. Which was just as Dia had predicted; boring as hell. The stock rooms were densely packed, and most of the lesser-used ingredients were in boxes, jars and barrels which were layered in dust.

"Oh yeah, because we didn't need to breathe at all," Dia coughed as she pulled out the items on one shelf to clean them.

Lily hummed softly in agreement. They had yet to be taught the spells that would help with cleaning and tidying, however, Lily figured that they wouldn't have been allowed to use them anyway.

"Ewww, look at these." Dia giggled, holding out an open box to Lily who found herself looking at string-thin tentacles that still wriggled where they lay in the box.

Lily pulled a disgusted face "What are they?"

"Tekalima tentacles" Dia stated, continuing at the raised eyebrow that showed on Lily's face through the dim lighting "Little creatures in the water that lose their tentacles about five times throughout their year. These probably were collected from the ones in the pond behind the Blue Dorm."

Lily's expression turned to confusion, and to give her credit, Dia was beginning to know just what went unspoken from Lily's lips.

"I had a wander around the back of all of them one of those times you were determined to stay in the library all Saturday." Dia chortled. Lily's lips formed an o-shape while understanding dawned over her. "There are a few other cool things, like the dancing shrubs behind the Green Dorm which are good fun to watch, and the singing vine fish that hang out in the Red Trumpet vines."

Lily paused in her cleaning, looking around at Dia who was chattering away. They were such little mundane things, but they sounded glorious to her compared to the dead ends she had discovered in the library each weekend. "I should go see them…" She mumbled.

"I'll show you tomorrow!" Came the immediate reply "Unless you're going to the library again?"

Lily frowned at the jar she had just cleaned; she should have been going to the library again. There were so many more books that she needed to go through, with the chance that maybe one, just one, had something in there that would give her any hint that she was even in the right place to be finding the information that was required from her. But six weeks of searching had led her to nothing…

"No," She mumbled before clearing her throat and speaking more clearly. "No, I don't need to go to the library."

"Really?" Dia sounded gleeful. "We should maybe go into town as well. We can go shopping or something?"

"I… I don't have any money." Lily couldn't keep the scoff from her voice.

"Me neither, but we don't need any to go look."

"What about food?"

"We'll figure something out."

"But…"

"Oh, come on. It'll be fun to get out for a day!" With an amused sigh, Lily gave in and nodded which was met with a small but genuine cheer from her curly-haired friend. "You won't regret it, Lil!"

Shaking her head unable to fight a smile, Lily turned back to the glass boxes on the next shelf. The smile instantly vanished, replaced with her eyebrows furrowing in confusion. Reaching out to take the top box, she dusted the entire thing and focused on the label *'Fae Wings'*.

"Those aren't fairy wings" Her words left her lips without thought as she pulled open the box and glanced at the thin glowing glass-like wings inside.

"Well of course not," Dia had walked over to look around Lily's shoulder at the box she held "Why would there be actual fairy wings in here?"

Damn. Lily gulped back a shudder before making herself force a chuckle, motioning to the label.

"Oh, yeah karai got the nickname of Lake Fae's some time back. You know, because they glitter over the water's surface like the way fairies skin glitters in the light?" Dia continued sounding a little odd, as though this was another piece of information that Lily should have known "Did your parents never take you to the lakes? I thought all of us at some point had been taken to the winter solstice lights over the lakes."

Slowly, knowing she had to tread carefully now so as not to give herself away too much, Lily shook her head. "My parents never thought to take me," Obviously, they would never have risked the witch's world even for something that sounded beautiful, "They never could leave the farm for long."

"Hmm..." Dia still sounded suspicious. "Your childhood sounds like it sucked almost as much as mine!"

"Well, inside the house it was great, I just never really got out much." Lily countered, a little too quickly as she couldn't bear to give her parents a bad image. Dia simply smiled.

"Well, if you stay here over the holidays, you can come with me! I always go. My mom used to take me when I was a kid, but I've snuck out to go every year since she died too. It's really cool! I think you'll love it."

With that, she went back to the shelf she had been working on, humming a soft song in her wake that sounded like the ancient winter solstice songs from when humans once existed without magic.

Lily looked back at the wings in her hand; replaying the genuine confusion that Dia had shown at the thought that they would have real fairy wings here. Did they not use fairy wings as a potion ingredient? Wasn't that the whole point of this endless war, that they were determined to harvest the wings from fairies for the uses in potions? Lily had found any of the potions listing them yet, but she had only been through a couple of the simpler potions books and still had many to go through. Would she not find any potions that involved anything more than these karai wings?

Frowning, she placed the box back on the shelf. Were they wrong about this whole thing? But if they were, why were the witches so determined to come for them every time the barrier weakened?

Later that night, she sent Kiki with a message to the Elders with this information. But she would have to wait for their response. She lay in bed, staring up at the ceiling listening to Dia's light snores, knowing what they would come back with. There was bound to be another reason then, the taking of fairies' wings when they invaded was a cover for some other motive.

It left her head reeling, and she barely slept.

Part of her wanted to head back to the library the following day, but she knew she couldn't without raising questions from Dia. Lily had to keep her promise to Dia that she wouldn't need to go to the library.

So, she followed Dia to the singing vine fish, the tekalima pond, and the dancing shrubs. They also found that at a specific time of day, when the sun was at a certain angle in the late hours of the morning, the grass behind the yellow dorm bloomed with light as though the sun was glowing beneath the ground. It was beautiful to behold. Lily could not resist removing her shoes to walk through the glow barefoot. It had the warmth and softness of an area of black fur which had been laid in the sun for a long time; it made her want to lie down on the grass and bask in it for the brief time that it would glow that way.

Dia had simply laughed at her, but not with any malice. The sound was fond, and it only made Lily more relaxed, the confused and concerned thoughts from the day before flipping to the back of her mind.

"So, town?" Dia asked nonchalantly as they walked back through the walkway between the dorms towards the main building. "If we pick up lunch we won't have to worry about trying to figure out how to get food when we are there."

Lily smiled. Her smiles were becoming easier and more genuine as the days went by. "Good idea." The lunches were often sandwiches and finger foods, so it was easy for them to load up their arms with however much they thought they would eat on the way, and they headed out of the front doors, passed the sentinels at the gate who, once again, made no movement to suggest they knew what Lily was, and walked out into the world.

The town was pretty boring all in all, there were quite a few shops, but all the owners shooed them away before they could even cross the thresholds. They all seemed to have a nasty glare on their faces when they looked at Dia.

"Are people not allowed to go inside to look?" Lily questioned after the fifth shop door was slammed in their faces.

"Well, they are..." Dia started awkwardly. "But my pop lives a couple of villages out and he's not got the best of reputations, so it's probably because of me. Sorry." She added lamely.

Lily blinked and tilted her head in confusion.

"I didn't think they'd be so cruddy about it even if they did know who I am." Dia kicked at the ground beneath her. "I mean, it's not like I've ever done anything. My old man, he's just not that great with other people, you know. And he drinks a lot which gets him into fights when he is out of the house. And he's..."

"Dia." Lily interrupted, unable to stop herself at seeing her first friend tense up more with each word. It wasn't anger. Maybe fear? Lily associated that kind of tension with the kind she felt in her own body when nerves took over as her mind ran over too many details to keep track of. Dia blinked her wide eyes up at Lily who felt a reassuring smile move over her face. "It's ok."

What else could she say? Lily had never needed to soothe another's turmoil like her parents had often soothed hers as a child. In the end, she opted for a light-hearted approach; she wasn't sure she knew Dia well enough to poke at what appeared to be family-related wounds.

"How about we go for a walk outside the village, the fields and stuff? Maybe even the very edge of the woods?" Lily didn't want to get too close to the fairy homes, but she always felt better watching the wildlife, perhaps Dia would too.

Dia smirked a little, likely relieved for the opportunity to change the subject. "The woods? I never pegged you for a daredevil, bookwyrm." She teased.

"We wouldn't go far, but the non-magic animals are usually pretty docile if they are at the edges, right?" Lily shrugged, feeling rather uncomfortable at the idea of being a daredevil. To be a daredevil, you needed to be brave enough to do dangerous things willingly. Not wake up every morning and feel sick because the thought won't go away that this is going to be that day that it all goes wrong. Each day she felt that tension which was fading from Dia, anxiety that she was going to mess up and be discovered for what she was. That she was going to fail. That she was going to either get a death sentence here in the witches' world or a social death sentence back home.

She'd managed six weeks, but nothing showed up as wrong on the surface. Even this town seemed completely normal with nothing that would hint at an upcoming continuation of the war. Lily needed to dig deeper to find the information she was here for, and that meant more risk.

Feeling a little sick, Lily followed Dia back towards the town gates, hoping that the woods would soothe her as well.

The woods did do wonders for her nerves, it turned out. The whisper of the plants and the aroma of tree sap gave her a sensation of her home she could never describe to her friend. She watched Dia walk along, kicking her feet through the fallen autumn leaves on the floor. After a few minutes, Lily found herself subtly copying that behaviour. It was odd how relieving and fun that juvenile act was, it brought a light sense of joy to her and made her walk more like a skip.

"So, you're a bookwyrm, but you also like nature?" Dia asked after a while of comfortable silence. "Did you do anything exciting growing up?"

"Erm, I'm not sure what you class as exciting. I spent a lot of time climbing trees and hanging out with the cats, but I can't say I did much else." Lily sighed, realising as she spoke it out loud that she didn't have any exciting qualities about her.

Dia let out a low whistle, "Damn. At least the climbing trees must have been good fun?"

"It was, you get to see some amazing sights from the top of trees," Especially when you're in a magical barrier that makes you a few inches tall. The world was so much bigger when you looked out at it from that size.

"I bet! I used to go the other way, out into the wide-open country so I could just see for miles and wonder what it'd be like to go over the horizon and over to the mountains."

"I've definitely never been to the mountains." Lily couldn't lie about that; she'd only ever seen them at a distance from the tops of the trees.

"Probably shouldn't either, I don't think it's safe. But still nice to fantasise about it!"

No more could be said as they heard a shriek of fear and angry yelling coming from outside the town.

"What the...?" Dia started, confused. "Come on."

"What?" Why would Dia want to go towards a sound like that?! Every instinct in Lily was saying to stay away from it so they didn't get caught up in something bad. But her feet seemed to follow Dia automatically after six weeks of following her whenever Lily wasn't in the library.

A crowd had gathered at the entrance of the town and had begun to follow a small bundle of people in the direction of the school, veering off to walk around the back of the high wall perimeter surrounding it.

"Whoa" breathed Dia as she pulled Lily to the front of the crowd so they could see the bundle better. Four large burly witches walked with heavy feet, one at the front leading and one at the back. The two in the middle both had hold of an arm, twisting it painfully into a position that couldn't be fought against. The arms in question belonged to a creature Lily had never seen before. Ultimately, the female looked human enough, the same number of limbs, the same facial features. Her dark eyes glinted with purple as she glanced at the gathering crowd before letting her head fall forward and her deep violet silk-like hair cover her face. That hair, however, did nothing to hide the scaled horns which curved up from the top of her head. Her hair was also not long enough to hide the patches of purple scales covering areas of the dark skin of her upper and lower arms.

Mostly, though, it was the large, scaled wings that sat folded without struggle protruding from her shoulder blades that could never have been hidden. Those wings seemed to be getting the most mumbling about in anger and insult.

Lily couldn't understand such a response. All she could feel, looking at those wings was awe. They were so powerful compared to the wings of fairies. The silver scales seemed to ripple with each very minute flex of muscle beneath the surface of the wings. They looked like they would be able to throw the witches off without any effort, and yet, the female walked along with tense, angry obedience about her.

"I've never seen one" Dia mumbled beside her.

Lily couldn't find words for a moment or two. Then, as the female was led further past the stone boundary of the school, one question came to mind. "Where are they taking her?" Lily didn't even stop to think if that would be an odd first question.

"The Lock Up obviously" Dia deadpanned.

"Why?"

Dia looked at her like she'd gone a little crazy. "Because draconians are warriors, vicious and merciless." She spoke like she couldn't fathom why Lily would even consider not locking one up. "If she's here, it's bad news."

"She's not even struggling though?"

"They've got rid of her weapon, so she probably realises she's lost."

"But they don't have a weapon?"

"Probably destroyed it."

Lily frowned at Dia, who met her gaze with a concerned expression Lily hadn't seen there before. It looked as though Dia was seriously considering whether Lily was in her right mind. But as a few whispers had now turned on them, *'Dragon sympathiser'* being the one to catch Dia's ear, she grumbled slightly and began to pull Lily away from the scene and back to school.

"Look," She hissed, "I get you're from a sheltered life, but you go around questioning something like that and you'll soon be more unwelcome in this world than I was in town today." Lily bit her lip, she couldn't help but wonder if the witches had been fighting a war against draconians too, ripping their wings from their backs in a similar fashion. She said nothing, much to Dia's relief, but glanced over her shoulder in the direction the draconian female had been taken.

She needed to find out if draconians were victims too. If they were, maybe the fairies would have some allies in the coming war.

Once Dia was in the bathroom that night, Lily whispered to Oscar that she wanted him to check out the so-called 'Lock Up' during his next few day ventures away from the dorm. It was the first of anything she had found that could give her any information at all. She had to follow it.

Chapter 9: The Draconian

Talk about the capture of the draconian female was all that anyone could talk about.

"Do you think she was here to attack us?"

"Maybe she was a scout."

"There could be more of them out there?"

"My mom wants me to come home."

"You'd think nothing interesting ever happened in their lives," Dia commented four days after the incident as she sat down across from Lily in the canteen for dinner. In response, Lily motioned to the pages of homework in front of her alongside the potions book she had. "Ok, point taken" Dia laughed "The dragon-lady is more interesting than writing up the uses, and complications if not brewed correctly. I mean, are you seriously planning on doing every piece of work given to us on the night it's given?"

Lily blinked away from what she was writing and swallowed the mouthful of delicious key lime pie she was enjoying.

"Why wouldn't I?"

"You're such a bookwyrm." Dia's voice was strangely fond, though it quickly turned mischievous. "Can I copy it when you're done?"

This was becoming a habit, but Lily couldn't find it in her to care. It made sure that Dia didn't bug her about her immediate solving of homework, which wasn't solely to do with the work itself. If she didn't have to worry about the homework, then Lily had more time to sit and read other books. This time, she was trying to find any book in the library that could tell her something, anything, about the draconians and their relationship with witches.

So far, she had found nothing. All she could go off were the whispered rumours that were rattling through the school after the draconian female's capture.

Lily was finding the stress of confusion building up in her like a fist twisting every muscle fibre under her skin until even the hot water of her baths couldn't relax her. Nothing she was coming across here was making sense. Kiki had returned with the reaction Lily had predicted; things were obviously hidden deeper under the surface than the Fairies had predicted.

"Don't you always?" Lily replied with a twitch of a smile.

"You're a star! Love ya, Lil!" Dia grinned into the sickly-sweet dessert she had called a treacle delight.

"You just like my brain" It was scary how easily Lily had relaxed around Dia enough to even begin to tease her. It was fun, and Dia never reacted badly. In fact, just like now she would just chortle softly and offer up a less-than-innocent grin.

"Nah, just your work ethic." Dia retorted.

"Oh, I'm sure she likes you for more than that, there's so much to like." Came the voice of the growingly-familiar voice of Finnigan Byrne who sat down opposite with a charming grin.

Lily couldn't keep herself from laughing lightly, even when she shook her head in disagreement.

"You're such a flirt Finn," Dia pointed her spoon at him in an accusing fashion "Anyone would think you were popular and likeable."

Finn gasped in mock offence. "How could anyone accuse me of such a thing?"

"I know," drawled Rainer as he sat down, taking a huge mouthful of his roasted beef before smirking at his friend "Everyone knows you're just an idiot with a good family name."

"You know me so well," Finn cooed in mock tenderness. He then turned to Lily and raised an eyebrow at what she was still writing despite the subtle look of amusement on her face. "You never get distracted, do you?"

Lily flicked her eyes up for a moment before shrugging. "I can still do my work while I listen to you all."

"You could join in?" He suggested though his eyebrows quickly furrowed in confusion at the frown that appeared on Lily's face.

"I could. But I'm not used to having interactions like this, so I don't know how" She replied honestly, her eyes downturned in embarrassment while her cheeks flushed slightly.

The silence that followed that was a little awkward.

"Well..." Finn started "You've got plenty of time to practice."

"Yeah, don't think Finn could leave you alone at this point. Ow!" Rainer whined as he received a light punch to his upper arm. Lily glanced his way, and then to Finn who, to her surprise, was flushing slightly.

"You're very kind," she said with an obliviousness that made Dia snort in laughter.

"And you're very dense"

"What? How?"

"Doesn't matter, we still love you" Dia reached out to mess up Lily's hair with a playful ruffle. Lily glanced around confused, Dia looked amused, while Rainer looked exasperated and Finn looked somehow embarrassed. They were all making as much sense as everything else she had discovered from this place.

The quick jibes and charming atmosphere lingered for the rest of the dinner and during the short walk back to the dormitories.

"Finn so has a crush on you."

The cheeky statement from Dia as she shut the door of the dormitory behind them short-circuited Lily's brain. She turned her head so fast that her neck cricked painfully.

"What?" Lily's confusion and disbelief couldn't be masked "Don't be ridiculous!"

"I'm not, you really are dense when it comes to social stuff aren't you?" Dia laughed good-naturedly.

"I…" Lily could feel her cheeks flushing, but she wasn't sure if that was because of the pointed comment on her lack of social skills, or the idea that Finnigan Byrne liked her. Shaking her head, she turned away from Dia. "He wouldn't like someone like me." She finally said, confused by the pang of disappointment in her stomach.

She quickly pushed that feeling aside, allowing the logic of her father's lineage to come through. Finnigan Byrne was not a romantic opportunity, he was the ancestor of the people who had built this school. He was a high up family name, and therefore a complete danger to her and everything she was here for. It didn't matter that he wouldn't like her anyway; for the exact same reasons why he was a danger to her.

It shouldn't matter. But Dia wasn't about to let it go.

"Oh, come on! So, you're quiet, big deal. You can still be liked despite that!" Dia protested.

"Dia, please." Lily sighed "I'm not… interested in that kind of thing."

"Sure, sure. If that's true, make sure you let him know" Dia waved off Lily's words with a shake of her head, perhaps realising not to push it.

"He's not going to need telling," Lily mumbled as she placed her homework on Dia's desk "Here, you can copy that when you want. I'm going to take a bath."

"Awesome! Thanks, Lil!" Dia chimed, not noticing the avoidance of the subject. With a flick of her eyes towards Oscar on her own desk chair, Lily trudged into the bathroom with the cat hot on her heels mewling happily as though he just wanted to be with her after a day of her being out of the room.

The running water from the faucets covered the low words from Oscar who hopped up onto the side of the bath like he usually did when he followed the fairy inside. "Everything ok, Lils?" He asked softly, his black ears twitching at the close sound of water falling.

"I've been thinking," She began, hesitant to voice something that kept visiting her mind "I want to speak to that draconian girl."

Oscar paused, his mind struggling to register the statement much as Lily's had a few minutes before. His fur bristled in discomfort as he shuffled his front paws to sit himself up straighter.

"Why?" He asked at last.

"Because nothing makes sense so far." Lily murmured, cautious of being overheard even with the taps running and the thick walls of the bathroom. Even with how many times she had gotten away with talking to the cats, this was a different topic rather than empty reports. "We've found nothing on what is going on here with the witches, and what we have seen doesn't match anything we were taught. A draconian would have another story, and a reason for being here; maybe she is here for the same reason."

Again, the cat shuffled, obviously choosing his words carefully. "I get that you are confused and probably frustrated that we've not found anything yet but doing something like that is too risky. How would you even get her to speak to you? If she thinks you are a witch she'll never talk, and if you tell her you're a fairy, she could rat on you and then you'll end up in the same situation as her. Or worse."

"The longer I'm here, the riskier this gets." Lily reminded him logically.

"I know, but you need to think this through."

"All I do lately is think about what I've found, and what I've not found. Nothing is adding up; these people are far from evil. This is just another school setting, with teachers and bullies and childish laughter. Not one thing could be used in a war, there's nothing that suggests we are right in what we are taught."

"Kiki and I could maybe search the town?"

"And if that's just a normal town like it looked when I visited?"

"Then we'll look deeper."

"Which is just delaying the risk until a later date."

"What's wrong with that?" Oscar half hissed in demand "Surely it's better to play it safe for as long as possible?"

Lily frowned before looking towards the locked bathroom door. She knew why Oscar was asking such a thing, normally she would never have dared do anything risky for fear she would fail at it.

"I'm scared, Oscar." She whispered, sitting on the edge of the bath and running her fingers over his soft fur. "If I don't find something soon, I'm scared…"

"Of what? That we won't have enough time to protect ourselves?"

"Well, that…" Lily sighed with a look of despair seeping into her disguised eyes "And that I won't want to find something."

Oscar's eyes widened at the crack in the girl's voice. Quickly getting to his feet he hopped onto her lap and nuzzled her chin. "Oh, Lil." He mumbled.

Admitting it out loud hurt. It filled her with an illogical and aching feeling of failure. She had fun here, and she was growing a substantial soft spot for her roommate along with others. Some of the teachers had managed to elicit fondness from her through their encouraging treatment unlike many of those had back at home. But the longer she allowed herself to have friends, to feel valued, the more it weighed on her mind. She knew she would fall into this easily, lulled into it through pleasant feelings. And in doing so, she would be failing her own kind, her family!

"I need to find something, Ozzy." Lily sniffled.

"It'll be ok." Oscar licked at her chin gently, "We'll find something."

The sound of water stopped behind them, the bath recognising the right time. Neither the fairy nor the cat moved for a few minutes; Oscar nuzzling her chin to comfort her.

"I'll start checking out the Lock Up and see if there's any way to get in there. For now, you should get in that bath and relax for the night. If you are too worked up, questions will be asked."

Lily nodded in defeat, waiting for Oscar to jump down from her lap before getting rid of her clothes and settling into the bath to do as he suggested.

It took the best part of the following week for Oscar to come back to her. Days which were filled with the same lessons filled with slow progress, and laughter between friends. But when Oscar finally did come to her, Lily's fears were conflicting with her mind more and more in the night hours.

"There are some hours in the small hours of the morning where there are only sentinels on the door, no guards or anything inside." Oscar was saying while Dia was in the bathroom. "There's an upper window which you could get into if you use magic."

Lily's eyebrows furrowed in confusion, but she didn't need to speak before Oscar continued. "I can only guess that it's arrogance that leaves it without too many guards, though I think the rooms themselves are magically protected without the keys. I saw a few insects zapped into non-existence when they got too close."

"So, how would I get in through a window on the upper floor? It's not like I can hover with those boots let alone fly."

The cat stared up at her with a look that told her Lily was being stupid. Lily's mind ticked over slowly, painfully slow. Until finally... "Oh, Fairy Magic." She realised sheepishly, watching Oscar roll his eyes.

"That was slow," He teased.

"Shut up," Lily pouted.

"At least you got there in the end," Oscar chortled. "If we get some plant matter, you'll be able to create enough vines to climb up to the window and get in. The draconian is a couple of floors down, in room nineteen. She's the quietest one there. Some of them seem a bit insane, and all of them except her are witches of various ages. You'll have to make sure none of them sees you if you are going in there, if one of them decides to shout about an intruder, people might look into it."

Lily nodded in agreement.

"Should be easy enough, the doors of the cells only have half windows, so you'll have to crawl through the corridors and be silent down the stairs. She's thankfully at the end of a corridor away from others, probably so she cannot talk to anyone else, but that means no one will hear you once you are there unless you scream and yell."

"Have I ever yelled?" Lily asked with a raised eyebrow.

"Not since you were a kid and you got that wood piece stuck in your leg. So, you'll be fine so long as she doesn't stab you through the window."

"She doesn't have her weapon?"

Oscar chuckled and shook his head "No, she doesn't. I'm pretty sure that is locked away in the basement, but I couldn't get in there to confirm."

"Well, that's ok. I just want to talk to her anyway."

"What are you going to say?"

Lily blinked in thought, her mind trying to focus on some of the questions that were bugging her. She knew that wasn't what Oscar was talking about though, he wanted to know what she was going to say to make the draconian even willing to answer those questions.

"I don't know," She mumbled honestly.

Oscar sighed, looking up at the bathroom door. They were running out of time for this conversation. "Well, think it over. You should go Friday night, Dia sleeps heavily and always sleeps in so you'll be able to lay in and catch up on sleep when you are back."

"Yeah. Ok."

When Dia opened the door to walk back inside, Lily was sitting with her potions book open, acting like she was reading up on that day's lesson of changing lead to silver with an Argene potion.

Friday was only a few days away, but they were difficult to get through without her mind wandering. Lily had no idea what she could say to convince the draconian that she wasn't there to fetch information for the witches. She only had one idea, but it was her riskiest one yet.

Lily did not take the potion that hid her true appearance on the evening of Friday, and she was woken by hissing in front of her face.

"Are you insane?!" Kiki hissed down at her in anger.

"What if Dia woke up and saw you like this?!" Oscar joined in.

Lily's blue eyes blinked through the darkness at them, sitting up so as to force them from snarling down at her face.

"This is my best chance; no one will see me," Lily whispered, quickly swinging her legs off the side of her bed and stood silently. "You guys are my lookouts, and I have a vial with me in case I need to quickly alter my appearance and make some excuse."

"I can't believe you!" Kiki growled as she trotted to keep up with Lily as she left the room. "This is so dangerous!"

"They won't see me," Lily assured her. To make a point of this, she raised her hand and black shadows licked around her fingers before spreading to the lights in the corridors, causing them to dim and shield Lily from the immediate view of anyone who could leave their dormitories. "It's not my strongest element, but I can still make good use of the darkness for something like this."

"Hmph." Kiki scoffed.

"Good thinking kiddo." Oscar piped up before running ahead to check out the stairway down to the entrance.

"And how are you going to hide if there's anyone outside when we go through the statue?" Kiki was still growling lightly.

"It's two in the morning." Lily sighed "How likely do you think that will be?"

Kiki clicked her tongue but said no more.

Lily was right, though. No one was outside this time of night. She shivered at the temperature change as the cold night air hit her skin. The cold wouldn't settle in, the ice magic within her veins wouldn't allow that, but the difference between temperatures wasn't something she could immediately ignore.

"We're going over the back boundary," Oscar informed Lily as he led the way behind the dormitory buildings, so they were secluded in darkness as they moved. As she walked, Lily plucked a couple of vine roots from the ground. At the boundary she knelt to plant the first vine in the ground, placing her hand beside it and concentrating. With a low creak of quick growth and a glow of green beneath her hand, the vine shot upwards, curling tendrils into the gaps of concrete for stability. Her silver eyes watched the vine reach up until it was lost into the darkness above, the breeze causing her white hair to sway back and forth in the ponytail she donned it in.

"You guys will need to fly up while I climb," Lily instructed; her words met with a small fluttering of the cats' wings springing from their shoulder blades. They flew quickly and silently upwards into the darkness.

"I really wish I could do that," Lily grumbled to herself, grabbing the vines with one hand and starting her climb up. At least he was used to this, climbing up and down her home had given her plenty of practice. She was slow though, almost two months of no practice made her muscles ache as she climbed. Every few feet a glow of green showed on her feet to grow thicker vines up under them to take her weight. Once at the top, her job was easier as she could hang from the end of the vine and have it grow towards the ground.

She had picked a place that was in the centre of two custophinga sentinels, hoping that they wouldn't pay her any attention if she still didn't have wings. Thankfully, her assumption was correct; neither moved even remotely.

"We'll have to leave it there and hope someone doesn't see it from that side," Oscar stated close to her ear in the darkness. "If we need to get back over quickly, this is the best way."

Lily hummed in agreement, reaching out to take gentle hold of his tail so he could lead her to the next wall she would need to climb. It was pitch black to her eyes this side of the boundary, the moon shone from the front of the Lock Up, leaving them behind it cast completely in shadow. She trusted the cats wholeheartedly though; she knew that Kiki had vanished her wings and gone to sit at a vantage point a little way off to keep an eye on any movement around the front.

Oscar glided to the ground, guiding Lily's hand with it until she was met with a very thin slice of dirt between the concrete ground beneath her bare feet and the stone building. Placing her hand on the ground, she planted the second vine with the other. This climb was a few feet taller, so Lily made sure to increase the shadow that laid across her, unmoving and deceiving even if a light was shone their way. Oscar flew up first to nudge the loose window he had discovered open, and noiselessly, Lily dropped herself inside onto the child of metal lined floors.

The material felt cruel against the balls of her feet, claustrophobically so. At least with stone, she could still feel a sense of freedom with weeds, vines, and moss growing up and through it. But this metal interior made her feel oddly exposed and powerless, more so than anyone had ever made her feel. Swallowing back the wish to leave already, and the fearful doubts that this was the right call, Lily slipped to a crouch and began to gingerly make her way down the hallway.

It was difficult to move silently in a crouch, but there were snores and grumbles from a few of the cells they passed which covered any minuscule noise that came from her. Lily still couldn't figure out exactly why there was a jail of sorts directly behind a school; it was the only threatening thing she had come across so far.

Down two flights of stairs and Lily found Oscar guiding her further and further down the corridor, towards the end where the moon was barely shining through from its high angle.

"I can smell you out there even if I can't hear you." A rough female voice sounded from inside the room at the end. Lily stood rooted to the floor. Oscar shared a look with her that seemed to be defeat; we've come this far, he seemed to say.

Letting out a shaky breath, Lily raised to her full height and walked towards the door until she could see inside.

The Draconian inside was bathed in a strip of moonlight, making the purple scales on her face glitter like obsidian glass. The purple glint in those eyes that met hers seemed to glow in the darkness.

"A fairy?" The Draconian didn't mask her confusion.

"Yeah. Long story." Lily replied awkwardly "They, erm, they call me Lily."

"Xalina."

An awkward silence fell, Lily really should have had a plan of what to say. She knew that. But she was not well versed in conversation, her time at this school had proven that enough times. It would have been easier if Dia had been in on everything with her. Lily thought she would know exactly what to say.

"What is a fairy doing in the Lock Up but not in a cell?" Xalina broke the silence with curiosity.

"I wanted to speak to you" Lily found her voice saying with honesty. "I'm here looking for information to help us protect ourselves in the coming war. I thought maybe you were here for a similar reason."

"We do not take part in your ridiculous wars." Xalina growled softly.

"Ridiculous wars…" Lily repeated, surprised by the tone. "There's nothing ridiculous about slaughter."

"There is when you all remain in darkness about your reasonings and merely follow the whispers of pasts long gone."

"What do you mean?"

"That's what we are taught about you. Fairies are so cut off from the world they live and die through their own ignorance."

Lily frowned deeply. Her chest ached in confusion and frustration. A low rumble of a laugh filtered through the door, Xalina was amused by this reaction.

"Let me guess," She started "You've come to find information only to realise that there is none to find?"

Lily nodded.

"I did the same once, I met a young witch when she holidayed with her parents. I thought I ought to fear them, but she was, and still is the greatest thing in this world. They were taught that we draconians are savages, and we, in turn, were taught witches were dangerous. But I could never harm her, and she wouldn't harm me." Xalina sat herself down and rested her head against the wall of her cell. "I don't know what your kinds have against one another, but there are good witches."

It wasn't the information that Lily had been hoping for. It pulled a sigh from her lips.

"I know there are." She admitted, "I never expected to come here and make friends."

"You should show them mercy."

Lily sighed again. "When the war starts again, they won't show us any."

"All the more reason for you to show it, no?"

The purple in Xalina's eyes burned as they directed themselves straight into Lily's. It wasn't a plea for the race as a whole, but for the one which the draconian had spoken about previously. Something dawned on her then.

"You were here to visit your friend."

It wasn't a question, but Xalina smiled sadly, "More than a friend, but yes. It's her birthday soon, so I wanted to give her a gift. I didn't expect to be caught, now I will only be causing her sorrow."

"But, why let them imprison you if you weren't here to attack?"

"They would imprison me no matter my reasoning for being here, as will they do to you if you are discovered. Besides, if I told them a witch had come to care for one of my kind, my witch would be locked in here with me. So, I will rot in silence." Xalina's tone was full of finality, she had accepted her fate and she dared Lily to contradict her.

Lily couldn't. She could merely stand in awe of a love that crossed races despite the way they had been brought up. Perhaps such things were possible between fairies and witches; perhaps the war had gone on long enough and it could be stopped with the right proof that witches were not inherently evil.

"You're braver than I," Lily whispered into the silence.

"You're kidding right?" Xalina snorted when met with a sceptical look her eyebrows raised in wonder. "Seriously? You're wandering around in a witch community after living the sheltered life of a fairy, and you think I'm the brave one?"

"I was ordered to come here." Lily countered "You came here on something pure, a wish to see a loved one."

"You should give the individuals here a chance, some of them might look past the whole race difference. Though, not many I suppose." Xalina added in an afterthought.

Lily glanced to Oscar who gave her a look of exasperation. "Such a thing would be way too risky!" Xalina glanced around in confusion, her eyes widening as there was a flutter of wings and Oscar twitched his whispers in the moonlight. "Hey!"

"Ah, so it's true that fairies have companions that can talk and fly?" Xalina sounded impressed.

"You don't?" Lily asked.

"Nope. We don't have any companions at all, not even ones like witches without powers."

"I wouldn't survive without mine," Lily said honestly, scratching Oscar behind his ear as he hovered there. She couldn't fathom being stuck in a silent room without Oscar and Kiki. The thought itself made her sigh softly. "I wonder if we could get you out of here" She mused.

"Don't be daft, you'd put yourself in more danger." Xalina chuckled.

"At least I'd have another ally somewhere."

"You have your kind, don't you?"

"Well..."

"Hardly," Oscar scoffed "Every time we send a message back, they just say the same thing. Witches must be hiding the secrets, keep looking."

"Hiding secrets?" Xalina laughed again. "They're just living their lives."

"We can see that, but if they aren't preparing for a war why will the war continue in five years again?"

"It's not making sense, but the council isn't willing to think about any other ideas." Lily sighed.

"They sound a bit... well, small-minded." Xalina deadpanned, though at the silence she was met with she coughed awkwardly "Sorry".

"It's ok," Lily mumbled. "I suppose it's true, we've been secluded for so long. It would be good to have someone who knew the truth about me as well as the outside world."

"We should go, Lil," Oscar informed her, glancing to the moonlight position to check how it had moved.

"Already?"

"They have magic scans throughout the night, staying too long would be way too dangerous."

Lily sighed and looked back to Xalina. "I'll try and find a way to get you out. It was nice to meet you, Xalina."

"Hmm, don't worry about it." The draconian female waved her off lazily, obviously not believing Lily would come back.

Both Lily and Oscar dropped to the floor and noiselessly crept back the way they had come. The vines carrying them back down and vanishing into the ground and then the second vine carrying them back over the wall.

After taking her concealing potion, Lily struggled to get to sleep, her mind whirling with more thoughts than she'd had before the visit to Xalina.

Chapter 10: Bonding of Music

The following week brought a torrent of wind and rain which lashed at the windows and had the students running from their dormitories to the main building. Each entrance had been enchanted to dry them off as they walked through. Despite this, both flying and creature handling lessons were cancelled, much to Lily's disappointment.

"Stop sulking, come try this out for size!" Dia grinned, slapping Lily's left knee to get her attention. The fairy looked up from *Aquatic Creatures: Care and Uses,* tearing her attention from the detailed description of the Karai's lifestyle.

"I'm not sulking, I'm reading."

"You're always reading." Dia retorted, reaching out to snatch the book from Lily and hold it out of reach. The grin that spread on her face was full of mischief and amusement, never wavering even when met with an irritated pursing of Lily's lips. Dia had recently discovered that she could extract a slight reaction from Lily when she stole her books, and she seemed to delight in the infrequent but growing obvious emotions that rose to the surface of Lily's being.

"If I don't do the reading, you wouldn't have any homework answers to copy."

"You calling me lazy?"

"If the shoe fits…"

It was very strange, talking back in a way that would sound mean if not for the smile that wound her words in a jest-filled embrace. It always brought tension to her shoulders, an underlying instinctive fear that she'll lose a friend for her words. Dia, however, simply threw back her head, curls swaying and laughed brightly. Lily felt her lips twitch into a traitorous smile, her own laugh only kept at bay with the biting of her tongue.

"You're a quick learner even when it comes to wit I see," Dia beamed "One day, maybe you'll do it outside the dorm room."

"I wouldn't hold your breath." Dia was the only one so far that Lily felt comfortable enough to let herself speak some of her mind. Holding out her hand for the book's return, Lily sighed when Dia merely raised an eyebrow at her. "What?"

"I said stop reading and check this out, I've found some pretty terrific magic."

Lily noticed at that moment that Dia was motioning to a second book, her eyes widening a little in befuddlement. "Since when do you study books?"

"I don't, I skim read for anything fun looking." Dia shrugged. "But this one, brilliant! It says here you can create music out of nothing."

"Seriously?"

"Yeah! It's a Distortion spell, though I don't know whether we'll actually get taught it in class. But you're damn good at picking up stuff like this so..." Her words trailed off as she looked up expectantly at Lily.

It took her a couple of moments, but quickly a twitch of a smile pulled on her lips "So, you want to use our free period trying to do that instead of our actual cover work?"

"Bingo! I always said you were clever!"

Rolling her eyes with a smile on her lips, Lily flung her legs over the edge of her bed to sit up. The book was handed over to her and she was given silence while she read through the page on the spell.

> 'The Caelicantus spell manipulates the sound waves in the air. The caster can either reproduce symphonies they have within their memory or create melodies of their own slowly over time; adding one layer of sound over the other.'

"You're right, this sounds amazing. We never had that much music at home, only on special occasions." Lily mumbled.

"Really?? I love a good dance."

"I wonder if I can remember them enough to recreate them." She mused before reaching out to grab her wand from the desk. It was strange to automatically reach for it now; she would never have expected the wand to feel natural there. It channelled her fairy magic to a more direct result than she had ever seen before, though of course, she could only test those out in the dead of night where no eyes could see. It wasn't even a real wand, so she wasn't sure how it managed to channel the magic, but she couldn't deny the results.

Raising the wand before her, Lily moved the end in small clockwise circles slowly. *"Caelica."* Immediately, she winced at the sound that shot from it. A loud, screeching noise that made her drop her wand quickly.

"Please tell me that wasn't the music you knew!" Dia whined, rubbing her ears.

"No, I just didn't quite get it right."

"Any tricks in that spell book you're constantly reading?"

"Basic Spells: Incantations and Their Tricks? It could do, hang on." Lily picked up the wand from where it had clattered from the floor and walked over to her desk to find the large encyclopaedia of spell help. She flicked through to the Distortion chapter of the book and scanned through until she found the little section about the Caelicantus spell.

"Ah, here!" She prodded her finger at the page before reading it out for Dia's benefit. *"Keep the tune in mind clearly and make the first two circles of the wand quick and sharp, then slow the circles to a steady gentle pace.* Ok, let's try that one."

It took many more times of creating either awful noises or nothing at all. But finally, around an hour after they had started, Lily managed to produce a very faint sound. It was like far off music, muffled by doors and walls.

"What kind of music is that?" Dia frowned "Why's it so far away?"

"It's the closest I ever got to it. I wasn't usually invited to wherever it was being played. The other kids didn't exactly like me."

"Can't see why not!" Dia grumbled as the faded music came to a stop with the lowering of Lily's wand. "Well, I better get the hang of it so you can listen to some proper music!"

Despite the determination in her voice, her next attempt produced nothing more than a static crackling.

"Oh yes, I'm sure we could dance to that," Lily smirked.

"I'll just poke you till you dance." Dia laughed before continuing her attempts.

If Lily had thought the comfortable feeling of a wand in her hand was strange, it was nothing compared to how bizarre it was to spend hours on end happily and contentedly talking, laughing and practising magic with Dia.

"*Caelica*" Finally, music filled the air. It was nothing like Lily had ever heard even from afar. It had a quick beat and a liveliness to it; instruments that Lily had never once come across were combined in a joyful song. There felt like no escape from the sounds, but it wasn't something Lily ever thought she would want to escape.

The lightness of the sound, the chirpiness of its feeling, made her soul soar and her lips twitch upwards. There was a tension growing in her right leg as the urge to bounce it in time. Dia had begun humming along to the tune she obviously recognised, looking very proud of herself while sitting on her bed.

"Man, I love this song!" She exclaimed after a moment "When I was a kid, my pops used to drag me and mom down to the tavern and they used to play this one a lot. Pops never joined in, but my mom would get me to stand on her feet when I was little so I could dance with her. Either that or we'd twirl and flail like it was what we were born to do."

"That sounds great fun, your mom likes to dance?"

"Liked" Dia corrected, smiling despondently causing Lily's expression to change into troubled "She died a while back. Illness."

"I'm sorry." Lily cringed, remembering that Dia had in fact mentioned her mother's death before and scolding herself mentally for bringing it up.

Dia sniffed a little and shrugged. "Yeah, it sucks. But being able to play the music we used to listen to will be nice. I refused to go to the taverns after she died; the old man wasn't exactly any fun to be in them with." She continued to turn the wand as she spoke.

Lily felt lost. For the first time in her life, she felt like she had to say something, but she had no idea what that would be. Swallowing loudly in thought, her eyes dropped back to the page describing the spell they were working on.

"You could teach me how you both used to dance to this music?" She suggested slowly, turning the book to show Dia what she was looking at.

> *The caster may extend the music to keep it playing in turn with the songs they think of. While circling the wand, utter the word* **'Epektei'** *to extend the time, and* **'Finiri'** *to bring the sound to a close.'*

"Try it out" Lily urged with a gentle smile. Dia glanced at the book, a small tentative smile pulling at her lips. She seemed grateful that Lily wasn't prying into the subject further, or maybe she was simply happy for the chance to share something of such a precious memory.

"Epektei!"

Slowly, Dia lowered her wand and placed it on the bed next to her, a Cheshire Cat smile making her face brighten. "It worked!" Dia cried gleefully as she hopped up from the bed. Within moments, her arms were spread wide either side of her and she swayed and spun on the spot with an entirely childish giggle. She bobbed from foot to foot in time with the underlying beat. Not a couple of seconds later, she had turned to Lily with a fiery glee in her eyes and linked their hands to pull Lily to her feet. Dia moved Lily's arms like she was the string master of a puppet giving Lily little choice but to let her body move awkwardly, though her feet remained planted in one spot on the floor.

Lily had never danced before; it wasn't really done in the fairy kingdom. Dances were for weddings, mostly, and she had never once been invited to those. Her father had taught her the wedding dances, from the waltz to the quick-paced swing, but they all had specific steps and this dance which Dia was doing didn't look like any of them.

"Just relax" Dia giggled at the awkwardness in front of her. "You don't have to think, just move; wiggle, sway, hop, bop, whatever you feel like doing when you listen to the sounds."

The instructions only made her feel more like a fish out of water. The more she tried not to think, the more she seemed to do just that. Dia kept moving Lily's arms for her, but they were so uncomfortably out of time that she couldn't ignore them and focus on the music. Her only saving grace in her embarrassment was that Dia's laughter was not unkind, instead, it appeared fond. Perhaps she was happy that Lily was trying a little too hard even though she didn't need to.

Lily wasn't even close to getting the hang of it when their dormitory door opened, making them both jump, heads snapping around to look at the intruder. Were they about to get told off for the noise?

The girl who entered didn't seem annoyed though. She walked with a sultry swagger and a smirk that could make people both wary and hot under the collar at the same time. Her short black cropped hair bounced a little by the base of her long earrings and her dark blue eyes twinkled with adrenaline. Lily could picture her in the old stories she had read as a kid; pirates on the distant sea, finally laying their hands-on treasure and delighting in the discovery of the legendary Sky City which, of course, didn't really exist. This girl had that wild, explorer feel about her.

"I love this song!" Were the first words she spoke, her voice surprisingly deep for a female Lily thought. "How'd you get it playing in here?!"

Dia didn't seem phased by the lack of knock before entering, nor the lack of introduction. "Found a spell that lets you play music out of thin air! It's great right?!"

"Hell yeah! I thought I was going to have to break the age rules and sneak into the taverns in town to hear these again. Not like my fam is around to go in with me so I can get away with it." The girl sighed dramatically as though it was a sin against all that was powerful that taverns had age restrictions. Her grin told the world she was only kidding, though. "I'm Tanith, living in the room next door. My roommate doesn't get on with me though, so I won't go get her to introduce ya."

"Dia, honoured!" Dia half saluted in response before glancing at Lily who had still had hold of Dia's hand with one of her own. "This is Lil, she's quiet as hell, but great fun once she warms up to you. It's like living with three cats."

Lily absently glanced behind her at the two cats sitting on her bed, a small twitch pulled at the side of her mouth. However, she quickly looked back and smiled shyly to Tanith and raised a hand in quiet greeting. "Nice to meet you."

"Wow, polite too. None of my mates back home are that polite" Tanith chuckled.

Lily flushed "Sorry?"

"No, don't be. It's nice." Tanith waved away the apology "I should apologise that you probably won't get the same courtesy, I've been told I'm too casual for my own good."

"I'm sure we'll be able to handle that!" Dia laughed. "Wanna learn this music spell?"

"Yeah, that way I can play some of the stuff my parents like to play!" Tanith half slammed the door in her excitement and shrugged off the long witches cloak she was wearing.

"Whoa, is that a snake?" Dia gasped in awe. Lily followed her eyes and saw a thin black creature coiled around Tanith's right arm, its head resting on her shoulder with eyes closed.

"Yeah, my mom freaked out a little when my companion turned out to be a snake, she says the lack of legs is creepy. But I love my little Hebi." Tanith tilted her head to kiss the tip of the snake's nose, its forked tongue lazily flicking out in acknowledgement.

"I've not seen anyone with a snake companion yet, they're pretty rare, aren't they?" Lily piped up, remembering a snippet of information she had read on companion lore in witches. Tanith looked proud at the statement as she nodded.

"Yeah, because of that they've got the reputation for being unfriendly because not many people get chosen by snakes, but she's just a warmth addict and lazy as hell." She laughed fondly. "I think they're just too lazy to actually turn up at companion rituals, so other animals beat them to it."

"That would take a lot of the mystery out of them" Dia chortled before holding out the book they had been learning from. Holding up her wand and muttering "*Finiri!*" to silence the music in the air.

Tanith was much quicker at getting the spell to work properly, and the music she played was so much like Dia's. It was quick-paced and jolly; it made her grin immediately and it wasn't long before Dia was dancing again. This time, thankfully, she did not insist on Lily dancing with her; Tanith took up that role instead. She didn't need guiding though; in fact, her style of dancing was considerably different. She rocked her head back and forth, making her hair flail around her face and ears. It looked like it would end up hurting if she moved her head too fast, but when she started shifting her shoulders as well Lily guessed it was less of a risk.

They spent the rest of the night that way, talking and laughing over the music. Lily would never have guessed that there were such simple ways to make friends.

Chapter 11: The Mediheim Festival

Though Tanith wasn't in any of their classes, she took to descending on them during breaks and evenings. Between Dia, Tanith, Finn, and Rainer; the seasons turned from cool and damp to frozen without much acknowledgement from Lily. She barely thought of the reason she was sent here, of the messages she absently sent home that she hadn't found anything still, and of the draconian female who had only given Lily more confusing thoughts to think of.

The only thought that really plagued her, was a growing wish that everything she had ever known was wrong. They were all such good friends to her, and never had a single one of them uttered a word of dislike towards any other race.

Maybe they could understand why she was here. Maybe they would accept her.

"Come on! We'll be late meeting everyone if you don't get dressed now!" Dia smacked Lily's shoulder, jogging her out of her thoughts.

Dia was standing already wrapped up in the thickest piece of clothing that Lily had ever seen. It seemed to be lined with some kind of fluff, or fur and was padded in such a way that Dia looked puffy on her torso while her legs were wrapped in soft, thick linen and her feet stuffed into warm, water-proof boots. She had made them for Lily as well, but Lily had managed to convince her that she didn't need the layers to be as thick. Lily had told her it was because she was used to the outdoor lifestyle, so she had acclimated to the colder weather of winter.

However, the layers were still too much. With her lineage being of ice fairies, Lily could have laid in the snow bare to the skin without feeling cold. And after living her life wearing thin layers and no shoes, so many layers felt even more claustrophobic than when she had first put on a pair of shoes.

Still, she got up and pulled on the layers, knowing if she protested too much she would get that suspicious eyebrow raise that Tanith had displayed the first day it had snowed, and Lily hadn't put the coat on.

"So, we're going by carriage?" Lily asked absently, zipping up the coat and shoving her feet into the thick boots.

"Yup! None of us has mastered flying for that long yet, plus it's freezing out there. I wouldn't want to be in the ice wind flying around, would you?" Dia chuckled, checking her three rats were safely in their cages before opening the door.

Lily had to bite back a comment that she would give anything to be able to fly through the snow and hale. It would be her strongest element surrounding her and she would be doing what she had always dreamed of. It was just a shame that her only chance would be with the help of some enchanted item. Instead, she shrugged lightly and nodded. "Point taken. Let's go, I'll just leave the window ajar for the cats."

Outside the front of the school, there were carriages upon carriages waiting in line to pick up students. The Mediheim Festival was something that apparently witches still celebrated over the winter solstice period. It was an ancient celebration from before magic existed in the world; and one which had died out in fairy lore. Fairies didn't allow their kingdom to go through the seasons like the outside world, so they never dealt with the ancient seasonal celebrations. The witches used the festival now to celebrate the memory of those they had lost over the years in the Great Ongoing War.

The way her friends spoke of it though, it sounded amazing. Tanith had joined them outside the dormitory building, and they met Finn and Rainer at the carriages themselves. None of them seemed to bat an eye to the fact the carriages were just floating balls with steps rolling out of them like a tongue. Were they enchanted to float? Or was there something weird holding them up? Lily couldn't ask, or at least, she didn't feel like she could.

"You alright there?" She was pulled out of her thoughts by Finn who stood beside her with his head tilted. He looked a little like an intrigued kitten, and she couldn't help but smile a little at that thought.

"Yeah, sorry. I've never really seen these before."

"They are more of a between town transport, you don't get them in the further afield areas." Finn smiled with a patient understanding before stepping up into the carriage and holding out his hand to help Lily up. "It's a very smooth ride, the Avesibil keeps the ride steady so it should be comfortable."

Lily smiled in thanks, encouraging the idea he seemed to have that she was nervous about the travel plans, not just confused over how it worked. She would have to look up Avesibils later as well. Honestly, trying to keep up with all the things in the witches' world was painfully difficult. All she could be thankful for was that her quiet demeanour let her get away with a lot, including the shy flush that dusted her cheeks as she felt the warmth of his hand close around her and the strength of his arm pull her into the carriage.

The interior of the carriage was cosy, filled with soft cushioned seats and more legroom than Lily would have expected even with five people sitting down. She was grateful as it turned out the journey was further than Lily had expected, and the carriage only had tiny windows for her to watch the world from. So instead, her entertainment for a couple of hours was the conversation of her four friends, most of which went completely over her head.

They continued to speak of the Mediheim Festival mostly, which at least allowed Lily to stay quiet and just listen. Nothing they said, not one single description, could have prepared Lily for what she saw in front of her when the carriage came to a halt and the five of them clambered out.

Snow fluttered to the ground and settled into mounds at the side of walkways. Where it sat on the ground it glittered like a white fairy's skin under the lights that floated in the air all around. They were tiny little lights, much smaller than the lights Lily was used to hanging in the main trunk of the city hall at home, and they shone with different hues of colour with seemingly no pattern. Hanging suspended from nothing just above head height, they held the promise of illumination when the sun would set later in the day.

Beneath them could be seen pop up wooden stalls with items of material, food and drink origin being sold to members of the thin crowd which milled through the walkways. The stalls had enough space between them for the crowd to continue moving even when people stopped to peruse the wares, and by the look of it, many people did stop even if they didn't buy anything. Lily immediately felt curiosity and excitement spread through her chest like a warm pressure that threatened to bring a giggle past her lips. She didn't have any of those weird little metal things she had come to understand worked for trading in the witches' land, but she still really wanted to look at everything.

"Come on, we'll show you the best stuff." Tanith grinned, waving a hand in front of Lily's apparently stunned face.

"The mulled wine is the best here," Rainer chimed in, gaining a smirk from Tanith.

"I was thinking the honey brewed mead." She countered.

"Or we could maybe not go for drinks that might make her memory of her first festival fuzzy?" Dia interjected sternly, though the small smile on her lips suggested she wasn't going to stop Lily if she decided to go with those ideas.

"How about we just go for Spiced Mint Fusions?" Finn suggested finally.

Rainer shot him a suspicious glare before sighing and nodding in acceptance and letting a smile pull on his lips "Alright, I suppose that's a decent enough welcome. These are the best ones around."

Lily blinked from one friend to the next, wondering what Spiced Mint Fusions were; though as she had never heard of mulled wine or mead either, she wasn't sure what ballpark she should be trying to imagine. It did occur to her in the next moment that maybe that didn't matter.

"I... I don't have any payment for them though." She commented quietly, feeling oddly inadequate.

"We know," Finn smiled, "Dia told us, so I bought extra."

A moment of silence fell as Lily's eyes looked to Finn as though he had said something in a completely new language she didn't understand. "Wha...? No, it's ok. I can't ask you to pay for me." Lily protested with a much too vicious shake of her head. "I'm happy just to look around."

Finn's smile became a little wicked "I wasn't offering. I'm going to buy stuff and either you have them or they are going to waste."

"But..."

"No buts" Dia nudged her with a weirdly shy smile and a blush creeping onto her cheeks "Just accept it. Rainer's making me accept the same from him."

"Well, can't come here and not enjoy the produce!" Rainer claimed as Tanith nodded enthusiastically.

"I'd offer, but these guys have more than I do." She chortled, sounding as though she got the best deal out of everyone present.

Lily still looked like she wanted to protest but with a mockingly frustrated sigh, Finn simply took hold of her hand for the second time that day and began walking in the direction of the crowd. "Don't argue, none of us are going to listen. Just smile and try everything we stuff in your hands."

The pout couldn't be stopped, but at least it covered up the intense feeling of gratitude and guilt that spun a tight web in her stomach. How could she accept such friendships when she was living a lie right in front of their eyes?

The answer to that was easy; when she let all of them take the pace of the day, Lily forgot that she was living a lie. She forgot that her brown hair was supposed to be as white as the snow they walked on and her green eyes were supposed to be an icy blue. She forgot that the freckles all over her skin weren't real. She forgot that she was a wingless abomination of her own kind and that she was actually here to fetch information that would help fairies end a war quicker than usual. When she was laughing at the antics of these four that had adopted her into a friendship, she forgot everything else.

It was a bliss she had never known before. A bliss she couldn't face beginning to let go now.

Finn let go of her hand as she fell into a non-protesting step just behind him, leading her and the others through the crowd to a specific stall which was covered in cups and mugs with the initials M.T. written across the sides in swirling font. The banner across the top of the stall read 'MEDIHEIM THIRST' in bright orange lettering that had fire dancing behind the glass fronts.

"Two Spiced Mint Fusions please!" Finn called up to the lady behind the counter.

"Size?" She asked with a very soothing voice.

"Largest you have."

"But… what if I don't like it?" Lily attempted to interject, finding herself faced with Finn's hand as he waved over her shoulder.

"No one has ever not liked these" He dismissed, counting out some shining silver pieces into his hand. "Besides, if you somehow don't like it, that means there's more for me to drink. I love these drinks, but the rest of the year you can only find poor imitations."

Lily frowned slightly but resigned herself to not arguing back. Instead, she could do little but sigh in defeat and take the drink that was handed to her. It was green, a soft pale green with steam billowing up from its heat. There were specks of brown littered through it like some kind of powder had been mixed in but had yet to fully dissolve; perhaps it had been sprinkled on top and was sinking through the liquid.

Other than milk, water and fresh fruit juices, Lily had never had many types of drinks, but this one looked the strangest yet out of the ones she had discovered in the witches' world.

"It's mint, cinnamon and energy granting herbs that I can't remember the name of." Finn chortled at the look of suspicion on Lily's face.

"Why would you need energy from herbs?" Lily mused while sniffing the drink.

"To… give you more energy?" Finn deadpanned, a small smirk pulling on the corner of his lips at the disapproving pout that spread over Lily's face.

"Obviously…" she shook her head finally lifting the drink and taking a sip. It was unusual, being a hot drink, it warmed her from the inside, but the mint left her tongue feeling cool with each breath that followed. The cinnamon and herbs heated her cheeks while the heated milk settled in her stomach in a soothing way that reminded her of being bundled up in a fur blanket on an ice-cold night. "Wow!" Lily breathed finally.

"Good, isn't it?" Finn sounded borderline smug.

"It is. I don't know how, but it all just works." She conceded, taking another sip. She would have loved to have gulped it down, but she couldn't deal with heat like she could the cold. There was the great temptation to use her magic to cool the drink, but with Finn looking at her and the others moving to join them with their own steaming mugs Lily didn't think she would get away with it.

So, instead, she blew breath over the surface of the Spiced Mint Fusion while they set off to look at the other stalls.

The stalls were covered in so many different things, it was mind-blowing for Lily. There: clothing designed for the winter months, jewellery that glittered in the light of day, round glass balls that had snow swirling inside with little figurines being covered in that snow, and food of so many different smells and flavours.

Lily couldn't help but look at each stall with wide-eyed curiosity, though quickly moving away from them when Finn asked if something had caught her eye.

"Dia makes clothes awesome enough for me." She had replied after the fourth clothing stall.

"Charmer!" Dia had called back over her shoulder.

The day was jovial and relaxing. Lily caved on purchases when it came to food, partially because of hunger, but primarily out of interest for what these outlandish mixtures of sweet, spiced and savoury would taste like. Her favourite by far was the Spiked Chocolate Strawberries. They were exactly what they were called, strawberries dipped in chocolate, which was dyed blue to fit the winter theme, and spiked with a choice of liquids. Lily had tucked into a whole selection, Dia and Finn recommended sugar syrup spikes while Tanith and Rainer recommended things that gave Lily a very warm feeling that spread through her quickly and made her wobbly as she walked. When asked, neither would confirm what they had chosen for her.

Lily's arm was hooked with Finn's for stability by the time the sun was lowering, and they stood by the lake waiting patiently for what her friends described as the greatest show she would ever see.

"So, what is the show?" She asked.

"You'll see." Tanith grinned, sipping on a tankard of honey brewed mead.

"You'll love it. By the sound of your house, it's not been close enough to see anything like this before." Dia smiled eagerly, bouncing on her heels as she glanced out to the lake where little fluttering of glass wings skittered over the centre where the water remained unfrozen.

"It is honestly beautiful," Finn added "The guys who created it are genius'! They are always brought into any big event and this is their yearly bonanza!"

"It's always epic!" Rainer nodded over his mulled wine.

Lily smiled at the growing excitement in her stomach, or maybe it was the warm giddiness that the sweets she had eaten had given her.

That feeling vanished in an instant, replaced with a shocked fear as Lily felt her body thrown forward.

"Lil!"

"Oh, Crick!"

"What the...?!"

"Lily!"

The voices of her friends overlapped one another before being muffled completely as her body tipped over the edge of the ice she had skidded to and sunk under the surface of the water.

Everything was quiet under the water, but Lily could practically hear her mind screaming in the panic she felt while being pulled down further from the light above the water. Instinctively, Lily held onto whatever breath was left in her chest while she moved her arms and legs desperately trying to reach the surface again. Swimming wasn't her greatest strength, and with the weight of the sodden clothes fighting against her, she was not going to win with her physical efforts alone.

She was torn between two thoughts of fear. If she didn't use her magic over water, she was going to drown. If she did use her water, she would probably be found out and she would likely be jailed or killed. Either way... either way, she failed her parents. Either way, she lost her friends.

Her tears joined the water around her as her lungs and limbs began to burn with a frantic need for oxygen. There was a mist of spots beginning to descend over her vision. She felt faint in the pain. Her lungs couldn't hold out any longer and urgently, automatically, unwillingly, she parted her lips to try and take in the oxygen she craved. Nothing but water filled her lungs.

If she had thought the pain from a lack of oxygen had been bad, it was nothing compared to the suffocating choking that came with breathing water into her lungs directly. She couldn't cough it back out, because more water rushed in to replace it. The water around her began to move, her instincts replacing any and all fear in her mind and created a current under her to push her up towards the surface.

As her face reached the surface, the movement of water she felt wasn't beneath her but within her. The water in her lungs moved up through the trachea past her larynx causing her to gag and retch.

A hand sealed itself around the collar of her coat and wrenched her up onto the ice allowing her body to convulse in its confused attempt to both throw up the water inside and breath in the oxygen her whole body screamed for. There was no strength in her limbs now, she could barely see anything let alone register what was happening around her, but strong arms held her head up away from the ice so that the water could fall away from her lips.

"Lily? Lily, can you hear me?"

The voice seemed so far away, drowned out by the sound of her rattling lungs and thunderous heartbeat. The moments ticked by with her body calming itself while remaining limp against whoever was holding her steady. She could have slept for days, but the voices around her kept talking. Lily couldn't tell what they were saying, but they kept her conscious while the magic moved the last little drops of water causing discomfort from her lungs to her mouth.

"Come on, we got you."

"That's it. Just breathe."

"I'm going to kill that liche next time I see her!"

Lily groaned a little, finally taking the weight of her own neck and turning to look around at the concerned faces of her friends. It turned out; the warmth that held her steady was Finn. He had her torso elevated a little against his lap and kept her neck and shoulders supported with his arms. The others knelt around her with fear and worry etched into their expressions, though Tanith looked angry as well.

"Lil! Oh, thank Nocto! You ok?" Dia cried, tears spilling onto her rounded cheeks.

She tried to speak, but all Lily could do was nod. Thankfully, that seemed to be enough as Dia choked back a relieved sob as she launched herself forward to hug her friend despite the awkward angle. Lily reached up an arm to return the embrace, the world slowly becoming clearer.

"What happened?" Lily croaked.

"Kelsie Fulton" Tanith growled darkly.

"She hit you from behind with a spell that propelled you forward" Rainer expanded. "I don't think she intended to drown you, she looked a bit shocked when you didn't come back up so her and her friends scarpered."

"I wish I could have got a good jinx in on her" Tanith snarled.

"She better watch out when we get to the advanced lessons," Finn nodded, helping Lily up to a sitting position. "She's on her way to becoming a test dummy."

"Guys, it's fine. I'm ok." Lily spoke weakly, not wanting to cause more trouble. This wasn't the first time a bully's antics had become a close call, but she didn't like the idea of facing off against Kelsie any more than she had with River.

"You could have drowned!" Dia scolded.

"But I didn't."

Exasperated sighs surrounded her, but no one questioned how she hadn't drowned. Lily was quietly grateful for that.

"We should dry you off," Finn diverted the subject, noticing the tremor in Lily's hands, assuming she was cold. "Did anyone manage the *Siccalidum* charm without setting fire to their objects?"

He looked to all the girls, suggesting that when he and Rainer had learned the Drying Charm with Master Ova neither had managed to do it successfully.

"Lily, obviously." Dia chortled, knowing that Lily spent every evening practising the spells they had been taught until they worked how they were meant to. Despite how many weeks had gone by, Lily had not lost that enthusiasm to complete the tasks.

"Can you do it for yourself?" Rainer asked.

"I assume so?" Tanith shrugged watching Lily search for the wand she had grown so used to in the interior pockets of her sodden coat. "Though, you sure you want to try while shaking Lil?"

Lily pulled the piece of wood from her pocket and nodded slowly, trying to calm the adrenaline shakes in her hand long enough to turn it and point it at herself. Thankfully there was no hand movement involved with the incantation, so with a soft muttering of '*Siccali'*, the area in front of the wand tip shot hot air across her torso.

"Better?" Dia asked once Lily had guided the charm over her whole body.

Lily nodded with a small smile "Yeah, I'm very tired now though."

"More S.M.F's?" Tanith asked, "It'll warm you up more and maybe give you enough energy to see the show." She wasn't really asking. Before Lily could so much as think about the option, she had grabbed Rainer and Dia and started pulling them off back to the stalls calling over her shoulder. "We'll grab them, you and Finn go get a good spot to watch from."

Finn, who still had an arm hovering behind Lily in case she needed support, blinked after them. "Well, I suppose sitting on ice probably isn't a good idea. Here," he pushed himself to his feet and immediately took Lily's hand to help her up. They didn't walk far but settled against a couple of trees at the side of the lake. Finn never let go of Lily's hand while they walked and kept hold when they came to a halt. It was as though he wanted to make sure Lily didn't get cast back into the water.

"Um…" Lily started, flushing as she looked down at the hand that felt so warm in hers.

Finn quickly dropped her hand with a timid smile "Sorry."

"It's ok" she replied quickly though they both fell into an awkward silence. It wasn't uncomfortable, it just made Lily feel like she should be more interesting than she was, that she should have great things to say to keep the male beside her happy. Every now and then she caught him glancing at her as though he was trying to work something out, but he always looked away in the direction of the little market quick enough that he could have just been thinking in general.

"Are you sure you're ok?"

"Mhmm." Lily nodded more confidently than before, leaning against the tree subconsciously to keep her back covered. "I've had similar problems in the past so…" Why was she saying that? It just enhanced the fact she had always been the odd girl that got picked on.

"Someone almost killed you before?" There was a wave of quiet anger behind his eyes as Finn looked back at Lily.

"Not intentionally." Lily paused with a frown "I think?"

"Why?"

Lily couldn't answer that. She knew why River and everyone back home had such an attitude against her, but she didn't know why Kelsie seemed to have the same problem. She shrugged lightly "They just don't like me I suppose."

Finn huffed out an annoyed laugh "Well, they must be blind or stupid then."

The blush on her cheeks felt one hundred times warmer than the *Siccalidum* charm had done. "Maybe" she mumbled, unable to fight a smile again.

"You know you're pretty amazing right? Quiet maybe, but I'm glad I helped you with those books" Finnigan Byrne really did ridiculous things to her heart and stomach. That sweet smile looked so genuine it made his handsome features even more charming.

"Oh, so now you try and flirt with her" Rainer's voice made them both jump, Finn's cheeks rising in colour to match Lily's already pink ones.

"Dude!" Finn whined, snatching his Spiced Mint Fusion from his friend while Tanith handed Lily hers. Dia was shooting Lily a look that translated roughly as 'I told you so' which Lily promptly shook her head at and thanked them for the drink.

"Oh look! They're setting up!" Dia exclaimed, pointing out to the other side of the great lake where a few tiny figures were moving back and forth, carrying stuff and placing it down in a specific order.

"How are we meant to see it from here?" Lily's question was met with giggles at her ignorance.

"You'll see. Just trust us ok?" Dia grinned excitedly.

Trusting them was completely worth it.

The first burst of colour was all it took for Lily's face to light up in childish glee. A shattering of lime green lights broke out and swirled in different directions, bright against the darkening sky.

"Oh my god! That's so beautiful!" Lily yelped.

"It gets better," Dia snickered.

Colours of all hues exploded in the sky and formed shapes that danced across the sky like stars coming alive. First, red and pink roses bloomed above them glittering, while small blue hummingbirds flitted around them. Second, came orange cats pouncing on one another, then flames danced all yellow and red, trees bloomed, and leaves fell and sprinkled down onto water and ice of the lake. The images the light show created was a spectacle to behold.

The light show changed its tune, from pretty images to vast expanses of people with their wands held up into the air, the end of the shimmering wands glowing brightly. They glowed brighter still until the light shot further above the array of glittering witches. In a beautiful icy blue, which reminded Lily of her father's eye colour, a shining phrase came into view *'Never Forgotten. Forever Honoured'.* Cheers and hoots erupted from the crowd of on-lookers that had gathered.

It was heartachingly nice to witness. The fairies never did anything like this; individual families would remember their ancestors within their own homes, but, as a whole society, they never celebrated their memories in such a communal fashion.

"That was gorgeous" Lily whispered as the cheers and applause dissipated and the lights flickered out of existence on the sky.

"Hmm. My family are all represented up there. Well, not my parents obviously, but they vanished not long ago when they knew the war was coming closer again." Finn muttered softly as their hands bumped together. Lily didn't even think before she linked them together, squeezing his hand in a way she hoped was comforting. The way he looked down at her with a soft smile suggested he had got the message, closing his hand tighter around her fingers.

"They left you?" Lily frowned, her eyes meeting a sad smile and a shrug.

"I could have gone with them, but I always wanted to go to school properly. I want to build my own house one day when I'm older, so I need the Elixirs and Maceration lessons."

"Building your own home; that sounds like a wonderful thing" Lily smiled, a warmth tightening her heart gently in her chest.

"Hopefully."

There was a peaceful quiet between them where their hands lingered for a moment before breaking apart as Tanith turned to them. "We all done and ready to head back? It's still a long ride home."

Lily nodded, knowing she would be grateful for sleep after everything that had happened, and pushed herself away from the tree trunk she still leant against to follow her friends back towards the carriages.

Chapter 12: The Escape

"Are you sure you're ok?!" Oscar demanded of Lily the following morning in the bathroom. She had gone straight to bed the night previous when they had reached home so now was the first chance she had got to tell the cats about the events of the Mediheim Festival.

"I'm fine, Ozzy."

"It's another incident like back when River sent you off that branch!" Kiki hissed.

"And this little liche is going to get away with it as well." Oscar huffed.

"Guys. Come on, I'm ok. And no one discovered what I am either. We're safe." Lily reached to scratch both of their ears in the attempt to calm them down.

Kiki bristled a little in annoyance. "I'll scratch her to pieces when I see her."

"Or just inconvenience her by constantly getting in the way or knocking her stuff over" Oscar chuckled.

"Please don't," Lily sighed. "I wouldn't put it past her to do something to you guys."

"Maybe you'd do something about it then" Kiki scoffed angrily, her words stinging a little.

"Even if I did do something, it would bring more attention to me and things would only get worse."

"But if you don't start doing something, we'll never find anything else out and it'll be worse when it comes to you having to leave." Kiki continued, beginning to pace up and down the side of the bath. It was clear she wasn't keen on the idea of living the lie for a longer period than they needed to. "I love that you have friends here, but if they react badly to what you really are, it'll hurt more the longer you are here."

Lily leant against the sink with a soft nod of her head. She was very aware of that, it was slowly becoming a fear that rivalled the fear of the oncoming war.

"Xalina knows what you are," Oscar started. "I think we should get her out, then you might have an ally when she comes to visit whoever it is she visits here? She could help get information from that angle?"

"You want her to break into prison again?" Kiki shook her head.

"We can get in like we did last time and get Xalina out the same way."

"And how do you suggest she unlocks the cell?"

"Steal a key?"

"Or I could use wood and have it mould itself to the lock so it'll work" Lily cut in, shaking her head to stop Kiki speaking as her jaws parted. "Ki, he's right. We're getting nowhere on our own, maybe the war stuff is hidden from all witches my age so we wouldn't learn anything in time to make a difference. But whoever

Xalina visits knows that she's a Draconian, it wouldn't be as strange for her to ask questions about the different races, especially considering her feelings for the person."

"Right! She could approach the subject through concern for her partner, not suspicion of foul deeds" Oscar encouraged.

"And if she tells her partner what you are and they know you?" Kiki hissed.

"Then I'm in trouble," Lily sighed. "But I'll be taking the same risks if we have to start searching in places students aren't supposed to go or start asking questions that label me as a 'sympathiser'. Just asking about why they were arresting Xalina got me looks of distrust and I need to keep a place here."

Kiki's green eyes levelled the fairy and fellow cat with a look of disdain but stalked off without further argument. And that was how Lily found herself ascending the side of the holding cell block the following night after Dia was snoring soundly at midnight.

The silence of the night was intense. Every tiny sound became thoughts of being caught. Every movement of the shadow caused by the cloud in front of the moon became the foreboding figure of a witch who would have her life.

"No one's here." Lily's recoil at a cough somewhere down the corridor had alerted Oscar to her mental strain.

"Sorry," she mumbled sheepishly.

The large cat nuzzled against her calf before leading her along the same route as before. Soon enough, they had come to a halt in front of Xalina's cell, and the shadow which Lily had kept up around her for concealment drained down into the dark void of the floor below.

"Xalina?" She whispered sharply through the bars, causing the woman inside to startle and turn a confused expression to the owner of the voice.

"Lily?" She questioned, eyeing the darker hair colour which Lily hadn't kept up last time.

"It's me." Lily confirmed with a timid smile. "I didn't want to let my disguise fade this time."

Xalina simply blinked and then nodded with easy acceptance. "No wonder they haven't realised what you are" she mused with a glint of amusement in her shining purple iris'. "You really shouldn't be popping in and out of here you know, you'll get thrown in the cell next to me if you aren't careful."

"I hope not. Well, I might get thrown in it, but we're here to get you out so I wouldn't be able to talk to you through the walls."

"You... what?" Xalina inched closer to the bars in the door with an eyebrow raised.

"We want to get you out. And ask a favour, but I'm going to get you out whether you agree to it or not" Lily shrugged.

"Lil! That's not a good way to make a deal" Oscar half scolded, though the delight in his voice was unmissable.

"I'm dealing with someone's freedom, not a bribe" Lily deadpanned.

"So…" Xalina started tentatively. "What's the favour?"

"I want to ask for your help with getting information about what this war's really about and what's going to happen. I can't openly ask a lot of questions without basically pointing to myself and telling people to be suspicious." Lily spoke briskly, not wanting to pressure Xalina, but not wanting to give her a chance to cut her off. "However, we thought that maybe you could ask your partner little bits without it causing too much trouble or suspicion? Then you could get the information back to me with one of my companions when they go out 'hunting'."

Silence followed her words, and Lily found herself beginning to ramble. "I've found nothing so far. And the friends I've made so far seem too good to be thinking of going off to murder fairies in five years. The people I knew back home may not have liked me, but none of them were being raised to be killers either. So, the idea that we're about to go to war is making less and less sense every day I'm here. It's like I'm missing something huge that's the driving force behind fairies and witches going to war every hundred years. I need to figure out if there's anything the witches are hiding and if there isn't, and the war is just some kind of recurring grudge then maybe I could go home and convince the Council there's no need for it."

"You're incredibly optimistic," Xalina snorted, cutting Lily off and forcing a flush to her features.

"Not really. Just hopeful, I guess. I don't want to find out my family or my friends are actually vicious and then fight against them." Lily sighed heavily.

Xalina nodded into the silence. For a couple of moments, neither of them spoke. Oscar did nothing to move away from the stairway where he kept watch for guards. Finally, Xalina broke the heavy stillness. "Well, I'd be a pretty big liche if I didn't help you out in exchange for my freedom. No one else is going to let me out of here other than to take me to the proper prison they've got."

Lily's eyes snapped to the purple ones which still glowed in the darkness of the cell. "Really?"

"Yeah. It's not like you're asking me to do anything risky for me, so it's the least I can do if you pull this off." Xalina chortled. "I'm looking forward to seeing how you're going to hide my wings."

Lily couldn't help the very tiny pull of a smirk on her lips. "You've never met a fairy, have you? I can hide you so long as we aren't directly close to people. It'd be too obvious in the day, but the night helps."

"Hmm. Sure." Xalina still didn't believe her, that much was obvious, but her voice was tinged with good nature. It seemed she was hoping Lily wasn't exaggerating.

Her scepticism vanished quickly the moment Lily held out the vine she had used to scale the building this time and slotted it into the lock in front of her. Three clicks echoed in the darkness of the hall and the cell door swung open.

"I thought magic set off alarms?" Xalina mumbled.

"Well, technically I just grew the vine into shape so it probably didn't register as magic" Lily shrugged.

"Witch prisons are arrogant if they didn't take into account that Fairies use completely different magic."

"Well, they probably think any Fairy would be inside the cells without anything to use for a key" Oscar chortled deviously. "Couldn't ever imagine one being able to exist beside them for months on end."

"That's because it's a death sentence!"

"She has a point" Lily agreed as they reached the window and glanced outside. "So, can we be quiet so no one catches us now?" Both Xalina and Oscar spread their wings a little as they nodded. "If you're going to glide down, try and go slow enough that I can keep the darkness over you smoothly."

Again, they nodded as the vine looped itself around the broken window frame they had been using to get in and out. Covering a second person with darkness moving in a different space was trickier than just extending it to cover Oscar's black fur hovering close to her. Thankfully, Xalina was controlled enough to keep just above Lily to allow the shadow to spread evenly and steadily until they reached the ground.

"We'll go around the side of the school, then head out towards the Densewood until we can't be so well through the dark. Then you can head further while I go back before someone notices I'm missing" Lily explained softly once they were safe on the ground.

"How am I meant to walk with this shadow basically making me blind?" Xalina hissed urgently.

"It is?" Lily glanced over her shoulder at those purple eyes in confusion.

"What? You can see through it?"

"Yeah. But I suppose I'm the caster so…" she trailed off for a brief moment "Why don't you hold onto the back of my dress, and Oscar and Kiki can sit on your shoulders to tell you what's happening around you?"

Without needing to look at them, the two cats hopped up to sit on both the draconian's shoulders. That relaxed her, and Xalina reached out to curl her fingers around the back of Lily's black dress.

"Is this how you sneak around the school looking for stuff?" Xalina whispered.

"Nah, she's too scared to do that but not scared enough to break you out" Kiki grumbled.

"Which you don't approve of?"

"No! The first major risk she takes and it's to free you, not to get information. We don't even know if you'll actually help us!" Kiki growled. "You could sell us out to that girlfriend of yours for all we know."

"Ah, so you're the cynical one" Xalina smirked.

"We usually call her reactive and prickly" Oscar teased from Xalina's other shoulder. "Though she's just hyper and cheeky when she decides she likes you."

"Shut it!" Kiki hissed. "You know I'm right, you're just hoping too much, so I'm trying to point out the other side!"

"We know Ki, we do. But searching through the library is only going so far." Lily sighed softly "We have to stick to enough rules to not get caught, but we also only have so long before things get too close to the war. We need help!"

"This is an ongoing conversation?" Xalina mused.

"It's starting to become more regular. The fairy council don't seem to have much input." Oscar breathed while glancing over their shoulder to check behind them. "We're still clear behind."

They kept to the edge of the outer wall of Quintegia school, allowing its shadow to help with their hidden movements. Only once they reached halfway did they turn to move diagonally towards the Archaic Densewood. The Densewood was many leagues further away than the Fae Greenwood, but the line of tall trees gave out a foreboding deep black while hiding the rising moon behind it. The distance also meant that within ten minutes of quick walking, Lily no longer needed to keep darkness around them, and it was no longer Xalina who was struggling to see so the cats had to lead the way.

"I should probably lead you all the way to the forest," Oscar thought aloud as he flitted along with Xalina's hand held onto his tail for guidance. "They'll be able to see any flames you use until then and might panic. Flying is probably a bad idea too as they'll spot you in the moonlight."

"Good idea," Kiki agreed.

"Do they make all your decisions?" Xalina chimed in a little louder now they were out of earshot from the school.

Lily coughed out a breath awkwardly at the forwardness of the question. "No! Well... Yes; I suppose they do" she conceded after a short pause. "I'd... never really thought about it."

"Well, you barely talk so we kinda have to do it for you" Kiki teased softly.

"True" Lily sighed with a shrug.

"It's nice that you have that" Xalina commented "Companions that are both part of your soul and your friends always sounded great to me. Never seen it in real life though."

Lily smiled into the darkness as they slowed to a halt "It is pretty cool."

"Pretty cool?"

"You know you love us."

"Always." Lily chuckled, turning to squint through the darkness at the draconian. "Are you going to be ok from here?"

"Yes. Thank you for this. So, if I get information, I'll let Oscar know every other week? I'll have to wait a little bit before I see my missus, but I'll be able to contact her at that time."

"Not getting caught again is a great idea" Oscar laughed.

"Exactly," Xalina agreed. "But still, two weeks would be good. If you don't show up I'll have to assume you've been caught and I have to come and bust you out."

They laughed softly into the silence of the night, Lily feeling the tension from the whole night loosen in her back. Even though she had been more than willing to free Xalina without getting the help in return, she was relieved that the dark-skinned female was organising the correspondence.

"Hopefully we'll avoid a cycle of just breaking each other out," Lily tittered.

"Deal. See you around!" Xalina clapped her hand against Lily's shoulder with a flash of a smile through the dark before following Oscar towards the Densewood.

"Stay out of trouble!" Lily called softly after her before allowing Kiki's insistent tugs to turn her around. "Ok Ki, let's go back." She whispered in amusement while her feet were guided by the cat in front of her.

The moonlight glittered off the snow that crunched under her feet. As they walked back, Lily shifted the ice to cover all the footsteps they had left behind. Manipulating two elements at the same time wasn't always the easiest, but manipulating three was one she had not done before. Keeping herself in darkness while removing footprints and pulling herself up over the wall with the vine, well, she was rather proud of herself when she landed on the ground inside the campus without messing up or harming herself.

"Now just sneak back! I'll go in through the window to make sure Dia isn't awake. If she is I'll meow at the door when you come up." Kiki chirped before scampering off towards the dorm building.

Silently, Lily walked back through the grassy areas behind the dorm buildings and circled around to the front so the statue of the Morequcor could let her inside.

As she turned the corner, however, she froze. Her face fell as she met the green eyes of Finnigan Byrne. His eyes focused on her through the darkness with his eyebrow raised in question.

"So, you're a fairy." It wasn't a question in his voice, and that somehow made the terror flooding through Lily much more intense. He'd already made the right conclusion and she had no idea how he had come to it, nor how she was going to convince him it wasn't true.

"W…What?" She said lamely, still frozen to the spot.

"You're a fairy." He repeated, a ghost of a smile playing on his lips. That made this even more confusing. It wasn't a cruel smile, nor was it forced or threatening; it was soft and almost amused. Lily stood rooted to the spot, wide-eyed and terrified. Half of her wanted to bolt back the way she had come and go meet up with Xalina. She could try and find out information from the outside. She could go home and tell them she failed. Though if she did that, there was no chance her own kind would ever allow her to feel like one of them. And she would have to leave the school where she had begun to feel at home with the friends she had made. Friends that didn't know what she was. Though one friend was standing in front of her in the silent night, and he seemed to be very sure of what she was.

"I don't know what you're talking about" Lily kicked herself at the squeaky sound of her voice which just made her denial an obvious lie.

Pushing himself away from the wall, Finnigan stepped closer to her, making her feel like a rabbit unsure whether to run from a fox. "Lil, I suspected after you got out of the lake. There was no chance you could have been so close to the surface still while wearing that thick coat, and you couldn't use any incantation underwater." His voice was soothing and patient, a hand raised as though to convince her not to run. "And I watched you cover yourself in shadow and the snow cover up your footsteps seemingly by itself."

Her mind was blank by now and all she could really register in her own head was the pounding of her own heart. No explanations, no words that would get her out of this. Lily glanced around absently hoping to find the solution somewhere in the cold air. There was nothing. Absolutely nothing to get her out of this. Lily paused, realising there was also no-one else there to bring her to the Lock Up she'd just broken Xalina out of.

"You didn't call anyone?" Lily whispered.

"Why would I?"

"Because... Fairies are the enemy right?"

"Are you here to hurt us?"

No!" Lily's voice gained some strength, her eyes turning to look at Finnigan's still curious face. "No. I don't want to hurt anyone."

"So why would I tell anyone?" Finnigan asked honestly, receiving an incredulous look from Lily who obviously didn't believe him. "Look." He sighed "You're my friend, right? I wanted to ask you about it, and maybe tell you to be more careful if you aren't here to kill us all from the inside."

The waggle of his eyebrows pulled a huff of laughter from Lily's lips despite herself. "I'm definitely not here to kill you all. I was sent here to find out where you guys would be attacking first when the war came around in four and a half years' time."

Confusion passed over Finnigan's face. "Where *we* would attack first? Witches don't plan attacks, we counter the threats we get before the fairies attack us."

"No. Witches attack us for our wings."

"Why would we want your wings?"

"For potions?"

"That's a bunch of zaloot! We don't use fairy wings in potions, the things we call fae wings are the wings of Karai!"

"I know!" Lily half yelled before wincing and looking around in case anyone in the dorms had heard. She then sighed, raising her hand to rub her face in frustration. "I know. The stories of why we go to war are completely opposite to each other, so it makes no sense how we end up going to war every hundred years."

Finnigan shivered a little in the cold of the night, but his head was tilted in interest. "So, wait, you're taught that we tear your wings off for magic and that's why we go to war with you?"

"Yes."

"That's... that's so wrong!" Finnigan exclaimed. "I assume this means that you guys don't attack us because you want to expand the area of the Greenwood?"

"What? We don't need to expand anything. We live in the middle of it inside a barrier that shrinks everything that goes through it. We've got spare space up the wazoo." Lily shook her head at the very idea of them going to war for something like more woodland space. "So, one's got to be a lie, right?"

"Or both?" Finnigan shrugged, looking at the ground with a mind-blown expression. There was nothing between them that suggested mistrust of the other. Instead, there was just a heavy silence where Lily knew her confusion and worries were not hers alone. She now had Xalina and Finnigan knowing the truth of her presence, and, so far, neither had reacted badly so far.

A few moments ticked by before Finnigan broke the silence. "By the way, how have you managed to hide your wings?"

"I don't have any to hide," Lily mumbled. "I was born without them. Which is why I was able to get in here, change the colour of my hair, eyes, and glitter and I look fairly normal so long as I don't put my hair up away from my ears."

A hum of thought left Finnigan's lips while he reached out a hand to brush the side of her brunette hair to the side. Lily tensed but allowed her pointed ear to be seen. Letting the hair fall back down to her shoulder, he smiled slightly. "Well, that explains the loose hairstyles you favour."

"Yeah…" Lily whispered.

Another awkward silence fell between them.

"Does anyone else know?" Finnigan asked, seeming to be the only one out of the two of them who could think straight enough to break the silences. But, Lily figured there was no change there. Finnigan had always been better at holding the conversation up than she had.

Slowly she shook her head "No, only you and the draconian girl I just sprung from the Lock Up."

"That's where you went?!" Finn barked out a laugh. "I thought you were the quiet, rule-following one?"

Lily blinked at him before a small smirk pulled on the side of her lips as she deadpanned her response "I'm a fairy infiltrating a witches' school while my companions' search everywhere for information and I learn everything I can from the library." Finn was laughing softly now which brought a light chuckle to Lily's lips as she admitted "Though, I think I've learned more from you and the draconian tonight than I have from anything else. But the magic has been fun, I never knew we could use witch magic."

"I bet no fairy has ever tried before. Can you do some of our magic without the incantations?"

"I've not tried, but I don't know if I would be able to. My natural magic is mostly tried to five elements but you guys can create all sorts with the incantations."

"It'd be fun to try though right?" Lily nodded to his question before he grinned. "Oh! We could go out of bounds as a social thing and you could see if you're able to get some of the spells to work?"

"What about the others?"

"You want to tell them?" The smile dropped from Finnigan's face at the idea as he glanced up at the sleeping dorm they were still standing beside. "What if they turn you in?"

"You're not." Lily pointed out hopefully.

"Yeah, but... I don't know them enough to know how they will react. Do you?" Lily shook her head with a disappointed exhale. She didn't know how they would react, but she really wished they would react positively. Finnigan smiled sadly as he reached to take hold of her hand, squeezing it soothingly in his. "Look, I can only imagine how much you would want them to know about this and accept it. But you've been hiding it for a reason, right? I can help you keep it hidden until we figure out what the liche is going on here with the whole war thing. When we have more evidence, we can get them on board; even if they aren't so cool with the whole idea of fairies being friends at first."

There was no arguing with that logic, even though Lily found herself disappointed that it wasn't Dia and Tanith who were telling her these things. She liked Finnigan, sure, and he made her stomach do weird twists and turns when he smiled at her so merrily. But, he wasn't the two who she wished she could tell everything to.

"Yeah" She resigned. "With more help, we should figure it out quick enough."

"Exactly! Especially as I can teach you the whole background of witches and you can tell me the fairy history and we can figure out where the discrepancies have occurred?"

"That sounds like a great plan!"

"Yeah? Cool, so we'll say I'm taking you into the town for drinks and we can call it a date so they don't feel the need to come with us?" That grin was back on Finnigan's face causing Lily to squirm.

"Wait... a date?" She squeaked.

"It's a good cover!" He defended. "It'll give us a reason to go off alone without them wondering what we are up to."

"What? But... but they'll ask questions" Lily felt a strange panic building up inside, even though it was going to be a cover, there would be questions and Lily had never even been on a date to know what they were meant to have done to make the cover work.

"So?"

"Well, I wouldn't know what to tell them. I've never..." Lily felt her blush grow on her cheeks, embarrassed by having to admit her lack of a social life prior to coming to this school. Finnigan tilted his head a little, raising an eyebrow but making no noise to pressure her. "I've, you know, never been on a date before" she mumbled finally.

"Really? Are you serious?"

"Well, yeah." Lily couldn't look at him, finding herself entirely too embarrassed. "I never even had friends back home, let alone anything else."

"Wow. Ok. We'll have to cover what you'd tell people when we get back from any outings as well. That's totally ok, feel bad that I'd be your first date would be a fake one." He chuckled, rubbing the back of his neck softly.

"Nothing wrong with that, I've never been too bothered by actually dating. It's just embarrassing when people judge me for it, you know? It seemed to be another thing for people to mock and avoid me over so I thought you were going to laugh."

"Never." Finnigan's reply was immediate, his hand squeezing hers again "They were all idiots, you're pretty cool in my opinion."

Lily smiled ruefully and squeezed his hand in return. "Thanks, Finn. It'll be nice to have someone to talk to about all this besides Oscar and Kiki."

"Oh of course!" Finnigan exclaimed with an excited smile "Your companions can talk, can't they? Is it true they can fly too??"

The smile was infectious and Lily found herself giggling quietly as she nodded. "Yeah, though they don't fly often because they don't like to rub my face in it."

"That's sweet of them."

"Very" Lily agreed. "Though I do feel bad sometimes, they seem to have lots of fun scampering around on four legs, much like I actually enjoy climbing trees."

"Maybe we should go climbing sometime then, while we're talking about the histories and stuff, obviously."

Lily laughed again but found herself nodding "That would be fun."

"So how about tomorrow we go get drinks then go climbing and we can catch each other up on all the history?"

Smiling lightly, Lily nodded and let go of Finnigan's hand. "Let's do that, meet you at breakfast so I can tell Dia and Tanith beforehand?"

"Good plan. Say I called you out tonight to ask you? Explains why we've been standing outside in the snow during the early hours of the morning too" Finnigan grinned.

"That helps for sure; I've been out a long time, Dia may have woken up at some point."

"Ok. I'll see you tomorrow then." With one last smile and a kiss to the top of her head, Finnigan turned and headed back to his dorm leaving Lily to go back to hers with a grin playing on her own lips. Two people knowing what she was, both of them being ok with it and willing to help her. Tonight had been a good night.

Chapter 13: The Fake Date

"He asked you on a date?!" Dia's voice echoed through the room, grating on Lily's tired ears. "When??"

"Last night. He got his companion to come up and knock on the window; surprised it didn't wake you up." Lily yawned loudly as she rubbed the sleep out of the corner of her eyes. She would never get a night of decent sleep during any of this year at the rate she was going. For the life of her, she could not imagine what Dia saw in getting up early each morning.

"No! I didn't hear anything!" Dia was so excited, bouncing on the end of the bed. "What did he say??"

"Finn asked you out?"

Neither girl even jumped when Tanith walked in wearing her baggy pyjamas with a tired grunt telling Dia to scoot over.

"He just asked to go to town and get some drinks then maybe have a bit of a walk," Lily grumbled.

"That's a date!" Dia half yelled, gaining a wince from the other two which she promptly ignored. "Isn't that a date?" She demanded, shaking Tanith's shoulder trying to get the answer to tumble out from her.

"I would consider it a date, he hasn't asked the rest of us," Tanith smirked while shoving Dia playfully off her. "So, you said yes, right? You are going, aren't you?"

They both looked at her so eagerly, eyes wide and excited, though Tanith's smirk was teasing compared to Dia's barely contained glee.

"Erm, yeah. We're going after breakfast."

Dia squealed loudly. Tanith responded by shoving her off the side of the bed with a yelp about bleeding ears which pulled a tired laugh out of Lily. "Is it really such a big deal?" She yawned.

"Oh please," Tanith smirked. "With how awkward you are, I'm betting this is your first ever date. So yeah, it's a big deal. Do you even know what you are doing? Are you going to actually be able to talk for long enough not to bore him to death?"

Dia looked at her with mildly offended wide-eyes. "Tani!"

"What? She's the quietest out of all of us" Tanith defended, sending a cheeky wink towards Lily who just shook her head while smiling. Tanith could have a harsh mouth, but she only ever mocked her friends with a good heart. "But then, other than you, Finn's the loudest so it should work out just fine."

"You calling me loud?!"

"You saying you're not?" Tanith snorted, nudging Lily who could only laugh quietly in agreement. Dia merely folded her arms and pouted, her curling red hair falling over her face. Tanith grinned in triumph. "We love you for it though, don't you worry your pretty little head for it."

"If you weren't so loud, you probably would have never adopted me as a friend" Lily pointed out with a chuckle.

"You suck!" Dia whined but bounced up to sit next to Lily, leaning against the headboard. "So, what are you going to wear?"

Lily simply blinked at her in response before raising an eyebrow "Clothes?"

Tanith barked out a laugh as Dia rolled her eyes. "What clothes? Like you've got to dress up for a first date! At least to look like you've made more effort than a normal day."

"Really?" Lily looked at Tanith for confirmation, getting a half-shrug half-nod in response.

"It's a good idea, especially as he sees you every day. Plus, if you like someone, it's fun to make an effort and see how they react." She agreed.

Lily frowned in thought as she glanced between her two friends and then over to her joint closet. "But, I only have like ten outfits." They were all black so no one seemed to notice the difference but they were similar enough that people probably thought she had more. Dia knew how few she had because Dia had made the ten outfits in the first place so she could mix and match.

"I'll take one of them and change it up into something new!" Dia sprung from the bed and began rummaging in the closet for which outfit she deemed worthy of changing.

Half an hour later, Lily sat finishing off her breakfast with a new black dress that felt a little tighter than she was comfortable with and had lace shoulders and half-length sleeves. It felt strange, and the way her friends kept smirking at her made her feel hot under the collar. She'd never really dressed up for anyone before, and it was difficult to keep reminding herself that this wasn't actually a real date. It was strategic and a way of gathering more information so she could figure out what was going on with this senseless war. The way Finnigan's bright green eyes sparkled a little as he saw her while being nudged by Rainer shouldn't have made the red on her cheeks darker either.

This wasn't a real date, she scolded herself in her mind. It was pretending. The fact she'd never been on a real date and was simply out of her depth could not be a reason to get pulled along for a ride by her own emotions.

"Hey, you look good!" Finn chimed as he reached the table and dropped down into the seat beside her, reaching out to steal some bacon off her plate as it all remained awkwardly untouched. His words didn't help. Lily ducked her head slightly, her brown hair shielding her face a little as her cheeks burned a bit more. Finn probably thought she was being ridiculous, making an effort with her clothes and acting nervous as hell. It was most likely laughable to him.

"She does, doesn't she!" Dia piped up, leaning across the table to steal the toast from Lily's plate. "Though I think she's a bit shy."

"Nothing new there." Finn chortled before looking at Lily as though studying her for a brief moment. "Though teasing may not be helping, how about we go now? Save you from any more torture."

"We're friends, torture is how we show love." Tanith countered with a laugh and a wave indicating that she was encouraging them to leave.

"It's a wonder you aren't more popular," Rainer drawled sarcastically as Finn took Lily's hand and pulled her away from the group and out of the canteen, the sound of the friendly bickering following them until they were a little way down the corridor.

"They really are loud," Finn mused with a chuckle.

"Yeah." Lily stammered as she looked down at her hand which Finn was still holding. It was just for show, but her heart was loud enough to hear in her ears! "Dia was louder this morning. And she insisted I wear this, so, sorry I look a bit weird." She flushed.

"Weird?" Finn quirked an eyebrow before smiling at the flustered look on her face. "I meant it when I said you looked good."

"Oh." Was it possible for her cheeks to grow any hotter at this point?! Lily seriously doubted it, especially as she was so pale already, it was only natural that the colour change would be so obvious. Finn didn't point it out though, he didn't say anything more as he led her from the school grounds and out passed the sentinels. Like the rest of their little group, they knew that Lily's silence often wasn't her being unfriendly, and it didn't mean that she didn't want to be there. She simply didn't know what to say.

"So, I was thinking we should go and sit down with a couple of Spiced Mint Fusions, where we can talk a bit. The Café that does them is really good, they've got booths that help reduce the carry of people's voices so we'll be safe. Then we can go for a walk after if it's not too cold." Finn broke the silence with a plan for the day which Lily was glad to hear. She had worried that he was going to ask what she wanted to do or where she wanted to go to talk about everything and Lily was awful at making decisions. Her friends would drag decisions out of her every now and then, but it was easier to just convince her that she was allowed to say if she hated the idea.

"I do like Spiced Mint Fusions," Lily replied with a smile on her lips at the memory of them at the festival.

"I had noticed," Finn chortled. "I imagine your drinks back home were quite different?"

"Oh yeah. I wasn't really lying about the whole being self-sufficient but usually having fruit and vegetable-based foods. We have a lot of milk-based foods too, but things like energy herbs and meat are non-existent."

"Really? No meat?" Finn looked incredulous. "You've been eating it here though?"

"Yeah, I didn't want to look strange not eating any," Lily admitted with a shrug. "It did take my stomach a bit of time to get used to it, but I still can't eat loads of it."

"Crick!" Finn cursed in amusement as they walked into town. "Good to know though, if we're going to date then I should probably know more than the others do about your preferences. My favourite food is meat though, so I'll end up stealing yours off your plate which will help you eat less of it."

Lily giggled at the thought "It'll be easier than me trying to take less so I don't get stomach aches."

"It probably would have been easier to just tell people you didn't like meat at the start."

"Yeah, but I panicked when I saw the food and just ate it without knowing what it was till later."

Finn laughed brightly while Lily rubbed the back of her neck awkwardly with her free hand. "The extent you've just accepted and adapted to so you blend in here is crazy. Surely there's so much you don't understand?"

"Tonnes, but if I ask questions I'll look suspicious."

"Didn't they, like, school you in what to expect before sending you here?" Finn asked as he pushed open the door to the café and stepped to the side for Lily to enter first.

"We had no idea what it's like here. I had long enough to learn how to make my normal magic move through a stick, and how to make a potion from the elements that made me look like this." Lily replied quietly. The café was quiet with people chattering to themselves but now words really carried. It was a cosy place with wooden décor and red hued flames flickering across the ceiling and giving the place a warm glow. It wasn't large, but the seats were spaced away from each other to give people privacy.

Finn headed over to the booth furthest from the door and sat down, pulling Lily into it after him. The seats were covered in soft cushions which Lily sank into happily.

"So, you just came here without any clue?"

Lily nodded at the question and shrugged. "It was a quick idea from them too, being wingless I was the only one who could get past the sentinels. But I'm also viewed as something that is wrong because I was born wingless, so they probably didn't worry about me getting caught or killed."

Finn looked horrified but paused as an older man came over and handed them a couple of small paper menus. "Drinks?"

"Two Spiced Mint Fusions, please," Finn replied with ease, waiting for the man to walk away before he turned back to Lily. "So, they just sent you in without any help, hoping you wouldn't get caught? That's insane!"

"I suppose it was a chance they couldn't pass up. We've never known anything but what we see in the battles every hundred years. We can't even begin to think about how daily life would be to witches." Lily frowned for a moment before adding more, "Well, we could. But as Witches are always painted as villains, the theories were always horrific and terrifying to think about."

"Like putting wings with dried blood on in cauldrons alongside live screaming animals perhaps just to make us eviler?"

Lily winced a little as the close accuracy he had guessed and nodded "Something like that. There were also theories that you're constantly being trained to kill us, and that's what the school actually is."

"Ha! I'd love to know how learning about pupuacrin would help us kill fairies." Finn laughed, pulling a soft giggle from Lily as well with a nod.

"Yeah, obviously everything I've been taught in the lessons, and all the books I can find, and all the potion ingredients I've cleaned has no threat to them in the slightest. But when I tell the council that, they just tell me to search further." Lily sighed with a shake of her head. "I'm beginning to think there isn't anything to find though, and I need to prove that to them."

"And knowing our side will help with that." Finn smiled brightly over at her as their drinks were delivered and he ordered a couple of snacks as well, knowing Lily hadn't eaten anything at breakfast.

"Hopefully." Lily shrugged again, feeling less confident in her little plan than she had done the night before.

"It's worth a try!" Finn encouraged as he sipped his hot drink, not as bothered by the heat. "If we find enough evidence then I could go to the city. I can try and get the council of witches to listen too."

"Really?" Lily's eyes lit up, heartened that she would not be the only one trying to convince her own kind to listen.

It came to light as they were talking that witches were taught that fairies would kill on sight and that they also had fangs like a predator of the forest. They thought that they didn't know about their magic over the elements and thought their magic was limitless and powerful. Which was probably true now that Lily had discovered she could use incantations for 'normal' magic as well, but the rest of the Fairies would only ever use one of their five elements. The witches also thought that they were tricksters and evil people who liked to watch others in pain and needed more space in the forest because they needed to feed their growing community.

It sounded to Lily that the witches attacking was more like a defensive cull to reduce the numbers of other races, they thought they were stopping the fairies from taking over their lands and leaving them for dead so they could watch on in entertainment.

Both sides had developed horror stories about the other and raised their generations on the belief that they were going to be a hell that descended on them one day. But no matter how they examined it, neither Lily nor Finn could figure out how the truth hadn't come to light sooner. Both species just went to war without wondering if it was something that really needed to happen, both believing they were in the right and that they were fighting against the evil in the world.

"This is crazy, the stories don't match up in the slightest!" Finn sighed as he let his forehead plonk onto the table in front of them, frustratedly chewing on a sweet macaroon he had ordered for them both.

"I wonder why the war even started in the first place." Lily placed her now empty cup onto the table and glanced around the café. Everyone was peaceful, getting about their day, living in the same way that her kind did.

"Who knows, I bet no one really knows either," Finn grumbled.

"You never know, I'll have to keep looking for something."

"I'll help. My family dates back quite far and I've got relatives in the city, they might have some older history books kept in their properties."

"The city?"

"Oh, yeah. There are quite a few towns for witches and then there's the big city where we have our council the same as you have yours." Finn explained with a small smile on his face.

"Oh. I suppose we have outer villages in other little bubbles, so I'm not sure why I expected this to be the only town." Lily chuckled with a hint of embarrassment, though it did mean that this war would be considerably bigger than she had ever imagined if they didn't convince the Elders and the witch council to not go through with it.

The café was beginning to get busier with the time trailing into lunch and afternoon hours; so, before they could discuss anything else, the pair decided to get some sandwiches to take with them on a walk. Lily chose the avocado and cheese mixture while Finn went for a spiced pulled meat.

"You weren't kidding." Lily laughed at the order causing Finn to shrug with a small blush on his face.

"I told you, I like meat. Of any kind." He tilted his head "Do you want to try and bite later? It's probably spiced differently to stuff you've had before."

"You sure?"

"I wouldn't offer if I wasn't," he teased.

Lily shook her head a little, knowing she really needed to stop triple checking for confirmation that the people around her were being truthful in their words. "True. Then yeah, thanks."

Once they had their little bags of sandwiches, Finn's hand found Lily's again and led her out of the café and out of the town itself. They headed up towards the edge of the woods just like Dia and Lily had done before. It was the only real place you would be guaranteed peace as fewer people were likely to walk towards the woods that housed their enemies.

"So, you said the fairies all have one element that's most prevalent in them, right? What's yours?" Finn asked as they walked, leaving footprints in the snow that covered the floor.

"Ice." Lily smiled softly, being able to talk about herself properly made her less anxious. "My natural hair is white, and my eyes are actually silver."

"That's so cool! So how does your magic work? Do you need incantations like us?"

"No, we just have to focus on what we want the elements to do. Some that are continuous are controlled by having so many of one prevalent set of fairies nearby that it becomes as automatic as breathing though." Lily explained. "We have light and shadow fairies who don't have to focus the whole time to keep our season as one continuous season because there are enough of them that have been trained to do it as naturally as moving their limbs, same with the storage of ice. They usually end up with other jobs like council work, or fabrics, or looking after the fugacapra. Water and plant fairies will always end up involved in the farming or housing upkeep of the kingdom."

"Does that mean you kind of know what training and work you'll go into from when you were born?" When Lily nodded at the question, Finn frowned slightly. "Well, that kind of sucks."

"Does it?" Lily tilted her head in confusion.

"Yeah. Like you don't get a dream of your own." The blank expression on Lily's face prompted Finn to continue. "Well, you don't get much of a choice. Especially if you are water or earth prevalent. Like what if you loved the idea of farming but you were born as a shadow fairy, you could never do farming because you aren't the right type?"

Lily mulled over the new way of looking at it in her mind. She had never met any fairy that seemed to be bothered by the work they had, but then, no one had ever pointed out that there could have been other options.

"I don't think anyone has ever looked at it that way." She admitted, finally. "We've always strived for a self-efficient and peaceful lifestyle, so I doubt anyone has ever been unhappy enough with that to think about other ways to do it."

"So, you never had a dream job?"

"My only dream was to be accepted by them even without wings" Lily laughed softly to herself. "That's why I want to be able to go back and save my people the losses that would come with war. One, I would ensure my parents would be safe, but I might also have earned a place in their minds. My future job is to work in the archives like my father, but I'd at least like it if people didn't avoid me at lunch."

"Archives?" Finn's voice showed he obviously didn't approve.

"Yeah," Lily giggled. "It's not that bad. I get to learn a lot from the papers and I don't have to deal with that many people."

"True, I suppose you couldn't be someone who needed to speak publicly." They both laughed softly at that though Finn's laugh was a little more pitiful. "But seriously, there's nothing else you'd want to do if you had the chance?"

Lily looked up into those serious eyes and saw her own reflection within them. Was there something she'd ever wanted to do? Back home there certainly wasn't anything that she thought about which made her feel the wish to do it forever. Nor was there any class particularly which gripped her in such a way either, though that could have been because of the pure focus she had to keep to make sure she didn't slip up. Classes made her constantly anxious.

"Maybe some kind of cross-race historian?" She tittered finally. "The more information I find about the past about this war alone is giving me enough questions to last years, I can only imagine how many I would end up with if I looked into other races as well."

Finn looked at her with a grin growing on his face which made Lily flush in embarrassment and shake her head quickly.

"Which is daft, pretty sure no such job exists."

"But if the war can be stopped, then maybe that job will become a vital one to build all the bridges between races?" He nudged her side softly. "And you're the one who's started this so you'd be the ideal person to carry it on."

"Yeah right." Lily scoffed.

"You need to give yourself more credit! Look at what you've already dug up."

"I've been here for almost four months and I've mostly got confusion and questions."

"Correction: You've only been here four months and you've worked out that both fairies and witches have been living with lies for five millennia which no one has questioned." Finn folded his arms stubbornly as he stopped moving through the snow to look down at the smaller girl. "Seriously, your willingness to see witches as good people despite everything, and draconians despite everything the witches say about them. I think you'd be the right person to ask the questions because you don't point blame."

"I kind of got adopted without much choice by Dia."

"Maybe, but you could still have remained suspicious after everything you were taught, instead you've gotten to know her and Tanith. And you started asking different questions rather than just searching deeper for the same thing you came for. You're now asking why, instead of where." Finn reached out and stroked the side of Lily's hair, revealing her ear for a second before the locks fell back down. "You're a really good person, Lil."

Lily flushed deeply and shook her head. Finn was giving her far too much credit, she was just confused and she wanted to know what was going on, but he made her sound like she was someone amazing for doing it.

"You may not believe me, but you are." Finn insisted, leaning to press one of those heart-destroying kisses to her forehead again before beginning to walk again. Even if this was supposed to be fake, there was no chance Lily was going to get found out with her blushing like this every time Finn did something gentle or sweet.

The rest of the afternoon was less talk about the two races and their differences and diverged into more talk about themselves. Lily found out over their sandwiches that Finn's favourite food was actually sweet pears with syrup on, but as that was more expensive he didn't get it all that often compared to his second love, meat. They laughed over the antics of their classroom time at school, both laughing loudly at each other's little stories from classes the other one wasn't in. Like the time Dia had spilled potions ingredients over her leg and turned her skin purple for an hour, and the time that Rainer and Finn got into a play fight while flying up on their charmed objects and both fell off and landed on Warlock Parvoz.

By the time they returned to the school, the atmosphere between them was light and joyful. Both knew that they had a lot of heavy questions to answer, but Lily felt like a huge weight had been lifted now she had a close ally in her search.

Finn took her hand again as they walked to their dormitories and Lily could feel a couple of eyes look their way. They were probably wondering what a boy from a good heritage was doing with the farm girl who spent all her time with her nose in books.

"Ignore them." Finn smiled as he felt Lily begin to pull her hand away. "It'll help us if everyone thinks we are dating. They'll naturally give us space when we are alone together."

Letting out an anxious breath, Lily tightened her fingers around his and attempted to move more confidently beside him. How did she walk around him previously? Was she walking funny now? The chuckle from Finn suggested that maybe she was and once more her cheeks flushed with colour.

"It will also help that you are really cute when you are nervous or get teased."

"Huh?" Lily snapped her gaze up to his amused features before quickly averting her gaze and pouting through her embarrassment.

"See!" Triumphant, Finn pulled her to a stop just before they reached the dorms and waited for her to turn her head before kissing her forehead again. "Now, remember to make it seem like it was a really good date."

"Well, it's the best one I've ever had?" Lily chuckled lightly.

"Still feel bad about that." Finn laughed, letting go of her hand with a wave so he could head back to his own dorm.

Lily tilted her head slightly as she watched him go, finding that she really didn't mind that this had been her first 'date' even if it wasn't real. She liked Finn, he made her feel things she didn't understand but mostly, he made her feel comfortable and he made her laugh. Even a fake date with him would surely be better than a real one with someone she didn't get on with?

Heading back into her own dorm, pausing only to let the Morequcor statue trot out of her way, Lily couldn't keep herself from smiling. She felt like she was finally making progress.

"She's back!!!" Dia's voice was loud in her ear as the curvy redhead launched herself at Lily the moment she entered their room.

"Whoa!" Lily stumbled back against the door facing a very excited looking freckled face.

"You're blushing!! Oh my god! Did he kiss you when you came back? What happened? Where did you go? What did you talk about? Did he hold your hand??" Dia grabbed Lily's face in her hands and half shook her in excitement and eagerness for answers. All her questions only brought the pinkness back to Lily's cheeks where they had only just begun to fade.

"Let her breath, Dia." Tanith laughed from Lily's bed where she sat with Oscar curled up on her lap and Kiki staring at Lily from the pillow. "But seriously, did he kiss you?" She smirked.

"What? No. Well... on the forehead." Lily mumbled through the crushing hug she received from Dia.

"Cute." Tanith chortled. "I did wonder if I'd have to beat him for making you uncomfortable."

"No! Not at all!" Lily rushed a little too loudly. "It was really fun and I felt really comfortable with him..."

"Eeeeee! Yush!! Our little baby got a boyfriend!" Dia yelled as she bounced back to her bed with Lily in tow.

"Our baby?" Tanith raised an eyebrow.

"Yup! I'm the mom who gives her the pretty makeovers! You can be her over protective dad!" Dia chimed.

Tanith considered the idea for a while before nodding her head with a serious face. "I better give Finn the 'dad talk' later then."

"The 'dad talk'?" Lily had no idea what they were going on about now.

"Yeah, you know. The one where I tell him that if hurts our precious baby then no one will ever find where I bury his body." Tanith grinned evilly in a way that made Lily genuinely believe her to be able to do something like that.

"Oh."

"We wouldn't really, but it's the protective parental threat that happens a lot." Dia laughed at Lily's unease. "Though, I will at least hex him into next week if he hurts you."

Lily laughed softly, feeling happier about her friends' protectiveness than she had done even when she was flustered and embarrassed over Finn's compliments. Maybe one day she would be able to tell them the truth too.

Chapter 15: Message from Xalina

Despite their intentions, for four months neither Lily, Finn, nor Xalina were able to find any information that they hadn't already known. Everything they found, and everywhere they looked proved to give the same unmatching stories that they had already discussed.

No matter what she had expressed to those back home, the council were adamant that the witches must be hiding their plans until the due time and that Lily ought to keep digging. They would not give her one ounce of their time to consider whether everything was all just a lie from history which did not need to be repeated again. Lily found that her efforts were being put foremost in finding evidence to support that this was a war that didn't need to occur, for she grew more desperate to be allowed to be a fairy with witches as her friends.

Her friendship with Dia and Tanith grew deeper with every day that passed, Tanith regularly sleeping in their room with them; on Lily's bed because Dia tended to wriggle and kick in her sleep. At least on Lily's bed, Tanith only has to contend with two cats who slept on Lily at all times; they hadn't beforehand, but Oscar and Kiki's protectiveness had led them to begin doing so after Tanith had started to join them. Something about being able to spot if Lily's appearance potion was fading through the dark and being able to wake her up quietly if they needed to.

They teased her regularly about her 'relationship' with Finn, calling them adorable for having done nothing more than the occasional peck of a kiss. Honestly, Lily didn't know what else they expected them to have done, but the last night of the spring months was no different in their talks after they had finished practicing the transmutation of objects into books with the *Liberatio* spell.

"How do we turn them back again?" Tanith asked as they looked over the pile of blank books they had created on Lily's bed out of every object they could find in the room.

"We do this every time and you still don't remember?" Lily looked slightly horrified at the concept. She had become more vocal with her thoughts in recent months, especially within those four walls of her dorm room. "Warlock Mayai will have your head if they find out!"

"You're still such a goody two shoes." Dia chuckled. Over the months, the pair had become more relaxed about lessons while Lily had gotten more uptight. She had shown an excessive amount of studying in the beginning and felt she now had to keep it up lest she raise suspicion. "Surely you can relax for a bit! At this rate, you'll have read every book in the library by the end of the year here. We've only got three months left."

"Three months which include exams!" Lily grumbled. She was terrified of tests. What if someone noticed she wasn't the same as the other witches here? The practical exams were supposed to be in front of the teachers only; Lily had to get it perfect so that no one questioned the fact her magic was deep in her blood as fairy magic.

"As if we could forget! We're constantly studying with you, remember?" Dia retorted. "It's any wonder Finn can get dates out of you these days. Or do you guys have study dates?" She added with a smirk.

Pouting slightly, Lily shook her head as she raised her wand to point at the first book on the pile. "*Novisatio*" she flicked her wrist and the previous spell reversed leaving a pillow in the space the book had sat. "We sometimes study..." she admitted quietly to a burst of ruckus laughter from the pair.

"Well, maybe he just likes a goody-two-shoes." Dia teased.

"He has to, otherwise you'd think he'd have brought up the fact she never goes to his dorm at night. Or asks Dia to stay in my room." Tanith snickered.

"I told you, I'm not interested in that kind of stuff."

"Offt! Poor Finn. He must have the patience of a saint."

"Or... I just really like her and respect her boundaries?" The voice from the window made them jump. Finn's face smiled at them from where the window was ajar. His stoat companion nudged through the gap ahead of Finn. He didn't come into the bedroom often, he was usually found venturing in the grass areas around the dormitories. Kiki joined him quite often to play in the green warmth. "Can you stop teasing my girlfriend and let me in?"

Lily didn't blush as badly now when she was referred to as such things, four months had increased her immunity. Instead, she laughed softly and moved over to the window to push it open further, realising as she did so that Finn was using a charmed board to fly up to their window.

"You really favour the boards, huh?" She murmured as she stepped back to let him in.

"They look coolest!" Finn defended as he hopped through the window and set the board against the wall beside Lily's bed. "Hey, babe." He added, kissing Lily on the cheek which did still cause her to flush softly.

"Lily prefers just walking through the air with the charmed shoes." Dia chuckled.

"It is the easiest way to do it." Tanith countered watching as Lily continued to turn the transmutated books back to their original forms.

"It's not as fun though," Dia grumbled.

"Being able to fly is fun no matter what it is making me fly." Lily sighed lightly as the final book switched back into the chair from Dia's desk.

"It's cute that she likes the simple things," Finn chortled.

"Obviously, otherwise she wouldn't like you" Tanith jibed as Finn gasped in mock horror, placing his hand over his heart as though he had been wounded.

"Tan!" Lily half laughed in surprise, gaining only a wink back from her dark-haired friend. "That was mean."

"Doesn't make it any less true!" Dia joined in the laughter as Finn pulled Lily back to half hug her and half hide behind her.

"Bullies!" He chimed with a lightness of joy in his voice. His arm around her waist still brought a slight flush to her cheeks, Lily still unable to get used to the feeling of being touched so casually with affection. She reacted the same when Dia jumped on her with a hug as well, and whenever Tanith gave her a cheeky kiss on the cheek followed by an innocent smile. It wasn't embarrassment, it was just sheer delight at the fact she had friends in her life who wanted her close. It had become a very addicting feeling.

"Don't use her as a shield," Dia laughed.

"Yeah, you know I'll side with them," Lily interjected as she glanced over her shoulder at those large green eyes which looked at her in mock horror.

"The betrayal!" Finn yelped as he pulled away from Lily and plonked himself down on the chair by her desk, folding his arms across his chest as he pouted. "I'll never get closer to you than those two, will I?"

Lily laughed softly and shrugged slightly "Well, I do spend all my time with them."

"Without complaint!" Dia chimed in.

"Definitely without complaint." Lily agreed fondly.

"Well..." Finn sighed in defeat. "It's a good thing I like your friends too, eh?" Reaching out to take hold of Lily's hand to pull her closer. "However, I am going to steal you for a while for a walk, if that's ok?"

Ignoring the long 'oo' sounds from behind her, Lily nodded softly with a smile on her lips. They did this every week at least once, letting their friends think it had become a weekly date so that they could talk over anything they had found out in lessons. So far though, they had found nothing, so the walks basically were dates; holding hands and talking about one another and laughing about their lives and the events in it.

"Take your tiiiime" Dia and Tanith sang in unison as Finn got to his feet and headed to the door with his charmed board in the other hand, dragging Lily along who waved back to her friends shaking her head at the kissing faces they were pulling.

"Considering we still haven't kissed in front of them, it amazes me they haven't started to catch on." Finn chortled quietly beside her once they were safely outside.

"Well, the idea of kissing makes me a little uncomfortable still, so I think they just think I'd too shy to kiss with an audience as I get overly flustered whenever they nag me about it." Lily shrugged softly, knowing well that Finn understood that Lily had no interest in physical intimacies. It worked well for the ploy they had going because she couldn't make him uncomfortable either.

"True. And even without it, you're the most fun girlfriend I've ever had." Finn grinned. "Like we actually laugh, and can actually be real with each other." His words and his smile brought a grin on her lips which got hidden as she ducked her head. She was real with him, everything about her was becoming common knowledge to Finnigan Byrne, and she felt safer every day that it was.

"And we don't judge each other."

"Well, we do. But never in malice" Finn corrected, joining her laughter as he pulled her a little closer while they walked through the corridors of the school and out of the gates. They always walked around the exterior, never far enough to cause suspicion, but far enough so their 'date' couldn't be overheard.

"That's true. I definitely judge how much time you spend on your hair in the mornings." Lily stuck her tongue out as Finn immediately reached up to check his messy style which was held perfectly in place.

"I don't take that long. I've almost perfected the spell for this." Finn whined a little as he pulled at the strands that reached his eyebrow. "Besides, surely you take longer as a girl!"

"I spend half my nights looking for information or studying so I can keep making sure I look like a witch when I perform spells. Do you really think I wake up early enough to do anything in the mornings?" Lily laughed at the look of surprise on Finn's face. "You seriously didn't think of that?"

"Erm... no, actually. Huh. Maybe Tanith was right, maybe you do get on with me because I AM simple."

His words brought them both into ruckus laughter.

"I like you because you're accepting, kind, you make me laugh and you make me feel good about being myself," Lily responded when she could breathe properly again.

"There's nothing you shouldn't feel good about." Finn squeezed her hand with a smile. "If you weren't different, you wouldn't be here. So, I'm pretty glad about it."

"Charmer."

"It's not charm if it's an honest truth, I think."

"If you two are done flirting..." Came a voice from behind them, making them both jump with a yelp. Spinning around they both saw nothing until a small cough sounded from the ground. Oscar sat with one fang on show while his mouth twisted into a satisfied smirk.

"You're such a believable couple even when no one is around."

They both flushed, dropping their hold on each other's hand awkwardly.

"And so easy to wind up" Oscar chuckled, pawing slightly at the floor. "Unfortunately, I have a more important message from Xalina so I'll wait to tease you next time."

"Xalina? Is she ok?" Lily asked, her tone changing quickly to one of concern.

"She's good, she just came to tell us that she heard something from the elders of her clan. It might just be folktales but it's something to look at." The fact that he was licking at his paw in between sentences should have given it away that it wasn't urgent and Xalina wasn't in trouble, really.

"Well, folktales are better than what we have to go on at the moment." Finn half scoffed.

"Good point," Oscar conceded. "Well, according to an elderly lady there, who; I must point out that Xalina made very clear, is known as the clan's crazy lady, said that she once heard that the secrets of history could be found hidden behind the waters of myth."

Lily blinked at the cat. "Huh?"

"That was what Xalina said. But the lady was apparently very insistent about it, and kept repeating herself while getting wound up until Xalina just called it quits and decided to pass on the information anyway." Oscar shrugged his shoulders lightly before readjusting to scratch behind his ear with his left hind leg.

"Hidden behind the waters of myth?" Lily echoed in confusion. "Is it a riddle?"

For many minutes, there was silence between them as their minds were racked for any idea of what that could mean. Lily had read all sorts of books in the library, and among those were books on legends and myths so that she could make sure she knew the stories behind the legendary creatures that the dormitories were named after.

"I don't remember reading any myths related to water..." she mused out loud after going through every story in her mind.

"Hang on." Finn held up a finger to show he was thinking through something. "What if it's not a myth, but she'd forgotten the full name of the old castle that's now become our city? Mythanissiam. Back then the castle was just called Mythan, I think."

"That could be it!" Lily exclaimed while Oscar hopped up onto his feet.

"It would be a good hiding place for the truth about anything as it's a place that has existed the whole time. But where would people have not discovered in five thousand years?" Oscar chimed in.

"Dunno. Old dungeons?" Finn shrugged.

"How is that behind water though?" Lily asked.

"Well, there used to be an entrance to the dungeons from the sea. Maybe that's still a possibility and the other entrances were sealed up?" Finn scrabbled for an explanation off the top of his head.

"Looks like we should focus our study on Mythanissiam, maybe the history section will give us better ideas of where water could hide something that old." Lily sighed softly, wondering where to start in the history section. So far, she had stuck to the broad history books about the races rather than about the settlements so there would still be plenty to go through. Finn, however, curled his lip with a long-defeated sigh.

"That's going to be a boring task. Searching history books about the castle is bad enough but having to try and find anything about water is just going to end up with us reading about water and waste systems." He groaned. "Reading is bad enough in the first place."

"It's not that bad."

"You're such a nicor." Finn rolled his eyes fondly as he spoke, though his words gained a blank expression from Lily. "It's just a teasing way to call a smart person. Came from the old unicorns having vast knowledge so people just took part of the word." Clearly, he had forgotten that the slang in one race was very different from another.

"Oh. I hadn't even heard about unicorns until I came here."

"True, though I'm surprised that you haven't heard of nicor already."

"No, so far it's been 'teacher's pet', 'brainiac', or 'bookwyrm'." Lily shrugged softly. "Though I quite like bookwyrm."

"Really? Why?"

Lily tilted her head at the question "Because, from what I've read, wyrm's were like wingless dragons. Still awesome, still powerful, just wingless... and I suppose it makes me feel cooler?"

"Isn't she cute?" Oscar piped up from beside her as Finn nodded with a strange smile on his face.

"Alright, forever bookwyrm it is."

"Lil is fine."

"Nope! I, now and forever, dub you bookwyrm. Soon to be the bookwyrm who took down an age-old war." Finn grinned at the pout that appeared on Lily's face, and while he continued to grin, she could feel that pout begin to break into a smile she desperately tried to fight off.

"And there you guys go again" Oscar sighed dramatically. "You should think about whether you are actually dating properly at this point!"

"Well, I wouldn't complain." Finn chortled as Lily picked up the large black cat and supported his weight as he rested on her right shoulder. Lily shot him a look that said she didn't believe him. "What? I wouldn't. You always make me smile."

"You're being charming again." Lily pointed out as she began to retrace their steps back to the main school grounds.

"We've already covered this. Not charm; just honesty." Finn's hand came to link into hers, and for a moment Lily actually gave it another thought. In the beginning, she had over thought everything, and she had thought that it would be a problem if they were too natural, but over the months, they had naturally fallen into this routine that maybe this was what it was like to date someone and begin to give your heart?

Dia and Tanith seemed to think that more should be happening, more physical displays of affection, but Lily couldn't think of anything else she would have wanted in a relationship. If she was honest, she wouldn't complain either, being with Finn felt as natural as breathing. They laughed together and talked about everything without any boundaries. She felt stronger knowing he was on her side and helping her with her mission and she felt safer being herself than she had ever done around anyone but her family. Sure, with Dia and Tanith, her personality was her own, but she couldn't be honest about her past, all her thoughts or opinions.

Finn saw and accepted all of it. But did that mean they were dating? Was that enough for them to be dating for real? And if it was enough for her, was it really enough for him?

Lily couldn't figure out the answer, so she pushed it aside in her mind. This new piece of information, which might lead to the information they wanted, was considerably more important.

"I found something!" She exclaimed as she placed a copy of *Modern Myth* on top of the three books Finn had been looking through in the back corner of the library. "Look here…" She motioned to the specific paragraph she had been reading.

> *'Water and mirage magic were utilised to create five regular changing pieces of art within the city walls and can be found in little nooks and crannies to give even the lesser walked streets a beauty.'*

"Could it be behind one of those?" She asked once Finn had finished mouthing the words to himself as he read them.

"It's a good start! They could have taken advantage of something that people wouldn't think to go behind." Finn agreed eagerly. "And it'd be easy to check if we can get some time to go to the city."

"How far is it?"

"Not a day trip, that's for sure. We'd have to go for the summer solstice break." Finn mused.

"That's two months away…"

"Yeah, but we can make a thing about it being a date and no one would question it. Means we can talk about it openly. Plus, there's a big summer solstice festival in the city so it wouldn't be weird that we wanted to go there and we wanted to look around the whole city." The logic of his idea couldn't be argued, but it was frustrating that seven months had already passed since Lily had started this journey and she was going to have to wait another two months just to chase something that could potentially just be folktale from a nutty old lady. As though sensing that frustration, Finn placed a hand on her cheek and forced her to look at him. "We have time. Even if it's a dead end, we still have time to stop this."

Lily leaned into the warmth of his hand with a defeated sigh. "Yeah, you're right."

Leaning to kill her forehead, Finn smiled and let his hand drop away. "Besides, I bet you'll love the city when we get there, so it won't be a wasted trip either way."

"Really?"

"Yeah. It's gorgeous! The stone is pristine white, and the main buildings have gemstones incorporated into them so they glitter and shine the most glorious of colours as the sun hits them at different times of the day." Finn couldn't keep himself from grinning as he spoke. "I'd love to learn the techniques for creating such high-level designs like that. But I imagine they glitter much like a fairy's skin with what you've told me."

Lily couldn't imagine something looking so familiar and yet be a city completely foreign to her.

"It does sound like something I'd love to see." She admitted.

"Thought so," Finn chortled. "Though, I may need a few minutes to fawn over the workmanship when we get there."

"I'm sure I can survive that," Lily laughed brightly. Finn never failed to bring a smile to her face even when they were focused on something that filled her with trepidation.

"If you can, I'll marry you on the spot."

"While I'm sure my parents will delight in being able to plan a wedding for me, I'd like to live in the trees which means you wouldn't be able to build the home." Lily shook her head, amused.

"Ah true. Well, maybe you'll come around if I give you a garden with some glorious trees for you to be in."

"I can't just make myself tiny to go up into the trees you know?"

"Wait, you can't?" Finn cast her an incredulous look as Lily laughed again.

"No. There's a magical barrier that's as old as the war that shrinks everything that goes through it."

"Oh. So, if I ever went there I'd be made tiny?"

"Yup, but everything else apart from the trees themselves are small as well so you don't feel that out of place with it all," Lily explained with a shrug. "I actually find it weird now to be so tall next to trees, it still feels weird to me."

"I bet! I'd love to see it one day."

"If we manage to stop a war, maybe you'll be able to." Lily smiled.

"You can show me around! You in your charmed shoes and me on my board." Finn encouraged the thought.

Lily hadn't really stopped to think about what possibilities there would be if they did manage to find the truth and get the two sides of the war to hold their fire. Would she be able to show her friends what she really was? Would she be allowed to show them her world and introduce them to her family? They could live with more freedom, only fearing the terrors of untamed beasts that lingered in the wilds of the world.

"I'd like that," Lily replied with a wishful tone in her voice. "I really would."

It did play on her mind as the days passed by, her heart encouraged by the hope that filled it. Dreams of having her parents and her friends in her life without having to choose a side made her extra attentive to any little details she could find out about Mythanissiam.

She hadn't expected it to be Wild Witch Agrios and her assistant Ferntide who gave her the extra titbits she had been looking for.

They were studying Angahaki, which were creatures about the size of a clementine with two front legs and a long extendable neck that lives its life in a long spiral shell. The shell was grown from the little creature's backbone and was fused to the creature which lives inside. The soft tissue of the body was a slate grey, leathery and looked like it had too much skin for the surface that needed covering. They were odd looking creatures that clung to wet surfaces near water to grab insects and small amphibians as their food.

"If you are able to get close, you can see the adhesive pads on the bottom of their two feet which allow them to grip perfectly even with the water acting to make the stone or tree slippery," Agrios explained as Ferntide carefully held the little creature still to walk around the students and show them the little pads which were surprisingly purple in colour. "They are an effective way to keep small animals from damaging your water features, so you may have seen them in your gardens or around ponds."

Lily's hand was in the air before she could really think about it. She didn't like drawing attention to herself, and even if she had a question she certainly wouldn't ask it out loud in front of everyone. The look of disbelief that both Dia and Finn cast her reiterated the rarity of her action.

"Miss Roselyn?" Agrios prompted.

Lily grimaced as she realised that the class's attention was now on her. She could feel herself curl in on herself as she glanced at Finn who raised an eyebrow at her.

"Sorry," she started, her voice cracking a little under her nerves. "I was just wondering if they could be found on the water features like those in Mythanissiam as well? Or would they ruin the mirage effect?"

Understanding dawned in Finn's eyes; Lily was using it as a way to learn more about the water features they would be looking for.

"Good thinking there, Rosalyn." Agrios smiled widely before waving a hand to the creature that Ferntide was still showing to a group near the back of the class. "As they would stick to the walls behind the water as it falls, and to the stone at the base of the feature, they wouldn't affect the mirage at all. And they would be a handy little addition as they would keep anything else from getting too close to the six mirages."

"Six?" Finn queried with a head tilt, glancing at Lily. "I thought there were only five?"

Lily shrugged as Agrios continued on to give them their tasks of retrieving an Angahaki from the mobile wells they had been standing around in groups of four and creating another detailed guide to the creature in question.

"Why are you so interested in mirages in Mythanissiam?" Dia butted in.

"She was reading a book on the city the other day." Tanith noted with curiosity dawning on her face.

Lily cast a sideward glance at Finn who let his lips stretch into a grin. "That one's on me. I said we should go on a date to the summer solstice festival there this year. Like an overnight getaway."

There was a heartbeat of silence before the two girls let out loud squeals of excitement.

"Girls! Please!" Agrios called across the class. Dia immediately shoved her knuckle between her teeth to stem her reaction while Tanith started to snigger.

"Sorry!" Tanith chimed cheekily as she elbowed Lily's ribs lightly before whispering to her. "How could you not have told us that yet?"

"Yeah!" Dia hissed.

"Well, it's not set in stone…" Lily started.

"The fact you are even *considering* staying somewhere over night with him when you never stay in each other's rooms means that you should be telling us that the thought has happened!" Dia looked like she wanted to shake Lily for some level of stupidity that she didn't understand.

"Well, it's not a trip that can be made in a day. So, we have to stay over" Finn commented from the side.

"Good cover" Tanith flashed him a knowing smirk that made his cheeks flush.

"That's... that's not the intention," Finn stammered. The way he shifted awkwardly seemed out of place until Lily finally realised why the girls had squealed so hard. They really thought it was a romantic trip with all the affection that went with it. Her face flushed a deep pink hue and her brunette hair ruffled as she shook her head desperately. She hadn't even thought about something like that!

"You know that's not me." She whined. "I've just never seen the city and it's supposed to be beautiful."

Tanith laughed lightly at the response and shrugged "Can't blame us for getting excited for you, and an overnight date is usually a big deal."

"I mean, it's still a big deal. They'll have a whole two days without us bugging them" Dia chortled.

"True, they might drive each other nuts." Tanith joined.

Finn's arm snaked around Lily's waist and pulled him away from her teasing friends with a pout on his face. "I don't think she could ever drive me nuts."

"Oh, isn't he cute?" Dia cooed as Lily leant back against Finn's broad chest without hesitation. She knew she was safe there, safe to be herself and safe to laugh just as she did then.

"Well this cutie wants to know where the sixth mirage is so he can show them all to his adorable girlfriend" Finn glanced over to where Wild Witch Agrios was now beginning to walk around to look at their work. She wouldn't be surprised that Finn hadn't drawn anything yet, even when he did no one could make out what it was supposed to be, but she would notice that the others had been distracted. So, the girls quickly picked up their tools and began sketching as Finn waved to the teacher with enthusiasm on his handsome features.

"Mr Byrne, can I help?" It was Assistant Ferntide who came over in response, a shy smile on his delicate features. Over the year he had become a little more confident with dealing with the students, but there was still a hesitation in his eyes that suggested he wasn't sure he was going to be enough. Lily recognised it from her own reflection, and such had taken a liking to the assistant as well as the Wild Witch herself.

"Oh" Finn started, looking a little sheepish, "I just wanted to ask about the six mirages that were mentioned. I only thought there were five."

"Nothing about the Angahaki, then?" Ferntide mused with a small shy smile pulling on the edges of his lips as Finn grimaced slightly. "Well, it's supposed to just be an urban myth, but having been so many places, Wild Witch Agrios tends to believe in those."

"Do you?" Dia chimed, tilting her head curiously to the side allowing her red curls to fall over her shoulder.

"Me? I like to, yes" Ferntide nodded. "It adds extra wonder to the world."

"Where does the myth say the sixth one is?" Finn pressed, his green eyes reflecting his eagerness.

"Well, rumour has it that there is one hidden somewhere in the gardens of the old palace gardens. But of course, the palace is somewhere used by those who govern us and the gardens are so overgrown that no one could go in and confirm it."

At his words, Lily glanced at Finn to find his eyes already looking at her. The same thought seemed to flash through their minds at the same time. If there was going to be an ancient secret, it was probably going to be behind something that everyone had written off as a myth.

"It's got to be there!" Finn hissed to her after the lesson had finished and he had linked their hands together and pulled her closer. Lily nodded in response, frowning a little at the teasing faces her two friends shot back at her as they sped up a little in front of them.

"Yeah… but how do we get past a garden no one is able to get through?" Finn merely raised an eyebrow at her query, waiting for something to click in her mind. Of course, when it did her cheeks did light up with pink hues. "Oh, yeah." She could manipulate the plants with ease to let them through. There were moments where she forgot the true magic she could use when she was constantly making her magic direct itself through the stick she claimed to be a wand.

"Idiot." Finn nudged her fondly before pulling her to catch up with Dia and Tanith.

They had a location and the beginnings of a plan.

Chapter 16: Mythanissiam

It was bitter-sweet to think that if they did uncover the truth, the following two months would be the last that Lily would spend in the school with her friends. She liked to dream that with whatever the truth was finally out in the open, the war could stop, and she would be able to visit them as and when she wanted. But even she knew she was being naïve. There was so much bad blood between the races that even if they did stop the war, it wouldn't make everyone friends straight away. There would be much work to be done to build relations and trust and there would still be boundaries between their people until that trust existed.

Of course, there was also the added risk that Tanith and Dia may not approve of who Lily was or forgive her for lying to them for so long. Lily let out a heavy sigh at the thought, rolling over in her bed to cuddle Kiki closer. Her falsely-green eyes picked out the silhouette of her sleeping friend through the dark; she couldn't imagine Dia holding her race against her, but Lily doubted that she would be willing to trust so quickly after finding out just how many months Lily had kept up a lie for. They would never really know whether she was being truthful or not to them in future.

In the dark of the sleepless night, she recalled words from a book she had read. It had been in the fiction section, but it had carried some heavy phrases.

'Lying may get you where you want, but it will never allow you the trust you need.'

It scared her that this quote was likely going to be very true in her life. So far, the one who knew the truth and the one where trust ran deep without worry, was Finn.

While planning their little excursion, the two spent more and more time together as just the two of them, and honestly, a lot of it became less about the excursion and more just relaxing in each other's presence. Frankly, Lily was reaching a point where she couldn't imagine going back to a life where she didn't have Finn next to her, laughing with her, encouraging her, learning with her...

He would sit in the library and practice spells with her while they debated how to go about the search through the city for water illusions. He would tease her over most everything. He would stand and defend her if Kelsie had anything to say against the fairy, to the point the girl had just stopped bothering.

Finn was a remarkably safe person to be around, and the fact his green eyes sparkled when he smiled was just an extra bonus. While there was still nothing particularly physical about their relationship, Lily had grown fond of the warm weight of his hand interlinked with her own and the arm that often settled around her waist or her shoulders when they were sitting or walking together.

Even in her mind, it looked as though their relationship was progressing smoothly and while to them, they both claimed it to be a façade, the behaviours of them both had become second nature. More importantly, Lily didn't feel like she would be against it becoming something that was genuine on the outside as well, she no longer felt like she was faking the dating affection she showed Finn and even shocked him a couple of times by pressing a kiss to his cheek when she had said goodnight. There was no real urge to do more though, and if Dia and Tanith were to be believed in their stories of love, then Lily couldn't have been in love with Finn… for it seemed to be expected and known that with love came the need for physical touch like kisses and holding the other close to you. Lily felt none of that, and she didn't think Finn did either.

So, neither of them ventured a conversation as to whether their relationship was deeper than they had said. And neither brought up what would happen when they did find out the truth and Lily went back to the Fairy Greenwood. Because whether she felt at home here or not, Lily couldn't not go back to her parents. But that didn't stop a small selfish part of her hoping that they didn't find anything in Mythanissiam so her time here would be extended. It was only ever a fleeting thought, one that she scolded herself for and never spoke aloud, but it was still there.

Unfortunately, life didn't slow down, or halt just as one wishes it. And when you have lessons, practice, friendships, laughter, sneaking around to share information with talking cats and your fake boyfriend... Well, time flies by pretty fast indeed.

By the last day when they were breaking up for the summer solstice break, Lily was sure they were ready for the search, but she was not ready to say goodbye if they succeeded. She had even found herself growing fond of the monotonous lessons of Warlock Mayai and the overly complex variations of what she would have just called potions once upon a time. In fact, she found herself wishing she had taken more time to pay attention to many more things in the school no matter how tedious or difficult they had seemed at the time.

Mostly though, she wished she had spent more time with her friends than with the books in the library.

"I'm going to miss you both," she admitted as she hugged the curvy redhead at the entrance to the school.

"I'm going to miss you too! You better be ready for loads of fun when we get back!" Dia sounded a little teary, but then, she hadn't seemed too excited for the summer solstice at all.

"And you better tell us everything about your overnight date" added Tanith as she wrapped her arms around them both.

"Oh yeah! We want all the goss!" Dia giggled.

"Don't worry, I'll tell you everything..." Lily lied, knowing that even if she came back after the break she still would not be able to tell them everything. But they were satisfied with the answer and with one last squeeze, they turned their backs and headed out of the school entrance with the little belongings they brought with them initially. All three of them had very little compared to the people leaving with crates of stuff hoovering along behind them.

"Are you ok?"

Lily jumped at the sudden voice beside her and she snapped her gaze to Finn's kind green eyes. He knew she wasn't ok, but she was grateful that he was allowing her to decide what she was willing to admit right before their escapade. Voicing aloud her fears, her worries, and her concerns would make it more difficult to stick to the resolve she had in the first place. So instead she merely nodded mutely and leaned her head against his shoulder in silent need for the comfort of his presence.

"Come on, we better get going too." Finn urged after a few moments, sliding his arm around her to give a gentle squeeze before steering her towards the entrance where he had arranged an Avesibil carriage to take them to the great city. Lily had suggested they fly the whole way, but Finn argued they would need to save their energy for when they were in Mythanissiam, especially, as they would have had to have carried Kiki, Oscar and Finn's stoat companion. This was no pleasure trip, after all.

"We've definitely got everything right?" Oscar asked as soon as they were all in the carriage, eyeing the single bag which Finn had by his feet.

"Couple of sets of clothes and some money for food. Do we need anything else?" Finn mused. Kiki chortled as she curled up in the spare space beside the male.

"I think we'll be fine." She purred softly, happily to finally be on track of a lead where Lily may take herself out of danger finally. "So long as Lil's got enough of her potion to keep her looking witchy, the rest can be done without, no?"

"Exactly!" Finn agreed, scratching the little feline behind her ear as she stretched out her white paws before relaxing further for the ride. Lily lifted the small satchel that was slung over her shoulder and smiled.

"I definitely didn't forget that," she laughed. Heading into the main city of witches sounded scary enough as it was let alone walking in there without plenty of her disguise potion on hand.

Within the privacy of the carriage, there was no need for the felines to keep quiet and conversation fell into an easy rhythm between them and Finn who had no objections about his conversation partners. Every now and then, just like the cats had always done, he would glance at Lily and pull her back into the conversation if she had fallen quiet again; but she couldn't help it, watching him with his fingers running through Kiki's fur and meeting Oscar sarcasm with just-as-quick wit was honestly warming her heart more than she ever knew possible.

Was it possible she was falling for this boy?

Shaking her head softly, she turned her eyes to gaze out of the little carriage window as they sailed smoothly above the ground towards the great lakes. She had to admit, this corner of the world really was quite beautiful, and the horizon to the east was always graced with the mountains that made up the border between them and whatever else laid further out in the world. Perhaps, if the war could be stopped, eyes could one day look out past those mountains and see what other beauty they could find.

That scenery and the thought of a peaceful future had lulled her into a sleep before Lily could even register she was going under. It was only when she felt a hand on her shoulder shaking her slightly and a deliberately gentle voice calling her that she stirred again.

"Lil, come on, wake up. We're here!" Finn called through her dream walls and pulled her back to reality.

Blinking her eyes open, Lily groaned very slightly, her back clicking as she sat up straighter in her seat and let out a large yawn. "Sorry..." she mumbled before turning to glance outside, realising that it was already dark.

"Don't be, I figured you would have been nervous so wouldn't have slept much. You got about six hours..."

"Six hours?!" Lily blanched at the information.

"Erm, yeah... that's how long it took to get here anyway. You were obviously in need of it, so I didn't want to wake you." Finn smiled softly at the raised eyebrow Lily displayed. "We've been planning while you slept." The two cats nodded in confirmation.

"You guys are going to go find the place we'll be staying in, get some food, and Kiki and I will do a quick scout to see if we can find some of the mirages." Oscar explained, while Kiki sat up straighter as though proud to have a part in the plan. "Figure, if we can find some, it reduces the amount of time you two waste walking around."

"As we only have two nights booked, it seemed like a good idea to make it more efficient." Finnigan added with a sheepish smile.

Lily nodded gently before answering, "Good idea."

The anticipation of a good plan and finally finding some answers gave Lily a small spring in her step as the Avesibil brought the carriage to a halt for them to step out.

"Oh, wow!" Lily exclaimed, tilting her head back to look up towards the top of the gorgeous white stone structure she was in front of. It was the walls of an old castle which had been spruced up and now glittered in the sunlight of the late afternoon. As Finnigan guided her through the front gates, her eyes darted to the ground which was made of the same white stone but had designs patterned into it with gemstones of all colours. Every step she took caused the light to create another angle of shine, though there was an array of colours being reflected onto the white. Looking up, Lily found herself further in awe. Floating above the buildings by a few metres were twisted spires of coloured glass, a different colour over the different sections of the city but still managing to create a dance of colour any way you looked.

It should have been too much, but the colours were gentle and soft on the eye, and rather than squinting at them, Lily found himself smiling softly feeling a deep happiness in her chest.

"Mythanissiam is gorgeous," she all but whispered, gaining a chuckle from Finnigan as he held her hand and playfully shoved against her shoulder.

"I thought you'd like it."

"I've never seen anything like it," she admitted even though that fact was obvious.

"You'll like the inn too I think." He smiled softly, spending perhaps a little too long looking at the glitter of green in her eyes before turning around and tugging her in the right direction. The cats trotted off in separate paths as they did so.

Because of the crowd of the city, Lily was forced to walk with her shoulder pressed close to Finnigan. Or maybe that was an excuse, she found herself not wanting to make space between them, and she smiled shyly when Finnigan let go of her hand in favour of wrapping his arm around her waist. Mythanissiam smelled of fresh flowers, a soothing scent that seemed to waft through the streets without source or end. Every now and then the scent of warm drinks or food would filter through.

"Oh, that smells good…" Lily mumbled as her stomach made her hunger known to the world around.

"Yeah? We'll come back when we've checked in then," Finnigan glanced up to the sign and mouthed the words *'The Perdi's Head'* to himself, casting them to memory. "I'm paying." He added with a smirk, knowing the debate they had had a few weeks ago when Lily realised that Finnigan was intending to pay for their stay here. It made sense, but she felt bad that she couldn't contribute. He had insisted this was for a good cause, and even if it wasn't and was just a date he would have insisted anyway.

It certainly felt like a date, but then, so did most of their time together these days. Frowning a little in protest, she bit back her arguments and leant her head against his shoulder instead. "Fine. When all this is done, I'm treating you to something."

"You can show me around your home." He commented with an easy smile. "Then we'll be even."

"Yeah, right. We don't even use money; how could we be even after that." Her only response was a grin and a shrug before she was pulled into a building that was tall, thin, and designed in a cloud grey colour with purple gems dotted around.

"Oh, it's cute!" She exclaimed without thought, looking around at the timber frames of the interior. It was like the wooden world Lily was used to had come together with the stone that witches liked and merged into something dainty and beautiful to behold.

"I thought you'd like it." The fondness of the tone caused heat to spread over her cheeks, though she didn't shy away when he took her hand and pulled her through the entrance hall to the reception desk. The blonde-haired witch behind the counter perked up as he set his eyes on them.

"Welcome!" His voice was high and a little nasal, but his face spoke of nothing but friendliness. "You two have a reservation?"

"Sure do. One room under Byrne."

Lily's eyes snapped to Finnigan in surprise. They were sharing a room?! As if sensing that panic through her fingers that gripped tighter around his, Finn smiled to himself before leaning over and whispering to her. "Don't freak out, I just couldn't afford two. It has a couch, I'll be on that."

How much more considerate was this guy going to get? Sure, they weren't actually together? Or were they? They'd both expressed that they'd be ok with it if they were... did that count as confessions? Glancing away from the beautiful male beside her, Lily attempted to quash the blush that stubbornly wouldn't leave her cheeks.

"You know, blushing brings out those freckles more," Finn teased, taking the key from the witch and laughing as the blush only gained a darker hue.

"Shut up..." Lily would never be proud of her quick responses.

"It's cute."

Lily groaned, her blush no doubt reaching her ears while Finnigan pulled her under his arm for a one-sided hug and pressed a kiss to the top of her head. "Alright, I'll stop. Come on."

The room fit the decor of the rest of the place, the grey and purple mixture creating a calming aura while the room itself seemed to have a faint lavender scent.

"Does everywhere here smell like flowers?" Lily asked without much thought as Finnigan dumped their bag on the bed and flopped onto the sofa to check out its comfort levels.

"Oh, yeah. The council thought it would offset any negative smells of so many people and companions living in one city. My cousin works in the council so she told me." He added at the raised eyebrow that Lily turned to him. "They were going to do food scents but just testing them out made them hungry more often."

Lily snorted a laugh. "I can see how that would happen."

"Just like walking past *Perdi's* brought your hunger to light," he teased. "Fancy going for food now?"

"Thought you'd never ask!" Lily chortled, her stomach grumbling again in agreement.

The interior of *The Perdi's Tail* was warm, likely from the open fire that was flickering to the side of the reception desk. There were a few people heading up and down the wide wooden staircase and into the adjoining room which had the scent of roasted meat filtering through the air. There was also the rich tang of mead which Lily recalled from the Mediheim Festival.

Following Finnigan over to a table in the adjoining room, Lily glanced around before asking in a lower tone. "So, what's a Perdi?"

"It's short for Perdiauxilio." Finnigan said as though that was enough of an explanation, quickly chuckling at the blank expression on Lily's face. Clearly, that was not a name she had come across in all her books. "They're thin cat creatures who appear only before those who are lost on a journey of which the destination is true and honourable. They are supposed to be a clear sign that the lost one should not waver on their journey as they are a good omen."

"Oh wow, they sound amazing."

"I suppose, there's been no record of them since the Great War though. Apparently, they were the ones who led all the refugee children away to safety - but no one ever saw them again so I'm guessing that wasn't true." He finished with a small haunted look as though the idea of hundreds of tiny children disappearing was a horror he'd been told about often. Perhaps it was a similar story to keep Witch children from wandering too far just like the Macellavir was for fairies.

"Maybe they are still out there?" Lily mused, "Like, back home, we had no idea that the draconians existed. So maybe the children were guided somewhere so safe they just thrived there?"

"That could mean there's non-magic humans out there still?"

"Imagine that, living without magic." Lily shook her head; she certainly would not have survived without using magic to manipulate her surroundings so she could merely move around.

"They'd have to come up with so many alternatives to things." Finnigan added with a mild excitement in his voice.

"Or everything would take a lot longer to do..." Lily reminded, causing that excitement to fall from the brunette's face.

"Ok, maybe that wouldn't be as fun."

"Or convenient."

They both chuckled before pulling themselves to sit straighter as a young witch walked over to take their order. Finnigan ordered for both, claiming he knew what Lily should be trying and that she should trust him. Of course, Lily trusted Finnigan. Though she didn't point out that that went a lot further than food choices.

Though his food choice was amazing. Lily wasn't quite sure what to make of the strange stack on her plate when it was set in front of her; but the layers of pasta, meat, veggies, all cooked with a mixture of tomato and cheese sauces came as a delightful shock to her tongue. It was warming to the soul and many times throughout the meal she ended up with some sauce on the corner of her mouth, blushing darkly any time Finnigan reached over without warning and stole it from her skin for a taste.

In between their talking and their laughter, Lily found there were just moments when silence fell between them in complete comfort and their eyes struggled to leave each other as though they were searching the depths for an answer to an unspoken question. It was peaceful, pleasant, and yet it set a strange fluttering alight in her stomach.

"Your white hair's starting to come through, we should go." Finnigan said after a long stretch once the plates were cleared. It was soft, so as not to draw attention, and Lily pulled her ponytail around to check. Sure enough, there were little white highlights beginning to show through the brown.

"Oh, I slept through when I was supposed to take it in the carriage!"

"It's alright, it just looks like a fashion statement." Finnigan laughed as he waved over the waitress to hand over payment for the food, adding in an undertone, "We'll be back before your eyes or your shimmer are a problem."

The darkness of the sky outside showed how much time they had spent inside, twisted spires glittering under the light of the stars above. The darkness kept her hair hidden well, and by the time the pair were shutting the door to her room, Lily's hair was half white.

"Oh dear," she muttered at seeing her reflection in the mirror over the dressing cabinet, immediately grabbing the overnight back from where it sat on the bed and rummaging for the potion.

A hand came to rest on her arm, causing her to pause and glance at Finnigan who looked almost nervous. "Can I see?"

Lily blinked at him in surprise. "What?"

"I want to see what you really look like," his voice was barely audible as he leaned in a little to touch a few strands of white hair. "This white is gorgeous. I'd like to see all of it. Please?"

There it was again, their eyes unable to tear away from the gaze of the other.

"Really?" Lily whispered, scarcely willing to believe her ears.

"Really." Finnigan chuckled, pushing her hair back to reveal her pointed ears which she had kept so carefully covered for so many months. The idea of Finn seeing her for exactly who she was gave her thrills shooting through her nervous system. After so long of being told to hate fairies, would he really be ok with all her features? A new fear spread through her. What if he wasn't ok with her silver eyes and her skin's shimmer? What if it made him pull away from her?

But what if it didn't?

Chewing on the inside of her lip, Lily nodded her assent.

There were still many minutes where the false colour appeared to leak out of her, and Lily couldn't help but fidget nervously while Finnigan watched her in a silence that was both comfortable and terrifying. It felt like he was judging, but his expression was soft, almost tender.

"You're beautiful." He breathed finally, stepping closer to run his fingers through the side of her snow-white hair. His green eyes danced with emotion that made Lily's chest swell and tighten at the same time. His fingers left her hair to skim over the skin of her cheek, entranced for a moment by the way her silver shimmer made her glitter in the fire light of the room. They stood inches from each other, but Lily found she didn't want to step away, if anything she wanted to be closer. Finn was looking at her as if she held more beauty than all the gemstones they'd seen that day. It made her stomach flutter and flip. As did the way his head dipped down and Lily let her body lean up to meet his lips with her own.

Her whole body lit up with delight at the contact, it was everything she had never known and it made her feel like she could fly. It was chaste, gentle, and his thumb brushed over her cheek.

"Oooo! Smooching!" Kiki's voice caused both Lily and Finn to jump and pull apart. Both of them turned to the window where Kiki sat on her haunches looking smug, while Oscar clambered in through the open gap behind her.

"Don't stop on our account," Oscar teased once safely inside.

Rolling her eyes, Lily pulled back reluctantly from Finn and turned to face the cats, ignoring the blazing blush on her cheeks. "Any luck finding mirages?"

Finn dropped himself down onto the couch with a small laugh, not interrupting as the cats launched into an explanation of what they had found and where. They had searched the sectors of the city that were closest to the inn. They had found three images; the Cantonitrua, Alesrex, and Morequcor.

"The legends? Just like at Quintegia?" Lily confirmed before tilting her head slightly. "That would make sense if there's a hidden sixth one; the six legends."

"True, and I'll bet the other two will be easy to find given that they aren't just basic images," Finn added.

"We'll ask the receptionist in the morning if they know the mirage locations and start with the two you guys didn't get to. For now, we should get some sleep." He ruffled Kiki's fur, eliciting a soft purr, before he headed for the bathroom to change into sleep clothes.

"I like him," Oscar sidled up to Lily's side, looking pointedly at the flush on her cheeks at the words.

"Yeah. Me too."

Chapter 17: Mirages

The mirages turned out to be a bit of a tourist destination. The receptionist not only was able to tell them where to look for but they were able to give them a map which gave them the exact location of the five of them in the main city.

"The only one missing is the Macellavir," Finn mumbled on the way out of the inn.

"Probably because it's the stuff of nightmares and they didn't want it terrifying children," Lily laughed with a shake of her head. All the books she had read about the legends in the witch world described the beast just as hideously as the scary stories she had been told as a child. There was no question that she would be put on-edge walking past the rot and moss-covered skeletal body, and it really would stand out against the beauty of Mythanissiam.

The Treanguis mirage was found in the furthest south part of the city, where botanists and apothecaries seemed to be situated every few buildings all treating or helping with specific things.

"Do people really want to change their hair so much?" Lily asked, leaning to look into a window which had vials of potions all with different colours as labels.

"Yeah; if it was only your hair that changed when your potion wore off, you wouldn't stand out as much as you think." Finnigan chuckled as he motioned to the lime green vial with a raised eyebrow. "Please tell me some green fairies have hair that bright."

"Some do, yeah."

"That's amazing. It's more of a city thing here - you don't see colours so much in the villages; and I don't think they allow it at Quintegia. I'd love blue hair."

"Really?"

"Yeah, I'd look so cool."

"Surely red would complement you better?"

"You think?" He sent a smirk her way before pushing the door open to let himself into the shop. "That's what we're doing tonight!"

"Are you serious?"

"Sure! We've got time out from school and I can always change it back. Besides, I think I'd like to stand out as much as you when your hair is white."

"I can't let that show though," Lily whispered in the quietness of the shop while Finn searched the shelves for a red colour he liked.

"Not yet, but you will be able to soon."

Rolling her eyes fondly, she stood back and watched as Finn bustled up to the owner with a vial of the brightest red he could find, offering over the correct money for them in a handful of silver coins. Once the vial was safely tucked in his pocket, they were back outside and heading towards the Treanguis mirage.

The mirage itself was gorgeously detailed. It spanned up a wall that was around ten-foot-tall and the three headed snake slithered up and down it in a slow motion. It was smaller than Lily had imagined the actual Treanguis would be, but it's green and brown diamond patterning rippled with the movement.

"Do you reckon it was bigger than that?" Finn asked from her side before walking over to the mirage and none-to-graciously stuck his hand through to the wall behind.

"I figured it would be a lot bigger," Lily replied, glancing around sheepishly at the strange look an elderly couple were casting at Finn. Thankfully, he only waved his hand around for a moment before jogging back to Lily's side looking unabashed.

"Not sending anything there... Where is the other one?"

Lily pulled the little map the innkeeper had given them and opened it in front of them. "It was the Noctosseus which I think was in front of the old keep?" Scanning over the map she quickly pointed to where she was talking about. They had decided to do the further mirage first, because if the Noctosseus was unsuccessful then they would be close to the keep where they castle gardens in the rumour would be.

Mythanissiam wasn't small though, it had taken a couple of hours to reach the Treanguis from the inn and it took a couple more to get back to the deep centre of the city. Finn was a little out of breath, but Lily had no issue with stamina.

"How are you doing this without wanting to sit down?" He demanded as they walked into the open space in front of the keep doors.

"I spent all my life walking and climbing and trying to keep up," Lily shrugged with a smile cast down to the smooth floor. "Plus, this ground is easy to walk on, so it's not straining me in any way?" Did that even make sense? She'd spent so long going up and down, walking over bark and through moss and around leaves that smooth marble was frankly very little resistance.

"Argh, you make me sound so old if I can't keep up with you!" Finn was chuckling though, coming to a stop to stretch his back out from where he had started to slouch while he walked. Letting go of Lily's hand he pressed both fists into the small of his back and pushed forward, encouraging the bend of his back and crackling a couple of bones. "Oh, that's better!" He sighed before letting out a small gasp.

"I don't think there's going to be anything behind the Noctosseus..." at Lily's confused face, he pointed upwards where the mirage swam over the sky above, likely trying to recreate the way the Noctosseus was said to move in the sky.

"Unless witches can hide things in clouds?" Lily ventured in jest.

"Maybe one day, but we can barely keep rugs and shoes levitating for more than a few hours at a time; I doubt we're floating an invisible mystery lair in the clouds." Finn laughed.

"True, that's more a fairy concept."

"You need to work on that!"

"Sure, once I've finished this job, that can be my next one" Lily chortled with a shake of her head.

"So, let's get this job done then." Finn took her hand once more and tugged her in the direction of the old keep where large steps of soft grey stone stood out against the white of the rest of the city.

"Are we going to be able to get in there?" Lily whispered, eyeing the witch guards at the front doors to the keep.

"Yeah don't worry. I have a way." Finn whispered back before enthusiastically waving at one of the guards. "Mikhail! How you doing, man?"

Lily shot Finn a horrified look. How was that going to help them sneak inside?!

"Lil' Finn! Good to see you." The man was at least twice their age but his smile brought a boyish charm to his previously stern features. Leaning down to wiggle his fingers to Finn's companion, smiling brighter as the little stoat trotted over to nuzzle his hand while the cats by Lily gave the stranger wary looks. "Here to see Essie?"

"Yeah, thought I'd drop in and say hi while I'm in town on a date," Finn smiled smugly while Lily flushed and turned her head away, missing whatever reaction Mikhail gave that made Finn bark out a laugh. Was it an actual date now? They were here for a purpose. But they had kissed the night before. Did that make this different now? Were they not fake-dating now?

"Well don't let me keep you," Mikhail chuckled. "You know where her office is."

"Cheers!" Finn squeezed Lily's hand pulling her through the main gates to the keep. Not wishing to be totally rude in her awkwardness, she raised a hand in farewell to Mikhail.

"Who's Essie?" She whispered when they were out of earshot.

"Esmaria, my cousin." Finn explained. "We're not actually going to see her but it's a good excuse if anyone asks why we are here. She works for the council, mostly in administration of records but it means her office is right at the back of the old castle because she can use the old library as storage space. So, no matter how far we go to get to the gardens, we have the excuse that will still work for us."

"Oh, yeah that will help," Lily visibly relaxed, glad that Finn had thought so far ahead and already had planned answers for any questioning that happened.

No one did stop them though, a few greeted Finnigan when they recognised him, one young lady commented that she thought Esmaria was in a meeting and Finnigan said they would wait in the library; that was a good enough response that she said nothing more. All rooms of the old castle had been changed into places of work, and, according to Finn, the old throne room from the old times of human Kings and Queens was now the vast meeting room where they debated changes and punishments to be put in place. Lily would have loved to see the room, but there was no reason to head into the centre of the castle when their goal was outside.

On the first floor, they found a set of glass doors that were unlocked and led out onto a balcony.

"Oh... That really is overgrown" Lily commented, looking down at the mass of plants that tangled together and grew in different colours and sizes beneath them. Shrubs, bushes, trees, flowers... she could see all of them knotting together and giving the garden a wild look that would be unpassable to most.

"Yup. But that shouldn't be a problem, right?"

Lily couldn't stop the tiny smirk that mirrored the one on Finn's face. "Oh yeah, I think I can handle some wild shrubs." As if to prove her point, she placed a hand on the edge of the balcony and encouraged the plants from below to wind up and around the stone structure, creating a thick blanket of vegetation for them to slip down into the undergrowth.

"Nocto," Finn breathed. "You're cool."

Lily's head shook despite the loud meow of agreement that Kiki let out as she batted at the stoats back end where they had settled near their human descendants. "Charmers."

Without letting them protest, Lily glanced around to check the hallway was still clear before hopping over the balcony and disappearing into the mass of vegetation, pulling the thick vines back down from the balcony once Finn and the companions were all down in the shadows with her.

"We'll go around the edge first," Lily commented quietly as she turned towards the left, plants untangling and bending out of the way to form an arch to walk under at a crouch. Every foot in front of them, more plants followed suit while a foot or so behind them, they knotted themselves back up into their original mess.

"This is amazing," Finn breathed, so close behind her that Lily could feel his breath on her ear. Lily had long since forgotten how cool it was to manipulate the environment at will; back home it was just second nature that barely anyone used any magic consciously. But with Finn's awed voice, she began to create little images in the walls of the arches as they passed through them. She bent and twisted the vegetation to design the shapes of woodland creatures, Finn's stoat skittering up his leg as Lily created its mirror image in thorny twigs on the floor and had it trot alongside them for a couple of moments.

Her antics kept them amused until they reached the far end of the gardens, sticking close to the walls which her plant critters utilised and danced over. At the far end, Lily let out a loud scream while stumbling back into Finn.

As she had moved more plants out of the way, she had found herself face to face with a rotting body curling over them from a height and a dragon's skull staring down at them, jaw ajar to show the razor-sharp teeth of a dragon from a long time back. Behind the skull was blackness that wasn't even remotely penetrated by light. It was like staring into a void. It had skeletal arms which reached out to them slowly and it's wide, trunk-like feet seemed to merge with the ground beneath it.

"It's just the mirage," Finn laughed softly as he wrapped an arm around Lily who's breathing had become laboured as she looked up at the horrific sight of the Macellavir. It even had strips of flesh hanging from the teeth as though it had recently finished feasting on a body.

"It's worse than I ever imagined" Lily whimpered softly, unable to tear her eyes from the nightmare of her childhood. Seeing it like this, she wouldn't be surprised if it became the nightmare of her adulthood as well.

Kissing the top of her head gently, Finn moved to stand in front of Lily and took her right hand in his. "Come on," he chortled, clearly tickled by her display of fear, and stepping towards the Macellavir with his left hand outstretched. Just like the other mirages, there was no resistance when he pushed his hand through the creature. So, Finn ploughed through the image, pulling Lily along who had opted to pick up Oscar with her free hand and hug him close while she squeezed her eyes closed.

Oscar nuzzled under her chin with soothing whispers reminding her that the Macellavir wasn't real and it was ok. She knew that logically, but that didn't make the cool sensation of the mirage feel any less like the ominous chill of death.

"There's a door!" Finn exclaimed, Lily's eyes blinking open in time to see his left hand try the door handle. It opened without issue. "Weird, I thought it would be locked..."

"Maybe someone's in there!" Kiki hissed from the ground, nudging ahead to sniff at the gap Finn had pulled the door open to create.

"If there is, then they can give us answers." Finn suggested, pulling the door open further. Lily recoiled a little at the damp scent that came from the entrance and squinted into the darkness to make out a stone staircase down into the ground.

"You don't think we should come back later?" Oscar piped up while wiggling a little to see better from the position Lily had him held.

"If we do that, we'd have to sneak through the whole keep…" Lily reminded him.

"I can't hear anyone." Kiki added.

"We'll be fine!" Finn stated, with a finality that settled the whole debate. Even if it hadn't, him walking through the door and pulling Lily into the darkened stairway certainly did.

The stairs were worn and uneven under her feet. The stairway was obviously ancient and not refurbished like the rest of the castle had been over the years. That was probably a good sign that this was not a common place for people to venture, and therefore a good place to hide truths. The damp scent grew with every step that descended them further past ground level. They didn't venture too deep, likely on the same level as old human dungeons would have been in the old days.

They emerged into a wide room with a low ceiling, a slight layer of moss growing through the gaps of the dark stone, each slab curved on the edges from where water and moss had worn them down over time. One of the walls had a set of shelves from floor to ceiling that was filled with all sorts of objects. Oscar hopped up onto Lily's shoulder as she approached for a closer look.

This was more what she had expected when she had come to the witch world. There were potions that appeared to sizzle and bubble where they sat, in the shelf above her head there were jars of varying sizes of hearts. Lily recoiled a little recognising a human heart within the collection.

"Ok; this truth might be eviller than we thought?" Oscar whistled as he jumped up onto the shelf to nose through the jars for a closer look.

"Yeah, these don't look like anything we've studied," Finn agreed, picking up a couple of the potions to look closer inside the glass containers. "None of our books told us about potions that sizzle."

"Or creepy leeches..." Kiki chimed where her and the stoat were sniffing at a large glass container that was filled with slimy creatures about the size of Lily's thumb. Moving closer, she saw that they were in a small layer of water and some seemed to have latched to one another.

"What are they?" Her question was received with naught but silence in return.

Turning away from the shelves that seemed to fascinate all the others, Lily headed to the other side of the small room where a desk sat with papers and journals strewn across it. There was no organisation, no filing system that would allow a stranger to know where to start. So, she started with the first piece of paper that sat on top of the rest.

'Q, my love.

There is a fairy being sent into your school by our woods. The council are sending her in to 'find information' but of course, our dear child will not allow the council to believe a word she says. Though, if you could find a way to prevent her from returning, that would add fuel rather than suspicion.

Our children here are all well, they come to speak to me often to see how you are. They all send their love, and I send my heart as always.

Love, C.'

Lily's eyes narrowed a little at the words she read. This C person had to be in the Fairy Kingdom to have known that she was being sent, and was requesting that Lily was prevented from returning all together. There really were people who wanted the war to continue. But why?!

Placing the letter down, Lily rummaged through the rest of the loose papers. They were all letters from the same person; but mostly seemed to be general conversation and terms of endearment. Whoever C was, Q was certainly a lover or more from the way they wrote to them and the reference to their children. Children who were always referred to as another letter and never a full name. From the letters, Lily could conclude that there were another seven who lived in the Fae Woodlands and saw C on a regular basis; their names apparently being L, Y, S, B, and O. Were they the first letters of their names? Or was it some kind of code?

One letter reported that one child known as R had been acting against the plan and so they had been taken care of. The phrasing was ominous and Lily had a horrendous feeling that she had just read the report of a death.

Pushing the letter aside, Lily went for the scroll next, rolling it open over the rest of the paperwork and finding her eyes scanning a family tree. Well, she thought that was what it was. In the centre there were two names. Each lineage only extended down to grandchildren maximum, and many names were crossed through with a blood red smear. Looking over the names, Lily spotted the name Riole smeared out. Was that the R from the letter she had read? Were these people really killing their own children?

Glancing over her shoulder to look where Oscar and Kiki were now browsing the top most shelf, Lily decided to make a conclusion before she called them over. All these pieces of writing made her more fearful than she had been in a long time, this whole thing was deeper than she could have figured out.

Her eyes turned back to the scroll, scanning over more names. Her stomach sank as she read over the name Esmaria.

And then... Finnigan.

A sharp intake of breath was all the response she got to give before something collided with the back of her head, knocked her forward and turned everything black as she fell to the floor.

Chapter 18: Truth

A dull throbbing and a sharp pain at the back of her head brought her into the land of consciousness. Panic raced through her the moment her mind became active and her eyes snapped open despite the protest of stabbing pain that occurred the moment light hit her pupils. She couldn't keep the groan from leaving her lips. Whatever had collided with her head had caused a heavy blow. Glancing down at her body, fear only crept deeper into her soul. She was bound to the wooden contraption that had been in the corner of the room, her wrists, waist, neck and ankles bound to it to keep her from moving. Her clothing was ripped and vacant in a lot of places allowing for her to see the numerous little leech-like creatures that were now littering her glittering skin as the magic disguise failed to work. Pain radiated from her skin wherever they were, it took now genius to know that they were biting and holding on.

Instinctively, she attempted to freeze them all until they dropped from her body.

Nothing happened.

Again, she tried and failed to summon up the magic she had controlled so perfectly from before she could ever talk.

The feeling of powerlessness and fear caused tears to prick the corners of her eyes.

A deep chuckle sounded from somewhere in the room and Lily's eyes snapped up to register that she wasn't alone. Finn stood against the desk she had been leaving over previously with his arms folded and a sinister smirk on his lips. He looked like a different being altogether from the one who had laughed with her and held her hand so often.

"Finn?" Lily's voice croaked, not trusting itself not to break. "What's going on?"

"What? You're too easy, that is what is going on." He laughed to himself as he watched Lily struggle against the restraints once again. "You actually believed everything I had to say. Man, do they not teach you fairies street smarts or something?"

Finnigan remained unflinching at the betrayal that dawned in Lily's eyes, tangling itself with fear and sadness.

"What?" She couldn't say anything else. Her mind wouldn't catch up with reality. This was a boy who had spent so many months helping her, who had encouraged her that the bonds between witches and fairies could be fixed, who shared his secrets with her as she shared her own...

His green eyes rolled in annoyance. "Thought you were supposed to be a quick learner." He clicked his tongue and shook his head, pushing himself away from the desk and moving to stand in front of her. "You. Got. Tricked." Reaching out one hand, he took hold of one of the little leeches and tugged on it. Lily gasped in pain at the strength it was latched onto her arm.

"Peyadu... They're my mother's favourite pets." He squeezed the creature lightly, gaining a wave across its skin of silver, pink, purple and blue in a pattern that could rival the beauty of the aurora borealis. "They're consuming your magic right now, so don't bother trying to use it."

Lily was still dumbstruck, shaken to her very core, and unable to find the words to respond with. A loud yowl sounded off to the side and her head whipped around towards it. Hanging from the ceiling were a couple of large metal claws, designed like the feet of an eagle, and clutching two struggling black shapes. Oscar and Kiki hissed and struggled against their restraints with no avail. Claws did nothing but screech against the metal, and their bodies were held tight enough that Lily wasn't sure they weren't having bone broken. If she could see closer, she would have seen one digit on the claw clamping the cats' mouths shut like a muzzle so they couldn't part their mouths far enough to make any noise other than the guttural growls and yowls that left their throats.

"Let them go." She croaked out, finally finding some train of thought.

"What, so they can attempt to scratch my eyes out while you all die?" Finnigan scoffed a laugh, pulling another Peyadu from the jar on the table Lily had been looking at when she had been knocked unconscious. "I don't think so."

"Why...?" She couldn't even think what to follow that with. There were so many questions. Why was he doing this? Why had he had to lie to her? Why was her heart seizing up like it had been shoved into a pot half its size? Why was her stomach convulsing in a way that made her feel sick? Why did she desperately want this to be a sick dream? Just... why? Why did the person she had decided to trust with the deepest part of herself have to be a person who could bind her and take her magic, her dignity?

Finnigan rolled his eyes again, letting out a small noise that suggested he didn't think this was all worth her whining. Shoving the hem of her dress up he placed the Peyadu against the skin of her inner thigh above her femoral artery. Lily hissed, a couple of tears escaping the corners of her eyes as the skin was broken and the pain ran up her core.

"The war has to happen. You're just an extra added bit of fuel to the fire." He shrugged as he stood back to admire his work. "A fairy came to infiltrate us and learn our secrets; it's a good spin." Reaching out he patted Lily on her left cheek, hard enough that it may as well have been a slap. "But of course, I'm the hero, so I caught you before you could do any major damage. At least that's mother's plan."

"However," He continued after stepping away from her and placing the lid back on the jar of Peyadu. "It'll take a few hours to drain you, and frankly, now I don't have to pretend to care about you, I'm not hanging around to talk until you die."

Those were the last words he left hanging in the air as he headed up the narrow stone staircase and out the door into the garden. No one else knew it was there behind the trickle of water. And even if they did, what witch was going to come and save a fairy?? In the silence Lily began to realise Finnigan was right. She had been too easy, too trusting, and this was her own fault. She had placed all her trust in him, she'd believed everything he had said, and she hadn't even gotten Oscar and Kiki to stay outside in case something went wrong.

She had absolutely asked for this to happen. She had brought herself to the place that would change her forever, and would kill the person she was.

The snarling from the cats seemed to fade into nothing as her magic and essence was drained from her body. She could hear the beat of her heart in her ears and she could feel the warmth of the tears on her cheeks. She'd failed. She'd failed everyone she knew. Her family would suffer loss and war. Her friends would be stabbed with tales of betrayal. Her soul bonds would die with her, their lives snuffed out because of her stupidity.

A loud clatter and a thud of paws on wood snapped her back to reality, straining in her confines to see that Oscar had managed to wriggle around enough to push the talons open with his legs and fall to the floor, not without knocking the edge of a small table on his way down.

"Kiki! Twist to your side then push them open!" he was instructing the smaller feline whose legs were flailing uselessly, sticking out between the talon shapes.

With no small amount of squirming, hissing, cursing and grumbling, Kiki managed to pull her legs inside and shift in the way she was instructed until she too was landing on the floor with a soft thud.

"Are you guys ok??" Lily called hoarsely, swallowing back her tears.

"Fine, but that son of a liche!!" Kiki hissed angrily "I'll scratch his eyes out!"

"I'll tear his tongue out. He'll never lie again..." Oscar agreed with a snarl as he hopped up onto the surface Lily was strapped to. Reaching out a paw he dug his nail into one of the peyadu and attempted to tug it off the fairy's skin gently. Lily hissed at the sting before shaking her head.

"I think it has hooks holding it there." At least that was how it felt.

Oscar glanced up to her before sighing "then, this will hurt." Without further ado he gripped his claws tighter and pulled hard until the creature dislodged from Lily's skin, leaving a small patch of bruise and blood. Lily yelped a little at the feeling, but the relief of having one less being sucking the magic out of her was delightful.

"Bloody things!" Oscar attempted to shake it off his paw as it twisted around to latch onto him in return. "Ow!" As it's hooks latched onto him, he brought his paw down heavily on the ground, squashing the Peyadu and ceasing its movements. A small array of colours glowed around it before dissipating into Oscar's paw.

"What was that?" Kiki queried.

"Magic. I felt it..." Oscar paused, picking his paw up to examine it. "Kiki, help me crush them all before we take them off!"

Immediately both of the cats were up on her body, smacking down on each slimy creature with full force that only made Lily flinch from discomfort. With each one, the array of colours appeared briefly before seeming to sink back into her skin. Oscar was right, she could feel it like a familiar warmth of family, like a dream she knew well and couldn't believe she had forgotten.

It was the relief of coming home.

She could feel the warmth of it spreading through her being, though it felt a little disconnected still. Perhaps it would settle soon.

Once all the Peyadu had been crushed, the cats began ripping them from her body, gaining at least a flinch every time from Lily. It left her with an abused body, cuts and bruises littering her thighs, stomach, chest, arms... you name it, there was a bruise with a bleeding cut in its centre. She still felt violated by it, but there was a sense of freedom now her magic was coursing through her.

"Can you use magic to get out?" Kiki chimed as she eyed the leather binds that would take some serious effort to chew through. Lily knew what she meant, if she froze them deeply enough, they would shatter if she used enough pressure.

However, knowing it and making it happen were two different things.

Panic blazed through her stomach when no ice formed.

She tried again, turning her head to look at the bind around her right hand as if focusing on it was going to help.

It did not. Nothing happened. The tears that had been fading came back to choke her again.

"It won't work." She whimpered; scared of the concept of being without magic.

"It's ok, we got this!" Kiki immediately chimed and dove into gnawing at the leather bind while Oscar took to the one holding her left hand.

"Yeah, your magic will need to settle. Leave this to us." He chimed in before starting; though Lily was pretty sure he was just using pretty words to keep her calm. Not one of them knew how having her magic leave her body would affect her going forward. It might never sync up with her properly again. Swallowing thickly, Lily pushed the thought aside, hoping that the feline's words would be the end result.

It took a few minutes, but soon enough the straps fell from her wrists and allowed Lily to reach up and remove the strap front around her neck, before sitting up and pulling the straps against her ankles and waist open. Each one left behind a bruised band around her skin but with all the others dotted around they didn't exactly catch the eye. Well, perhaps the bruises on her neck would.

"Let's get out of here," Lily mumbled as she stood, steadying herself for a moment before heading for the stairs back to the entrance way. She didn't know where she was going to go once she got out of the door, she was obviously a fairy with her hair and skin on show right now; but she just had to get out. She had to get home.

However, the door didn't budge when she reached it and her body collided into the solid open as her hand pushed the handle down. With a groan she pulled back to try the handle again.

"It's sealed" she sighed with a swift, frustrated kick to the wood before turning around. "We're locked in..." Walking absently down the stairs again, Lily raised her hands to rub away the dried tears that were beginning to itch her cheeks.

"We'll have to wait till your magic's up and running again." Kiki commented, hot on Lily's heels. "Or there might be a back exit or something; you know, for emergencies."

Lily couldn't find herself believing that but she didn't deter the female cat from venturing around the room's edge, trying to sniff out a hidden entrance. Her eyes, instead, took her back to the family tree that was still unrolled on the desk where she had been standing before taking the blow that still sent a dull throbbing ache through her skull.

It was nothing compared to the crushing ache in her chest as her eyes settled on Finnigan's name again. She still felt confusion assailing her mind as her eyes followed the lines up from his name to the two which all lines led back to.

'Quintina & Cyrus'

Her eyes narrowed a little. Now she focused on them, she knew those names. But where from? It wasn't Cyrus that was ringing the bell in her mind, but Quintina.

"Oh my...!"

Quintina! She was the founder of Quintegia! But that was more than five millennia ago! How could Finnigan be linked to her in a direct line that indicated she was his mother?

Pushing the family tree out of the way, Lily began digging through the loose pieces of parchment and the small journals under the ones she'd examined earlier and were obviously aged in comparison. When she found one that looked oldest, its pages delicate and crinkled, worn from the battering of movement and time, she carefully flipped it open to squint at the contents.

The writing for the first few pages was so old that she could barely make out the lettering, but as she reached the seventh page, the writing had been traced over with fresher penmanship but the handwriting matched the ancient dim letters perfectly. Lily may not have been the quickest or most accurate when it came to gut feelings but she knew that the writer was the same person... all those years apart.

"Quintina is still alive," she mumbled, catching the cats' attention as she ran her hands down the page before gripping the corner and turning to the next one which explained to her exactly how.

'Turning pure magic into life force:'

Ingredients:

☐ *Blood of the line to extend (Three vials)*
☐ *Magic drained from another*
☐ *Dragon heart*
☐ *Cantonitrua fur (Two strands)*
☐ *Macellavir rot (Two pinches)*

☐ *Note: The more magic obtained, the longer life is extended - (EASIER TO TAKE FROM THE FRESH DEAD)*

There was so much about those words that spread acidic discomfort through her body, but as her eyes drifted to the side, to land on the crushed Peyadu that littered the floor, bile threatened to rise.

"They drain magic from the dead..." she started, both cats moving closer to her cautiously. "He said the war has to happen. Because they need the bodies, the magic." Unrolling the scroll of the family tree again, she glanced over the other names that she'd previously ignored for Finnigan's.

Taking a closer look, all lineages were connected to the centre two names creating the shape of an exploding star. The names crossed through with blood red lines also had a skull lingering next to it. That took little working out to conclude that not everyone in the bloodline was still alive. But the rest... had the rest been surviving through the centuries without anyone noticing?

Following one line Lily gasped at another name she recognised. One she would never have expected.

Layla Linwood. And just below hers was *Jared Linwood,* though his name had an hourglass next to it.

Were they in on this?! Did the reality spread through the fairy kingdom too? Manipulating the races into war every hundred years without fail? But, witches didn't give birth to fairies randomly... her eyebrows knotted inwards in confusion as she scanned the two central names. Was Cyrus a fairy? Somehow hiding his long life while manipulating the council through children? It would make sense; council leaders were of the same five blood lines dating all the way back to the beginning. Did that mean the whole council was in on it?!

Scanning the names again but she couldn't see the others. Though she did recognise the name of one of her father's colleagues who was in charge of keeping their magic monitored.

"Lil?" Kiki ventured with concern at the tension rolling off the fairy's soul.

"I think... I think this war is set up. And officials in both races are fuelling it so they can funnel the magic out of the dead." Her voice was grim, disgusted even at the thought that so many lives could be lost for something so greedy.

"We have to take these to the other elders, we have to stop this!" She concluded, grabbing up the family scroll and the journal with the potion ingredients in.

"How? Your magic isn't working well enough to get us out?" Kiki commented, grumpy that she hadn't sniffed a way out.

"There has to be a way!" Her voice was desperate as Lily located and pulled out a small satchel from the bookcases to deposit the scroll and journal into.

"Maybe one of these could help?" Oscar chimed as he wove between vials on a high shelf, squinting at the for any sign of names. "Finnigan was big on maceration potions, maybe these are linked to that? Wouldn't be locked down here if they were normal potions."

"None of them have labels." Lily sighed with a shake of her head.

"Only one way to find out then, watch yourselves!" Oscar flapped his wings to take him to the top of the bookcase and began to wedge himself between it and the wall.

"Are you crazy?!" Kiki yelped as she was plucked from the floor by Lily who dashed over to the staircase immediately, satchel knocking against her hip.

"Got any other bright ideas?!" Oscar groaned with effort. By her silence, Kiki did not have any other ideas. And so, Oscar continued to wiggle himself into the gap so he could press his back feet against the wall and his front ones against the back of the bookcase to tilt it forward. He didn't have to be very big, as soon as there was enough of a tilt, gravity did the rest, pulling the bookcase forward and sliding all the vials and containers out of the shelves with a crash and a severe amount of pink smoke filled the room while sizzling echoed off the walls. A few moments later, a stench began to seep into the room that frankly could only be described as smelling like body waste.

"Genius! Now we choke to death instead!" Kiki coughed through the smoke.

"Oh, shut up!" Oscar snapped.

"Well! What did you think was actually going to happen?"

"I am hoping it will burn through the floor and we will be able to get out."

"Oh yea… because in the ground is where we want to be."

"Better than going through the damn door into the arms of all the witch officials!"

"Guys! Enough!" Lily yelled over them, spluttering a cough immediately afterwards. "This is going to help." Pulling up her tattered dress to cover her mouth with its collar she attempted to squint through the smoke to see what the verdict was when it came to exiting the room through the floor. The smoke had an upward movement to it, as though there was air coming in from below.

"We'll go down and see where we end up" Lily coughed, moving through the smoke, wafting it around with a wave of her hand while tentatively stepping on the ground looking for an opening that was hopefully big enough to get through.

"Careful of any of those liquids left!" Kiki called after her.

"Some way to clear the air would be great right now," Oscar sighed.

"Should have thought about that before you shoved everything over!" Kiki retorted.

"Yeah yeah, alright!" Oscar grumbled. Lily continued further into the room, bumping into the fallen bookshelf before she found a hole to speak of.

"Doesn't look like it spread wider than the bookcase," she called blindly over to the bickering cats. "Which means I gotta move this thing," she added with a sigh.

Well, at least it would be lighter now that everything had fallen off it. It was still a strain, but she managed to lift it enough to push it back against the wall. It shook a little but settled and the movement caused the smoke to waft further around the room, dispersing up the stairs and leaving the room mildly visible.

"I can see the gap, though I don't know how deep it goes,' Lily commented, trying to waft more of the smoke out of the way.

"My time to shine, then!" Kiki chimed, jumping into the air, revealing her wings and flapping them gently to take her down the hole in question. "Ho! It stinks down here! That smell is not the smoke!" She hollered back up to them.

A few moments passed before the little black feline flew back up into the room with a light gagging sound.

"Ok..." she groaned "You'll definitely be fine jumping down there. But that's a tunnel that's got, like, so much waste! Makes me wonder what fairies do with ours." She chortled before gagging again as the scent from below hit her.

"So... it's through a load of waste, or through a city of witches?" Lily concluded, her nose wrinkling in disgust.

"One way we vomit a few times, the other way we potentially get caught? I vote vomit" Oscar chimed while stretching out his own wings.

This day... was definitely the worst of the ones she'd lived so far. But she could still do what she'd aimed to do and stop this war. She had the truth hanging from her shoulder and she had a way out of the room. Even if she did exactly as predicted when she landed in the slush and stench below, immediately gagging and hurling up any food remaining from breakfast into the slush.

Oh. That made her retch further.

"This is gross," Oscar groaned, voicing Lily's feelings on the situation perfectly. The feeling of almost-solid liquid slid and squelched around the skin of her legs and she could feel it soaking into the hem of her broken dress. It reached her knees and made all efforts to slow her as she waded through in a direction she hoped would lead out of the sickening tunnel.

It felt like hours trying to get through, gagging now and then on the scent that surrounded them... but in reality, it was probably only around fifteen minutes. When they came to an opening, it felt like they had been freed from a live burial as they gasped for fresh, cleaner air. Coughing to clear her lungs, Lily straightened up, still distantly aware that waste still sloshed around her ankles now while she looked around the new open space. It was still underground; the high ceiling was still quite obviously earth below the city. Below the waste pooled down into a trough that circled half of the room with most waste pipes leading into it from different directions.

In the middle of the room was a large contraption that seemed to be whirring in sound though it wasn't moving. And past it a large pipe running into the furthest wall.

"How are we going to get over there?" Kiki grumbled, catching the raised eyebrow Lily shot her. "Ok, you. How are you going to get over there? Is your magic working yet?"

Looking down at her hand, Lily flexed her fingers and attempted to draw ice into being. No luck. Sighing, she dropped her hand back to her side and shook her head. Maybe the cats could take the evidence back to their home ahead of her and she'd catch up eventually.

"Try a spell." Oscar ventured before Lily could speak. "Witch magic has a lot of the power in the incantation, right?"

"And a wand, which I don't have now..." Lily pointed out.

"Oh, for wings' sake!" Kiki snapped, beating her wings so she could bring herself to hover in front of Lily's face, her canines bared in annoyance, "You've never had a WAND! You had a FANCY STICK!"

Lily blinked. Ok, the small cat had a point there. She'd almost entirely forgotten that her magic was only being guided through the stick rather than enhanced by it. Stepping back instinctively from the feline, Lily nodded her head before looking down at her shoes, her white hair falling over her shoulders. Focusing on the items of clothing she took a breath.

"Volantra."

The arches of her feet itched in her shoes and, for a moment, anxiety set in that it wouldn't work. However, upon sliding her right foot forward at an angle she found that it raised into the air as it was meant to. 'Walking' on air was more like ice-skating with this technique, but with a smile she pushed herself forward from the ledge and found that there was no weakness in the magic she had used.

That was going to be useful if she could keep spells in her memory.

One foot in front of the other she managed to skate gracefully across the cavern to the furthest pipe they had been aiming for, the cats making whooping sounds and skittering through the air with her.

"See! Knew it would work; I'm a genius!" Oscar chimed happily.

"Uh huh, and I'm a singing fugacapra..." Kiki rolled her eyes.

"Really?! How did you keep that a secret? I always thought you were an edaximae; weakening my soul with every breath you take." Oscar retorted. Their voices echoed a little in the room but there was no one around to hear them.

"Well now that's just mean." Kiki gasped, shooting forward to bundle into Oscar in the air.

"True though!" Oscar laughed as he batted her head lightly as she approached in an attempt to defend himself lazily.

Skating down to the pipe, Lily settled herself on the solid surface before looking up to watch the now playing cats with a fond smile. Even with her world imploding in on itself, they never changed. They were a constant and they were a reason to smile that even the heartache from Finnigan's truth couldn't touch them. Leaving them to it she walked along the pipe until she reached a small latch, likely used to get inside if anyone needed to check on the internals.

"Oh, thank the wings! It's clean this time!" She exclaimed, interrupting the play fight above her.

"Good! I don't want to retch anymore," Oscar chortled as he landed next to her and peered into the pipe. "It's deep though..."

"Yeah, it seems that we'll be swimming," Lily nodded. "Well, you might be able to hover above if you both are careful?"

Maybe.

Picking up the satchel with both hands Lily took in a deep breath, casting her mind back over the books of charms she had toyed with alongside her friends. She knew there was one which could keep the contents of the satchel dry; she just couldn't quite remember which one. Studying so much was supposed to be a benefit, but right now it felt like she was drowning in a library within her own head.

"Ah!" The sound left her when she'd finally reached an appropriate spell in her mind. She turned her gaze to focus on the satchel in her hands. "*Addari!*" A ripple of shine extended from the points where her fingers touched the satchel until it coated the whole object. It was a barrier spell that the girls had perfected one evening because they wanted to test out some mess-making spells but didn't want to stain anything in their room. If it could keep the ink that spilled over Lily's bed from staining it, she was sure it would keep the evidence dry in water.

"I hope this takes us far enough to not be spotted..." Lily sighed, pushing her hair back from her face, taking a deep breath before jumping through the open hatch and into the water.

It took a lot of willpower not to gasp at the unexpected chill of the water, or at the strength of the unseen current that dragged Lily along with the movement of the water. Thankfully her clothing was less bulky this time being underwater, and so the weight did not drag her down like the time at the lake. Resurfacing, she glanced around to see if the cats had been able to stay above the water, only to find them floating behind her with their wings splayed out wide to act like a raft. She regretted the small laugh she gave at the sight when the current pulled her down a little providing her with a mouthful of water. Thank all the myths that this wasn't sewage like the previous pipe.

The twists and turns in the pipe were unpleasant and soon they were twisting around a corner which opened out into the sunlight of the open world... and a sudden drop.

A scream escaped her lips as Lily was ejected from the pipe with the water, falling down until she ventured underwater once more. Her body had turned in the fall so she entered the water below head first, shoes being torn from her feet at the pressure, and her orientation messed up as she tried to find out which way led to air. Once she broke the surface, she gasped for air and flailed a little in place to keep afloat while searching for Kiki and Oscar.

"Lily!" Oscar called from above, drawing her eyes to where they flew down to her, obviously having caught themselves before they hit the water themselves.

"You're okay!" She called back as they moved down to hover above the water. Looking past them, Lily squinted up at the pipe they had vacated. It stuck out of the side of a cliff, where the city walls of Mythanissiam stood proud in the afternoon sun. "Well, that's one way out of the city..." she mumbled before adjusting her position by sweeping her arms through the water. She was in the Great Sea, she could feel the continuous flow of water pulling out from shore and pushing back in. Pushing some wet strands of hair from her face she turned back to the rock face. They'd have to follow that until they found a way back onto land.

Glancing through the water to her bare feet, she sighed. Walking on air wasn't an option now her shoes had sunk to the depths below, and her elemental magic was still growing in her veins. Risking wearing herself out with that was something she couldn't afford. She'd more than likely need more once she was on land than right now. Which meant she only had one option; she was swimming.

Such a feat wasn't easy; compared to most fairies she had a flare for so-called exercise, but she had always had magic to assist. Swimming to the east, trying to stay far enough that no one on land would spot her, and trying to move fast enough that she wouldn't still be in the water when the sun was gone from the sky, was more effort than anything she had done in the past.

That was something she just about managed, though it did leave her face down in the sand of the beach a few leagues away from Mythanissiam heaving breaths while her body screamed with aches and pains. "I can't move anymore," she complained, turning her head so her cheek rested against the damp sand and her eyes watched the caves in the distance.

"Yes, you can." Kiki chimed somewhere nearby.

"Nope. I need to rest."

"We might not have time for that."

Sighing in frustration, Lily closed her eyes and cursed internally. A year ago, she never would have expected her life to be how it was now, she would never have known that one day she'd experience an exhaustion both mentally and physically that threatened to leave her numb. Right now, she felt weaker than she had with her magic being pulled from her. She could have fallen into a slumber easily with her eyes closed like this. Oh, she should probably open them to stop them happening.

A figure seemed to be standing by the caves in the distance when she finally forced her eyes open. It wasn't a human figure, but a horse? No, it had large wings by the look of it and the air around it seemed to ripple with purple hues.

"What?" Lily pushed herself up from the sand, blinking at the spot in front of the caves. The creature was gone, but she could have sworn that it had been the Morequcor. Death's horse.

That was not an omen she liked.

Even if she was imagining it, what did that mean for the future that now lay ahead of her? Was she going to fail in saving her loved ones? The thought raised bile in her throat which she swallowed back, pushing herself up to her feet where she wobbled dangerously. Her legs felt so weak and tired.

"Come on," Kiki nudged her shoulder before dropping down to the floor so she could trot alongside Lily's feet. Oscar flew ahead a little to make sure they weren't going to walk straight into the chains of witches.

The first goal was to get as far away from Mythanissiam as they could. A few hours of walking up the beach towards the caves which didn't seem to want to get any closer, they heard an echoing sound that shattered and split the air. It was coming from the city. No doubt an alarm to warn the rest of the towns nearby that there was someone who was a threat.

"We'll take shelter in the caves and rest." Oscar commented once the sound died off. "At least we won't be in the open."

Oh good. Her wobbly legs just wanted to give in and her eyes wanted to close and let sleep take over. The sand was an effort to walk across, occasionally stumbling Lily when her foot sand too far into the soft substance. Every now and then a stone or a shell could scratch or cut the base of her feet and cause her to flinch.

The sun had long since set by the time they finally reached the caves, Lily grumbling with the effort to stay awake as she haphazardly made her way inside the first one to find a dark nook to lie in and sleep. The discomfort of rocks and the uneasiness of lying in the location she'd thought she'd seen the Morequcor wasn't able to last long as her body fell into a sleep state the moment her head rested on the satchel between it and the floor.

Chapter 19: Reality

Lily stirred once throughout the night. The sound of hooves moving past the entrance pulled at her mind, but not enough to truly bring her back to consciousness. It was early morning when a paw swatting her face became too annoying to ignore that she finally opened her eyes and groaned out a noise of protest at the ache she immediately felt in her body.

"You'll have to get used to that." Oscar commented as he dropped to the floor beside her, laying down a freshly caught fish. "By my calculations, it'll take us a good two days or more to get back home on foot."

The tired eyes Lily turned to him held a glare that said more than she would ever need to at that idea. Oscar merely shrugged his shoulders in response before glancing down at the fish. "Get up and see if you can cook it; if not, your breakfast is going to be cold."

With a tired grumble, Lily waved her hand towards the fish, "*Agora.*" Flames jumped to life around the fish and flickered healthily in the sea breeze.

"Your magic is looking better..." Kiki observed as she dropped a second fish into the fire before sitting next to it in an attempt to dry her fur.

To test the theory, Lily lifted her hand again and pointed it towards Kiki. "*Siccali*" she mumbled, shooting the familiar gust of warm air over the fur until Kiki was a puffed-up ball of fur and Oscar was howling with laughter on the floor. "You're right, I can't feel any hesitation now."

"Try some fairy magic!" Oscar chortled, avoiding the swat Kiki aimed at him as he finally started to calm down in his laughter. Lily nodded softly and glanced around the cave; raising a hand with her palm facing upwards as she closed her eyes to concentrate. From her palm, light erupted in the form of small glowing spores that drifted up and into the cave, shining a light on the damp grey stone. Immediately, Lily felt herself smile and a weight on her shoulders vanished. She could still use her magic. Somehow, in the adrenaline of escape, she hadn't realised how scared she had been of that outcome.

The smell of burning brought their attention back to the fish and with a flick of her wrist, some water, from where the sea was lapping at the raised stone of the cave, jumped up and extinguished the fire. The fish in question did not look appetising, their skins were charred and their eyes still staring sightless out at the world. But the growl in her stomach at the smell could not be denied, and there was no chance she would be able to walk for another three days without eating.

Picking up one of the fish she shuffled herself over to the edge of the rocks not covered in water and dunked her feet into the salty sea water. She hissed a little at the way it surrounded and coated the cuts on her feet. She'd have to do something about that too. Taking a bite out of the fish, grimacing at the odd crunch it gave she stared down at her feet thinking, absently noting that the two cats had tucked into the fish she had left behind.

Hopefully they would enjoy it more. At least she had the willpower to finish off every fleshy part she could find, if only because she realised she had not eaten in the last twenty-four hours. Flinging the remains back into the sea, knowing other creatures to pick it clean, Lily pulled a face at the lingering taste in her mouth.

"We should stick to the sea until we get up near the woods." She spoke knowing her companions would be listening, not sure if she was expecting a response.

Of course, she got one. Though it was muffled around a mouthful of food that Kiki was happily scoffing down. "That would extend the journey."

"Yeah, but less witch settlements; and if my magic is working, I can use the water to move faster and shorten the time," Lily shrugged, reaching up to pull her hair back from her face, watching as the light spores made her skin glitter as they caught the natural shimmer she had. It had been a long time since she had seen her proper colours. Beside her, she grew a flexible and tough vine, thin enough to be near ignored and plucked it from the ground. Once positioned near her hair, it snaked around the white locks and secured them back into a ponytail.

"Think they'll be searching for us?" Oscar piped up.

"It's a fair assumption that they will…" Lily sighed, finding a strange level of calm over her since she had woken up. The intense level of panic from the day before had faded and logical thought was a lot easier to process. "That alarm wouldn't have sounded otherwise. Probably best to assume we are in danger than not."

And that was a statement that set the atmosphere for the next few days, as predicted, it took almost three days to get back to the kingdom within the Fae Woodland. Utilising the water to move Lily along had a higher speed than walking had cut some time down, but they had found the area where the Fae woodland began was being guarded.

They had waited in the rockeries and reefs just out of sight from the beach until night fell before they made a move. None of them had been able to sleep while they kept themselves afloat, and the rising tension in waiting for sunset had left them all exhausted. When night fell, there were fewer guards around than there had been in the day - which honestly seemed foolish as Fairies could control shadow.

For the billionth time in her life, Lily wished dearly that she could fly. Then she'd just be able to go over them, instead of having to sneak through them. She got Oscar and Kiki to fly over; the less movement on ground level, the better. Once inside the tree line, Lily quickly pulled herself up into the trees with a couple of vines and kept herself out of sight from any eyes turning to the woodland.

From there it was a straight shot home. That thought brought down the weight of the last week down on her shoulders as a feeling of relief settled through her. She was nearly home where she could let the way her heart ached and stabbed in her chest overwhelm her. Maybe they would know what this feeling really was and how to make it feel less like it was suffocating her every time she thought back to the revelation Finn had given her. The closer she got to the area of woods that she knew well, the more the need to sink into her mother's arms and sob became. Everything was sinking in now; she'd lost her first friends who probably now hated her, she'd been used, manipulated and fooled by someone who had trusted with all her heart, and she was holding evidence of a cover up that made each war staged and a manipulated slaughter of so many people. On top of that, some of those who kept the stage going were trusted leaders of their kind.

She'd have to try and find Clara Lior first; she always seemed like the most understanding of them all.

Unfortunately, none of Lily's best laid plans seemed to want to succeed recently. The moment she climbed the tree on the outskirts of the kingdom and crossed the barrier which immediately shrunk her and the cats down, she felt two sets of hands seal around her upper hands and pull her back from the branch she had been reaching for.

"What...?" She yelped in confusion as she glanced around to find two shadow fairies gripping her tight with stern expressions on their similar faces. In the corner of her eye she could see their hawk companions take hold of Oscar and Kiki. The irony of them being held in talons again was not lost on her, but only lingered as a fleeting thought as they started to get dragged through the air towards the central trunk.

This did not bode well.

"Let go!" Kiki spat up at the hawk that tightened its grip around her causing her voice to hitch up to a squeak.

"You'd do well to hold your tongue; your fairy is under arrest and therefore you are detained" the hawk hissed back.

"Arrested?" All three exclaimed in disbelief.

"What for?" Lily demanded in a voice that was far stronger than she felt. She got no answer from the companions or the closed-lip fairies, one of whom released her to open the door into the city hall so Lily could be pushed unceremoniously through the entrance and down the halls as soon as their feet hit the branch below. Why they needed to keep the grip on her arm tight enough to add more bruises to her body, Lily didn't know. Anyone who had known her for the span of a mere five minutes would know there was no chance she was about to run. Even if she wanted to, there was no logical suggestion that said she would make it.

Besides, she had a story to tell.

Though, as she was shoved through the main council meeting hall, she realised that it was never going to be that simple.

Layla Linwood stood in the middle with an ominously calm expression. Livius sat at the usual meeting table with a blank expression marred only by a cruel glint in his blue eyes.

"So?" Layla started with a raised eyebrow, examining Lily who straightened up, rubbing the bruises on her upper arm, noting that Oscar and Kiki had not been thrown in the room with her. "Our sources tell us that you are back to get us to lower our guard, and that you've even been conspiring with draconians."

Lily's eyes flicked from Layla to Livius and back. "Well, yes. But it's just…"

"And you were dating a witch," Layla cut in.

"No, that wasn't…"

"And you've made no effort to change their minds, so by having us lower our guard, you are encouraging the massacre of your own people!" Layla snapped, ignoring the way Lily's head shook in protest.

"No; there doesn't need to be a war at all!" Lily exclaimed, darting past Layla who she knew she had no chance with and hurried to stand in front of Livius who was looking at her like she was something disgusting he had stepped on. "It's all a lie. They don't use our wings, they think we want their land."

"Preposterous!" He snarled with a dismissive wave of his hand.

"It's true! It's all a lie. Designed by some old couple so they can make sure of the dead." Lily could feel herself welling up in her desperation. Rounding on Layla, she pulled the scroll from her satchel and unrolled it to wave in Livius' face. "Layla's a part of it!"

The flicker of anger in Layla's eyes could have been missed if Lily's eyes weren't unblinking in her heightened state of fear and anxiety. Thankfully that meant she saw the movement of Layla's hand as it started and she lifted her own hand as vines shot out of the floor to detain her.

"*Agora!*" Fire burned the vines before they could get close to her. However, the gasps she heard from the door caught her attention.

"The witches have corrupted her! She's a traitor to our kind!" Livius was the one who spoke, though the cruel victorious gleam in Layla's eyes suggested that the idea of this corruption had been hers. Layla was never going to let her come back.

"Arrest her!" It was Clara from the doorway who spoke, stepping aside for the two previous fairies to come forth and shackled her wrists in a heavy metal that sizzled as it burned her skin. They were ancient, vicious artefacts, and Lily had never known anyone who had them used on them. They burned enough that the nerves struggled to utilise the magic within the body while they were worn.

Lily hissed as she was shoved into moving, the burn searing into the sensitive skin of her wrists. It hurt, but there was a rush that came with the feeling that kept her in the reality of the moment. It grounded her, even though she was certain they were going to scar, and the feeling kept the tears back that stung her eyes.

The door that slammed behind her once she was pushed into a room caused her to flinch at the sound. In the silence she could feel herself tremble but there was no control to be gained over her body which sank to the floor.

Just how naive and stupid was she? How had she not seen all this coming? She blindly trusted that the council would listen to her, blinded that the people who controlled their kind were going to be decent people, she had trusted Finn with everything; told him of her life, her fears, her loves... and she had loved him.

The whole world ground to a halt.

Oh. That was why her heart felt like it had been crushed. Lily had loved him, trusted him, and begun to plan things they could do in the future without a doubt that he would be in it. And he... he'd tied her, betrayed her, bruised her, lied to her, and attempted to take the very nature of what she was and leave her a dying, empty shell.

In the calm of the room, Lily couldn't stop the choke that sounded in her throat as the tears spilled down her cheeks. She buried her face into her hands as the sobs shook her body. What had she ever done to deserve this feeling? She'd give anything to only know the feeling of being the outcast; to know what it was like to love and laugh and then to be suddenly left in a kind of cold she couldn't describe, it made her stomach turn.

She wasn't even being allowed the luxury of going home and sobbing to her parents. But would she want to? They'd think she was pathetic for falling for such things, for being naive enough to not see the signs. Were there signs? Sliding her hands up to grip the front of her hair tight she tried to swallow the tears. She hadn't seen any. Finn had been charming, and fun, and made her feel like she was wanted.

Staring absently at her wrists, she noticed that the burn was beginning to draw blood under the shackles. It was only slight, but the way it oozed to the skin surface and dripped down her arms in one line, then two, was oddly fascinating. Once again, the pain grounded her; allowing her breath to catch up with her and her tears to slow.

This was just another situation where she hadn't been good enough.

The blood that ran down her pale skin was slow, leaving a pink hue to the shimmer in its wake. It became a focus as her mind became little more than white noise. The pain of her wrists was easier to deal with than the pain in her chest, the fascination with the red of blood tainting her skin was better to focus on than the dawning realisation she was likely going to be locked up and stuck in those shackles forever.

At least it would numb the other pains.

Minutes rushed by as her silver eyes stayed on the droplets pooling in the crooks of her elbows. only disturbed when the door swung open and a different fairy stood in the door. She has a narrow face and her blue hair was pulled back from her face in a bun that was clearly far too tight. It made her eyes squint and added to the glare that Lily received from her.

"The council will address you now." Her voice was colder than her expression as she turned to walk back out, "Follow me."

Blood dripped to the floor as Lily pushed herself to her feet, obediently following the female out of the room. Each movement caused the shackles to shift a little and the burn to spread. The route they took did not lead them back to the council chamber, but outside of the main trunk. Even in the brightness of the light, it was clear the whole of the local fairies had been called out to witness this. They hovered above and around, giving her no real view of the world beyond them. There was angry murmuring that raged like the buzz of an angered hive.

"Lily!"

Her eyes snapped to her father who was being restrained alongside her mother by the same shadow fairies who had grabbed her at the boundary. Glancing up she saw two cages made of vines holding both Oscar and Kiki in spaces that were way too small. A blissful cool feeling surrounded her wrists, causing her to blink in surprise, looking down to realise ice was forming between her skin and the cuffs. A wink from her father told her to quickly pretend the ice wasn't there.

"Lily Rosales" The crisp voice of the White Fairy Elder carried over the crowd, signalling them all into a deafening silence. All eyes were on the Elder, most judging, expectant, or angry. The only eyes that weren't were her parents, who seemed to be silently pleading against what was about to be said. "You have been found guilty of corruption via witch magic. You are also guilty of conspiring with races who would see us dead."

"But..."

"Silence!" Livius barked from where he stood just behind the White Fairy. The sound got a bored look from the Elder in question before they turned back to face Lily again.

"You are hereby banished from the Fairy Kingdom and all its outposts. This banishment will last your lifetime."

A wave of muttering and jeers rippled through the crowd. Lily's hands could do nothing but grip the strap of her satchel while the cats howled from their cages in protest.

"But, I...?" Lily started before the lump of terror in her throat silenced her. How was she supposed to survive without them? Where was she supposed to go to be safe? What would she do when unable to get their advice and support? Shaking her head, a little, pulling back a little to look at her mother's face, wishing she could reach out and wipe the tears that spilled down her cheeks. "I'll be ok." She mouthed, trying to reassure them and herself. Trying to convince herself that she was able to do this alone, that they didn't need to see her break down as well when they had enough on their plates right now.

"Now, hand over your belongings and say your farewells."

Her silver eyes snapped back to the cold ones of the White Council Member. Her belongings had to mean the satchel. She couldn't give that over to them. There was no doubt that Layla would destroy it or simply give it back to Quintina... or Cyrus. Lily glanced around, wondering if the ancient man was in the crowd watching this play out.

Stepping back, Lily pushed the satchel back a little to be shielded by her body. She may regret this. She wanted to hug her parents, but she couldn't lose the only evidence she had that something was wrong with their culture wars.

"No." Her voice shook a little but she stood firm. Glancing down to her arms where she tested whether her father's ice would give her enough of a barrier so she could use her own. The ice spread up to her forearms as her confirmation.

"Hand over the satchel!" Layla snapped from where she stood, looking ready to go on the offensive.

Again, Lily shook her head and straightened her back with determination setting a fire in her eyes. *"Sokari!"* Without warning she stamped her food down as the spell left her lips, rippling a shockwave through the air that knocked the crowd backwards either into the air or onto branches.

The ice on her wrists engulfed the cuffs and solidified until the metal cracked and snapped, only then did the ice fall from her, taking the shards of her entrapment with it.

"Come on!" She called up to the cats, causing the vines that held them to rip apart. They were quick on her heels as she ran to the west of the scene, knowing she had to get as much distance as she could before the crowd stabled itself and came after her. Escaping a hoard that quite literally controlled the environment that you were in was not an easy task.

Sure enough, she only had a few moments before the branch in front of her began to bend upwards so that she could no longer run along it and voices behind her began to ring out in anger.

Raising her still bleeding right arm Lily didn't pause in her movements. She just hoped this would work.

"Saritu!" She yelled over the growing volume behind her and motioned her hand to the branch. A sickening crack echoed through the air, giving the fairies behind a startling warning before the branch split down the centre and Lily forced them apart, one of them being guided downward so she could layer it with ice.

If nothing else, Lily's creativity may have saved her life that day.

Sliding on ice gave her speed which the fairies could not keep up with, and manipulating each branch into her path to give her a continuous slide meant that soon she was out of reach and not long after she was sliding straight through the kingdom barrier and barrel falling into the edge of the Archaic Densewood when the now tiny branch snapped beneath her.

"Think they'll follow us?" Kiki panted as she landed beside where Lily was kneeling on the harsh debris on the ground.

"I doubt it if we keep moving," Oscar nudged at Lily's leg, motivating her to keep going. He was right, they were still in the light, still easy to find and drag back to punishment unknown. The Archaic Densewood isn't a place that any fairy wanted to step foot into, and so, there they would be safest right now. Especially as the Densewood was also going to be a safer option than out in the open where witches could see her

The Archaic Densewood was nothing like Fae Greenwood. The branches locked together above keeping all semblance of light from reaching the ground. That which did survive on the ground had to do so via the sinister lighting given off by deep red moss that littered the ground and tree trunks in patches. It was incredibly difficult to see where one was stepping, but at the same time, the eerie feeling made you think the darkness was a friend... because you couldn't see what might be out there watching you.

Pushing herself to her feet and brushing the blood from the scrapes on her knees, Lily drew ice into place over those wounds as well as her wrists once more.

"Stay close." She whispered to the cats before forcing her feet to begin stepping further into the unknown darkness. An ominous shiver ran down her spine as the light from the Greenwood dimmed behind her with every step.

"What do we do now?" hissed Kiki who was glancing around with her tail flicking nervously from side to side.

"We find someone who will believe us..." Lily sounded less than confident.

"Who? Witches will probably kill us if we go back and we've just been banished." Kiki pointed out.

A brief pause. "Xalina," Oscar breathed. "We'll go to see Xalina and her people."

"That's a long way without wings," Lily motioned. "But I suppose it's our best option and it will be nice to see a friendly face."

Both cats nodded their agreement.

"So, which way?" Lily asked after a moment.

"Well, the mountains are on the other side of the Densewood... so, just keep going forward?" Kiki offered up with a slight chuckle.

"Right. That's easy enough," Lily let out a deep breath before doing just that and stepping forward.

The two felines glanced at each other in scepticism before humming an agreement to follow the plan. Though, their first task would be to find their way through the Densewood so they could head towards the mountains where the draconian were said to reside.

Oscar nudged Kiki forward, encouraging her to walk in front of Lily while he walked behind; both of their eyesight was better than Lily's and with the darkness so dense, the only light Lily could manipulate was that given by the moss. A dim red light was not all that helpful.

And so, in that formation, the trio took their next steps into the biggest unknown yet.

Artist Acknowledgements

I am not an artist. While I create and invent the designs of the Ryvalian world, I am not the person who could bring them to life in art form, though editing is not beyond my limits.

I wish to thank the following artists for the work they have done for me, portrayed in this series and others.

- ➢ Sillaen
  - ○ https://www.deviantart.com/sillaen
  - ○ https://www.instagram.com/sillaen_arts/

- ➢ Le Chat Lunaire
  - ○ https://www.deviantart.com/lechatlunaire
- ➢ Hisokacchi
  - ○ https://www.deviantart.com/hisokacchi0w
    0

Printed in Great Britain
by Amazon